The Bennets
Providence & Perception

K. C. Cowan

Meryton Press
OYSTERVILLE, WA

THE BENNETS: PROVIDENCE & PERCEPTION

ISBN: 978-1-68131-073-2

This is a work of fiction. Names, characters, places, and incidents are products of the author's imagination or are used fictitiously. Any resemblance to actual events or persons, living or dead, is entirely coincidental.

Cover design by Janet B. Taylor
Front cover drawing by Anne Timmons
Back cover drawing by Charles Edmund Brock, *Persuasion*, Chapter 10 (1909)
Edited by Ellen Pickels
Book layout and design by Ellen Pickels

Published in the United States of America.

To my mother, who never denied me a book
and told me often, "You are a writer."

She was right.

Chapter 1

"**M**r. Bennet!"

A shrill and familiar voice yanked Mr. Bennet's attention from the book he was peacefully enjoying and startled him so thoroughly that he lost his grip, dropping the reading material into his lap. He took a moment to compose himself and mark his place, then turned to the doorway of his library where his wife stood. Her tapping foot, he noted, clearly signaled her irritation.

"Mr. Bennet, the carriage has arrived. Are you not going to wish me well?"

Mrs. Bennet rarely set foot in her husband's library unless it was the only way to converse with him. Mr. Bennet knew that his wife, never a reader, found the room dusty and dull, preferring to spend her time in the family's sitting room or upstairs in her private bedroom. Her absence from his book room made it that much more of a sanctuary for Mr. Bennet, which is why he spent so many hours in it.

He took a deep breath and studied his wife who was wearing her new pelisse trimmed in swan's down, purchased solely for this trip. When he had chided her over the bill, she had thrown a fit, declaring that of *course* she must look her best on her visit, or what would the acquaintances of their youngest daughter think of her? No point in bringing it up again, however. He just smiled.

"I am, my dear," he replied calmly. "Have a good trip. Would that I could join you to see our Lydia and Mr. Wickham—not to mention the grandchildren. But I must devote myself to securing a new rector for Longbourn parish. We have been without one for nearly a month now."

"Yes, quite inconvenient for Mr. Dudley to die so suddenly. How could he be so vexing?"

Mr. Bennet suppressed a smile. "Well, the good Lord giveth and taketh away in equal measure, and I am certain He must have had more important things on His mind than how His calling Mr. Dudley home would force me to give up my share of the visit." He gestured to some papers on his desk. "Bishop Wilson has sent me applications for three highly viable candidates from which to choose Mr. Dudley's replacement. While you are intent on pleasure up north, I shall study them carefully. By the time you return, we very well may have a new vicar."

Mrs. Bennet made a scoffing sound. "What does Bishop Wilson have to do with it? You own the advowson. That gives you the ability to choose whomever you wish for Longbourn parish! Why should Bishop Wilson have a say?"

"It is true the advowson gives me complete and legal right to fill the living. As it stands, however, I have no particular rector candidates in mind just now, so I thought it best to ask for some guidance from our bishop." He chuckled. "It cannot hurt to stay on his good side, after all, and let him believe he had a say in my choice."

"I suppose you are right," Mrs. Bennet said peevishly. "Oh, if only Mr. Dudley had left us sooner when all five of our daughters were still available. Then you could have given the living to Mr. Collins, and he might have married one of our girls!"

"Thanks to Charlotte Lucas, that ship has long sailed, my dear, and I think it highly unlikely my cousin would have been willing to leave the distinguished patronage of Lady Catherine de Bourgh in any case. Besides, with three of our five daughters securely wed, we can have little reason to complain. Now, come—you have a long ride ahead of you."

Mr. Bennet escorted his wife outside to the waiting carriage. He inhaled deeply, enjoying the moist, earthy odor of new spring growth. A breeze sent white petals down on them from the nearby blossoming apple trees, causing Mrs. Bennet to brush them off her new coat in agitation. Their middle two daughters, Mary and Kitty, were standing by the carriage. Each gave their mother a hug and kiss, then Mr. Bennet helped her inside and gave her a peck on the cheek.

Mrs. Bennet fretted as she settled into her seat. "I should feel safer on the long journey if you were with me; I fear for my poor nerves! Are you absolutely certain you cannot join me?"

"Young Master Miles will keep you safe; have no worries. It is nearly mid-May now, and the roads will give you no trouble. Give my apologies to Lydia and Wickham, kiss the twins, and I shall see you in a month's time. Write if you like; I am certain Mary and Kitty would enjoy hearing all the news of their sister and nephews from up north."

"Well, I can try, of course, but I am certain Lydia will keep me far too entertained to write." Mrs. Bennet shot a sharp glance at her daughters. "However, I shall rely on hearing from both of you very often. Relay all the town gossip—especially if you hear aught of what is behind Miss Bailey's broken engagement. I could have told her that man was not to be trusted, and indeed, I *did* tell her mother so, but she paid me no mind—"

Mr. Bennet interrupted his wife's diatribe. "Yes, yes—well, you have a long journey ahead of you, my dear. Best be off now." He stepped back and nodded to the driver and Miles, the young man hired to travel along as escort.

The carriage lurched forward, prompting a little yip of surprise from

7

Mrs. Bennet who nearly lost her balance. Recovering, she leaned out of the window and shook her handkerchief, calling goodbye. Mary, Kitty, and Mr. Bennet waved back until the carriage turned off Longbourn grounds and out of sight.

"It will seem so quiet with Mama gone," Kitty mused as they reentered their home.

"No doubt you and your sister will fill the silent space with little difficulty." Mr. Bennet turned towards his library. "I have much work to do. Why do you not take a walk into Meryton? I shall see you at dinner, my dears."

BACK AT HIS DESK, MR. BENNET AGAIN REVIEWED THE BISHOP'S submissions of candidates for the vacant rector position at Longbourn. At present, all were curates in small parishes. Two came with stellar recommendations from the head rectors. But neither they nor the bishop had included copies of recent sermons for him to review, which indicated the curates likely read sermons from one of the established books available to ministers. That in itself was not unusual, but Mr. Bennet had hoped to see some original thinking displayed. He was also suspicious of the overly effusive praise of two of the candidates. It could be that the parish rectors were trying to rid themselves of their curates for some reason; perhaps, their writing or oratory skills were lacking. Or worse, there might be a case of dallying with some young woman in the congregation.

He set the two applications aside and picked up the packet submitted on behalf of a Mr. Robert Yarby. Thirty years of age, Yarby was fairly new to the ministry, having found his calling following the death of his physician father. Since Mr. Yarby had been a curate for fewer than two years in a small parish in Dorset, he was not the strongest candidate, but his vicar, Mr. Smethurst, had written quite a positive recommendation, saying that he would miss Mr. Yarby but would also feel guilty for holding the young man back as he felt his curate had learned much and was ready now to lead a parish on his own.

Mr. Bennet read the three sermons Yarby had included—all clearly original. There was an openness to his compositions that Mr. Bennet found youthful and refreshing. Unless his delivery were dreadful, they most likely would not put him to sleep. Besides, being eager for his first job as full vicar, Mr. Yarby would probably not balk at the modest living Longbourn provided, whereas the two more experienced curates might try to negotiate a higher wage. But with an estate that yielded a yearly income of only £2,000, Mr. Bennet could guarantee little more than £120 a year from the parish's tithes. More could be earned, of course, from the fees for such services as christenings, marriages, and burials; still, it was a modest living—barely enough to hire a cook and maid—no doubt another reason there were but three candidates.

His mind made up, Mr. Bennet took out a fresh sheet of paper, dipped his pen in the inkwell, and began to write an invitation for Mr. Robert Yarby to come for a personal interview on Thursday next.

ELIZABETH BENNET DARCY AND HER SISTER JANE BINGLEY WERE seated in the cozy parlor at Pemberley, enjoying their afternoon tea. Jane had come to stay for a week or two at Lizzy's pleading as Mrs. Darcy was nearing three months into her second pregnancy. Her first pregnancy had produced a fine, healthy boy, and Elizabeth had no reason to fear, but this one had been a little more stressful than her first, and these were things only a sister could understand.

"Thank you again for coming, Jane. Fitzwilliam thinks I am being overly worried, but I just do not feel the same with this baby as I did with Thomas," Elizabeth said softly. She stroked her belly, just beginning to show a small swelling. "Everything with him was so easy; I was hardly ever ill. But this child has been a trial every step of the way, and I have not even met him yet! Or her," she added thoughtfully.

Jane replied with a warm smile. "I am always happy to be with you, Lizzy. And a few days away from my youngsters is a nice break."

Her smile vanished. "Oh. Not that I do not love them with all my heart—I do! I just…well, I mean—"

"—it is nice to have a change of scene and society?" Elizabeth finished Jane's explanation in a teasing voice. Her sister, face now turning red, nodded and took a sip of her tea. "I understand," Elizabeth continued. "You and Charles had three children in the first four years of marriage, whereas Fitzwilliam and I have had only the one. Thomas is a delightful handful, but I can only imagine the stress of having to cope with three—even with the help of a nursemaid."

"I am sure Mama would have been most happy to come and help you had you asked," Jane said.

"In point of fact, I *did* ask her. Not because I thought she would be as sympathetic as you or that I desired her company to that degree, but mostly to prevent her from running off north to be with Lydia and her twins again. Lydia takes such advantage of Mama, you know, and it vexes me greatly. Just because they can never seem to keep a servant for the nursery is no reason for her to call on Mama every few months so Lydia can have a break."

"Mama could say no if she wanted to," said Jane gently. "But I believe she likes to be needed. And Lydia is the most similar to Mama in personality and has always been her favorite."

Elizabeth heaved a sigh. "I know. But there is one consolation: Papa gets to enjoy some peace and quiet when she is gone."

Jane giggled. "He will be able to spend all his time in his library, reading without any guilt. I feel sorry for Kitty and Mary though. They will likely be bored to tears without our mother."

"Well, it is only for a month or so. Then Mama will be back to disrupt life at Longbourn as usual."

Chapter 2

Mrs. Bennet longed to retire to her guest bedchamber and ease her frayed nerves. Her twin grandsons were cute but such a trial. They fussed and screamed if they did not get their way, and today they were fighting loudly over a favorite toy. The screeches and tears! Mrs. Bennet had no one to turn to for help as she was alone in the cottage, Lydia having left for a dress fitting earlier that day.

"Mama, I cannot possibly take Gerald and Edward with me; they will be far too disruptive," Lydia had said after breakfast when she announced her intention to leave the rambunctious three-year-olds behind with Mrs. Bennet.

"But this is intolerable. With your husband gone for days on end with business matters, you really must hire a nursemaid!" Mrs. Bennet had looked forward to a pleasant visit with her youngest daughter and son-in-law, making calls in the neighborhood, and shopping with limited exposure to the twins.

Lydia pouted. "If Papa would send me more than twenty-eight pounds a year, I likely could. But as he won't see fit to assist his only daughter who did *not* marry a wealthy gentleman as Lizzy and Jane did, I must do the best I can. I can only stretch our finances so far, Mama."

"But what am I to do with them while you are gone?" asked an exasperated Mrs. Bennet.

"They will be fine. Just give them some of the taffy George brought home from his last trip. That will keep them happy." And before the argument could continue, she had flounced out.

Or make them even more high-strung than usual, more like, Mrs. Bennet thought. Oh, why did it have to be all left to her? It had been some eighteen years since she had had to deal with children that young. She had forgotten how much energy it took. And she had been able to afford help.

She grabbed the toy the two boys were squabbling over and held it high.

"Neither of you can have this until you learn to behave! Get your coats. We are going for a walk." Perhaps a lengthy span of exercise out of doors would tire the children sufficiently to calm things down.

At least, I hope so. Yet I fear I shall wear out before they do.

Lady Catherine De Bourgh was in high dudgeon following a visit by her nephew Colonel Fitzwilliam. Not that he had done anything in particular to annoy her. On the contrary, he was as polite and well-mannered as ever. He even paid her daughter, Anne, several compliments when her normally reserved daughter read two newly composed poems to her cousin.

No, Lady Catherine was put out because of the news the colonel shared that her nephew Darcy and his wife—whose name was never mentioned if possible—were expecting another child. With a second child (possibly another son) to be born, there was even less chance of his regretting his poor choice and divorcing her. Lady Catherine's hopes of ever marrying Anne to Darcy, as she and her sister had once planned, seemed all but impossible now.

Her brooding was interrupted by a servant who announced that Mr. Collins had arrived unexpectedly. Ever since Darcy had married the best friend of Charlotte Collins, Lady Catherine had construed some of the blame for the match to be the Collinses' fault. After all, it was Elizabeth Bennet's visit to the Hunsford Parsonage that gave Darcy the opportunity to fall under the wily spell of that fortune-seeking hussy. Yes, technically she may be the daughter of a gentleman and therefore Darcy's equal, but in Lady Catherine's mind there was no way that upstart Elizabeth could *ever* live up to the standards that her sister, Lady Anne, had upheld at Pemberley.

The result of linking Elizabeth's advantageous marriage to Darcy because of her relationship with Mrs. Collins meant Lady Catherine had nurtured a sizeable grudge and had sent fewer invitations to the Collinses in the past few years. Whereas before the marriage, Mr. Collins would visit by himself nearly five times a week and the couple was invited to dinner regularly, ever since Darcy had wed Miss Bennet, such invitations had dwindled considerably. And she often instructed her butler, Jonson, to tell Mr. Collins she was "indisposed." But today she nodded for Jonson to escort the rector in.

As Mr. Collins waddled into the salon (he had gained quite a bit of weight in the past couple of years, she noted), his hands were clasped together, and his head bobbed in a subservient, albeit not displeasing, manner.

"My dear Lady Catherine," he gushed, "How good of you to see me." He bowed before taking a seat on the settee to her right. "I wanted to be the first to share the happy news with you."

Lady Catherine raised an eyebrow but remained silent.

After a moment, he continued, "I hope you will be as happy to hear my news as I am to deliver it. My dear wife, Charlotte, is expecting our first child! Is that not splendid?"

"Is it?" she asked dryly.

Mr. Collins gave a nervous laugh. "Well…that is…we have been married for nearly five years now without producing any children, and I feared my wife might be…I mean…it was entirely possible she would be unable to give me a child at all. So naturally, we are both enthralled at the prospect of parenthood. I pray for a son, of course, as every good man should, but if it be a girl, we are agreed to name her Catherine after you." He sat back, panting a bit as though the telling of such news had been nearly more than he could handle.

"I see. And I suppose you would wish for me to become godmother to the girl—should you have one—provide her with a substantial stipend, no doubt, or a fat dowry to attract a good match. I suppose you might even hope for me to leave her a legacy in my will—usurp my own daughter for yours!" Even as she knew her response was less than polite, Lady Catherine could not stop herself from berating the cleric.

"No…I would never presume to…my dear lady, I only wished to share the joyous news…"

"It seems everyone is having children these days!" Lady Catherine spat. "I just heard the wife of my nephew Darcy is expecting—"

"—oh yes, Elizabeth wrote my Charlotte that she is with child again."

"Do not speak her name in my presence!" Her face was beginning to turn a splotchy red, and her hands clenched the arms of her chair. "Worthless fortune hunter—securing Darcy's fortune that ought to have been co-joined with my daughter's!"

"Indeed, what a blessing it would have been to unite Rosings Park and Pemberley," Mr. Collins said unctuously. "A match made in Heaven. To see your daughter happily wed to—"

"—and instead, she is still on the shelf! At twenty-seven and with her ill health, who will have her now? My dreams of grandchildren decrease by the day. I shall die bereft of the sound of happy children in my home." She leveled a gaze at her rector. "And. It. Is. All. Your. Fault!"

14

Mr. Collins swallowed before stammering a reply. "My…my fault? But how?"

"*You* allowed that young woman to come to Hunsford and visit your wife four years ago. I was hoodwinked into inviting her into my home, showing her condescension far beyond her merit. And what was the result? My nephew fell in love with *her* instead of my Anne as my sister and I always intended. It is all your fault!"

Mr. Collins's mouth opened and closed, but no sound came out. Finally, Lady Catherine stood. He jumped up, still attempting to speak.

"Leave me at once!" Lady Catherine ordered. "I do not wish for your company at present. Nor can I say I ever shall again." She glared at the hapless cleric, who could do nothing but bow and scuttle out of the room as rapidly as his girth allowed.

Lady Catherine sat down heavily once she was alone. She felt the beginnings of a pain in her temple. She rang the bell on the table to her right. When Jonson entered, she told him to bring her a glass of water and her headache powders. He bowed and hurried to do her bidding.

Miss Elizabeth Bennet—for she still thought of her by that name— *you may think your dear friend Charlotte's life is so fine. But you will see that things can change when you least expect them to.*

"YOU ARE VERY QUIET THIS EVENING, MY DEAR," CHARLOTTE SAID to her husband as the dishes were cleared away. She wanted to speak before he could disappear into his study for the remainder of the evening. Not that she greatly missed his company when he did so. She had no problem coping with her solitude in this cozy house whenever Mr. Collins absented himself for work or visits around the parish. Truly, her life was more than she ever could have hoped for when she had accepted Mr. Collins's hasty marriage proposal. As she told her friend Lizzy, she was quite content with her situation. But she found William's mood this evening disquieting. He was seldom like this—so taciturn. Indeed, he had hardly spoken a word throughout dinner.

"Is something causing you concern?" she continued. "Perhaps I can help."

Her husband gave a wan smile and heaved a sigh. "I do not wish to burden you with my troubles, Charlotte."

"Your troubles are mine as well, of course," she replied as she rose from the dining table and came over to him. She took his hand—inwardly cringing a bit at its moist touch to which she had still not become accustomed even after five years of marriage. "I am your wife, and we are soon to have a child, so of course whatever affects our household should be discussed openly between us. Can you not share what is upsetting you?"

"It is just—well, I had a very discouraging meeting today with Lady Catherine."

"Oh?" Charlotte led him from the dining room to the front parlor, away from the prying ears of any servants, and pulled him down beside her on the settee. "What made it so? Is she displeased with something you have done?"

"More like displeased with me in general." Mr. Collins lowered his eyes, unable to meet his wife's gaze. "I went to share the news of our impending child. I anticipated she would be pleased—especially at the news that we plan to name a girl after her. Instead, she went into a tirade, accusing me of expecting her to all but adopt the child financially! And then it devolved into her anger over Cousin Elizabeth's fortunate marriage to Mr. Darcy. She quite blamed you and me for it!"

Charlotte sighed. "Oh dear. I am afraid Lady Catherine simply will not give up on the idea of Mr. Darcy's divorcing Eliza so she can foist her daughter, Anne, upon him. It is, as you know, her fondest desire."

"True. But what disturbed me the most was her final statement. As she asked—no, *ordered* me to depart. She all but said she never wished for my company again!"

"But, she has been similarly upset and said such things before, has she not? Then she forgets her rage and the invitations continue."

"I have never seen her like this." Mr. Collins shook his head. "I fear she may ask the bishop for permission to send us packing. After all I have done for her. To be so summarily dismissed! It would be more than I can bear to lose her patronage—the humiliation of it!"

"Well, she has not yet taken that step, nor is she likely to in my opinion," said Charlotte calmly. After a moment, she added, "However… perhaps…*just* perhaps it is time for us to consider another path."

"What do you mean?"

"I mentioned to you that I received a letter from dear Eliza this week, remember?" At her husband's nod, she continued. "Well, her father has not yet found a new rector for Longbourn. Mr. Dudley is proving somewhat difficult to replace, likely due to the modest living it affords. However, since there is still an opening and Mr. Bennet *is* related to you, why should you not take the living there? I am certain we can manage on the budget quite adequately. You know how economical I am with money."

She watched as an expression of wonder appeared on her husband's face.

"Indeed, that is quite a sensible idea, my dear. Since I am to inherit Longbourn anyway upon the unhappy occasion of Mr. Bennet's death, it would be so much simpler to move from the parsonage to the manor. Plus, the parish would already know me and not resent my becoming the new head of the estate. I would not be seen as an interloper. And, you would like to be back with your family too, I imagine, as you near your time."

"You must write to Mr. Bennet tonight."

"No. Tomorrow, first thing, I shall take the barouche and catch the Town Coach so that I may visit him in person as soon as possible. But should Lady Catherine ask where I am, you must be circumspect."

"Of course, my dear. You may depend on me. I shall go pack your bag."

She kissed him lightly on the cheek and left the room.

Mrs. Bennet was in a state of happy anticipation for the day. For once, she had convinced Lydia to hire a day nurse (of course, it was she who paid for the girl) so they could spend time in Trent without the twins. She eagerly anticipated the time alone with her youngest daughter and envisioned a lovely walk around the commerce thoroughfare, shopping, and a fine lunch.

She checked her reflection in the mirror a final time, satisfied at what she saw. The great beauty of her youth was long gone, she had to acknowledge, but she had kept her figure fairly well—even after five girls—and looked quite handsome for her forty-three years, she thought. She adjusted her new bonnet a final time.

"Mama, are you ready? The carriage is here!" Lydia yelled from downstairs.

"Coming!" Mrs. Bennet called and hurried from her room.

"Boys! Where are you?" Lydia continued. "Come meet Miss Drayson and then say goodbye to Mama and Grandmama."

Just as Mrs. Bennet reached the top of the staircase, Edward and Gerald bolted out of the nursery, racing each other to the stairs. Heedless of their grandmother's location, they ran too closely to her as they rushed down, knocking her off balance. Unable to right herself, Mrs. Bennet lurched away from the only source of stability—the railing—and with a small shriek, tumbled down the staircase to the bottom where she lay still, her neck at a horrible, unnatural angle.

Chapter 3

"Mr. Yarby is here, sir," Mrs. Hill said after receiving admittance to Mr. Bennet's study.

"Ah, very good. Please show him into the drawing room, Hill. I shall join him directly."

The housekeeper nodded but did not depart. "There is a second person, sir—a lady who arrived with Mr. Yarby."

Mr. Bennet raised an eyebrow. A lady? As far as he understood, Mr. Yarby was unmarried. He shrugged. "Very well then. Show them *both* in, please, and bring tea."

After Mrs. Hill departed, the master took a minute to collect himself, then taking the pages of Mr. Yarby's sermons to discuss with the applicant, went to greet his guests. He entered to find Mr. Yarby standing by the fireplace while the lady accompanying him perched gingerly on the settee nearby. The two turned expectant faces to him as he entered.

"Good afternoon, Mr. Yarby," Mr. Bennet said with a slight bow of the head. "I do appreciate your coming all this way. Very pleased to meet you."

Mr. Yarby bowed. "It is I who am pleased and honored by your invitation, Mr. Bennet." He turned to the woman who rose from the settee. "Sir, may I present my sister, Mrs. Withers? She was widowed two years ago and now lives with me."

Mr. Bennet turned his attention to the woman. Well groomed and handsome, if a bit on the plain side—certainly no one would call her a great beauty—she was dressed in a muslin day dress of light blue with a rust-colored spencer jacket that complemented both her complexion and thick, auburn hair styled simply under a modest, pale-blue bonnet. She curtseyed.

"Welcome to Longbourn, Mrs. Withers," he said with a bow.

"Forgive me for arriving unannounced, sir," she said in a warm, well-modulated voice. "It is unpardonable, I know, but I have never been to this part of the country before. Any new place is always a welcome diversion to me, so I begged Robert to allow me to join him. Do not fear, however, that I shall interfere or insert myself into your business with my brother. I thought to avail myself of a walk around your property while you two speak if that would be acceptable." She smiled, and Mr. Bennet noted how that simple act lifted her from plain to moderately attractive. He put her age at perhaps early or mid-thirties. Was she an older sister?

"No imposition at all, I assure you." At that moment, Mr. Bennet heard footsteps behind him and glanced over his shoulder to see his daughter Mary walking past, holding some music. Oh Lord, was she about to murder another piece on the piano? That would never do. He called to her, and she stopped and entered the room.

"Yes, Papa?" Although Mary addressed her father, her eyes were firmly fixed on the unknown gentleman. Mr. Bennet's eyes turned from his daughter to Mr. Yarby, who was now standing. Noting the direction of Mary's gaze, he cleared his throat to return her attention

20

to him. Her face colored as she lowered her eyes. "Did you need something, Papa?" she stammered.

"I wish to introduce you to our guests. Mr. Yarby, Mrs. Withers, this is Mary, the third of my five daughters. Mary, Mr. Yarby has come to interview for the vacant rector position. His sister, Mrs. Withers, has joined him. Would you be so kind as to take her for a tour of our park while he and I conduct our business?"

Mary curtseyed to the couple. "Very pleased to meet you both. I am happy to escort her, Papa. If you will come with me, Mrs. Withers, I shall get my jacket."

The two ladies began to depart as Mrs. Hill entered the room with a tray of tea and cakes. Mr. Bennet offered some refreshment to Mrs. Withers, but she said that, after the long ride, she would much prefer a walk. As she and Mary exited the library, Mrs. Hill poured for both men, and at last, the gentlemen could discuss their business.

MARY AND MRS. WITHERS WALKED IN SILENCE FOR A TIME. MARY did not wish to be rude, but her mind was still on the handsome rector she had just met—wavy, dark-brown hair with dark eyes to match. And when he smiled, Mary was sure she had seen two dimples. She could only hope he would get the job. Oh, to gaze upon such a face in the pulpit every week! But she broke away from her daydreaming and realized she must make some effort at conversation with her walking companion.

"How long has your brother been with the church, Mrs. Withers?" she asked tentatively. Was it proper to ask such a thing? She did not wish to appear rude or overly inquisitive. But Mary saw no sign that her guest noticed her nervousness as they continued along the garden path.

"He has been the curate at a parish in Dorset for less than two years, Miss Bennet, which is why we were quite frankly surprised to receive your father's letter inviting him to a personal interview. We assumed Mr. Bennet would seek out someone with far more experience."

Mary pondered this a moment before replying earnestly. "But…every rector must start *somewhere*, must he not? A minister is not born fully formed as it were. Every experienced rector was once a novice curate."

Mrs. Withers let out a delighted laugh. "Indeed, you are correct! It would be lovely if your father also feels that way and is inclined to give him the living. But if not, we shall return to Dorset and continue as we were. Robert's time for his own parish will come, I am certain. Although, if we had better connections, it would likely be settled sooner."

Mary nodded sagely. "I have heard it said that the surest way to acquire a benefice is to be related to the bestower. It does not seem fair that connections should play such an important part in receiving a living. Talent, compassion for the poor, and love of God should be paramount in my view." Mary glanced at her companion, hoping she was not speaking out of turn. "Not that I have much knowledge in these matters, of course," she added.

Her companion laughed lightly. "I see we have the same frame of mind when it comes to acquiring a parish. But as I said, I believe Robert's time will come."

The two continued to walk in silence a while. Mary again tried to think of some way to continue their conversation.

"Do you…have…" Mary fumbled to find the words. "Forgive me, I do not wish to pry. You are married?"

"Widowed. My husband passed after a long illness, and sadly, there was little left for me to live on. His business affairs had utterly collapsed. So, a year or so ago, I came to live with my brother and manage the household."

"How sad."

"I do not tell you this to elicit your sympathy. My brother and I have always been close, and we get along well. I am content to live with him and help him in his work."

"Have you any children?"

"Sadly, no. My husband and I were married for eight years before he died, and we were never blessed with a child. Now, of course, at thirty-three, it seems unlikely I shall ever become a mother. But I do adore children and very much enjoy the little ones in our parish. And perhaps one day Robert will marry and make me an aunt. So that must suffice."

"God's will is sometimes difficult to comprehend," Mary said seriously. "If you will pardon me for being so forward—you seem like someone who would make a wonderful mother, yet God chooses to let you remain childless. Why should that be? I often struggle with His decisions." She gave a small gasp, stopped short, and reached out to clutch Mrs. Withers's sleeve. "Oh, but pray do not think me disrespectful of our Lord. His wisdom is far greater than I can hope to comprehend."

Mrs. Withers gently patted Mary's arm. "Not at all, Miss Bennet. It is clear you are a most thoughtful young woman. I must say it is rather a refreshing change from some of the flibbertigibbets I have seen in Dorset. I do believe their heads are filled with nothing but ribbons, dancing, and flirting with single men. Meeting you has given me another reason to hope Robert is given the position."

Mary's heart soared. Such kind words. Mrs. Withers clearly favored her. Could it be she might—at last—find a close friend? Could this gentlewoman be a kindred spirit? Mary had never had one before. And she had often felt at odds even within her own family—what with Kitty and Lydia always together, and Jane and Lizzy inseparable. Mary had always been on her own, taking refuge in her books and music. She felt lonely at times though she had learned to hide it.

"I should very much like you both to come here," she said softly as the two continued their stroll through the park.

"Well, Mr. Yarby, I believe my mind is made up," Mr. Bennet said as they concluded their discussion about Meryton, Longbourn, and other parish issues. "If you think you could bear to move to

Longbourn, and if you can survive on tithes of £120 a year, I should very much like to offer you the living. My estate has no glebe to offer, so you will not be able to farm land for additional income although the parsonage has enough space for your own sizeable garden, and there is a shed for chickens or pigs if you like. Those will help stretch your salary."

Mr. Yarby let out a relieved breath, grinning widely. "I would be very pleased to accept your offer, Mr. Bennet. I cannot thank you enough for this opportunity!"

"Let us walk over to the church and you can see it for yourself, as well as the house you and your sister will share. I hope they will be acceptable."

"Oh, I am certain they will be."

The two men exited Longbourn House and walked up the lane to the church. After a thorough inspection and a few moments for Mr. Yarby to kneel and give a prayer of thanksgiving, they continued on to the rector's cottage on the other side of the church. Mr. Bennet had never paid much attention to the house or its contents; such things had always been more under his wife's purview. And time spent in the company of the late reverend—outside of church services—was usually when Mrs. Bennet invited him to dine at Longbourn House. In fact, Mr. Bennet could not recall having set foot in the parsonage more than a half dozen times in the past decade.

Now, he saw to his dismay that the furnishings were in far from top condition. The draperies appeared dingy. There was grime and wear on the arm rests of some of the chairs and—heavens!—was the carpet in the sitting room a bit threadbare? He felt embarrassed and cleared his throat.

"Of course, we shall make some upgrades and improvements for you. Mr. Dudley was with us for so long…and never complained… but I can see a bit of freshening up is clearly in order."

"That would be very generous of you, sir, but such changes would be costly. We can take it as it is. I am sure we would be content."

"No, no, I insist. Mr. Dudley was a widower, you see, so there was no lady of the house to keep things as fashionable as they might have been. I cannot have you and Mrs. Withers live in such a state. We shall consult with Mrs. Bennet about improvements as soon as she returns from the North."

"I am most grateful, sir."

"Well, let us locate your sister and my daughter and tell them the good news. I shall write the bishop at once to inform him of my decision. You were one of three names he submitted, so he can have no objection, and I own the advowson for Longbourn parish in any case, so it is ultimately my choice."

"Again, I thank you, Mr. Bennet. Amelia—that is, Mrs. Withers— will be so very pleased."

The two men left the vicarage and walked back towards Longbourn. As they reached the edge of the property, Mrs. Hill rushed to meet them, waving an envelope.

"Oh, there you are! An express, Mr. Bennet," she gasped, holding an arm to her plump side. "It was delivered just moments ago."

"Thank you, Hill." Mr. Bennet opened the envelope and scanned it. "Good Lord," he muttered.

"Mr. Bennet, are you well?" Mr. Yarby asked. "You have gone quite pale."

Mr. Bennet shook his head a moment, pulled out a handkerchief and wiped his face. "How soon do you think you can be available, Mr. Yarby? I believe I shall need your services very soon." He studied the message again, then raised a pained face to the new rector. "It appears my wife is dead."

Chapter 4

"Mr. Collins is here, sir. Shall I tell him you are too grief-stricken to see him?" Mrs. Hill spoke hopefully but softly, knowing that the rector who would one day claim Longbourn as his own—and perhaps be her new employer—was waiting just outside the book room in the entry hall.

"Thank you, Hill, but I suppose I must allow him in. He has come, no doubt, to condole with me about Mrs. Bennet's death. Although how he heard of it so soon, I cannot imagine."

"Sir William Lucas, would be my guess," she grumbled.

Mr. Bennet sighed. "Yes, he likely sent an express as soon as he learned the news. Very well then, send Mr. Collins in. But do not bring tea unless I call for it. I hope his condolences will be brief, and I am reluctant to extend his visit with courtesies."

Mrs. Hill nodded, then opened the door and gestured to the waiting rector to enter.

"Mr. Bennet, my good sir, how lovely to see you again!" Mr. Collins burst past Mrs. Hill with a hearty voice and took Mr. Bennet's outstretched hand firmly, pumping it several times. "How are you? You look very well indeed!"

"I am…as well as can be expected, Mr. Collins." Mr. Bennet was a bit startled at the effusiveness of the greeting. "It is good of you to call." He gestured to a chair for Mr. Collins and took his own chair behind his desk.

Mr. Collins plopped down and continued his exuberant address. "Well, as I told my dear Charlotte, it has been far too long since I have visited you all here at Longbourn. I am delighted to return, although I hope my unannounced visit is not inconvenient."

Mr. Bennet paused, trying to decipher the man's meaning. "Oh, no. No advance notice was necessary. I suppose I should have expected you by now."

"Oh, indeed—I am glad to hear you were thinking of me at this time." Mr. Collins give Mr. Bennet a wink, beaming with happiness. Then his expression turned serious, and he bowed his head, shaking it slowly as he continued. "Such a loss for the whole parish—a good old soul, depend upon it. Although getting on in years. It was not to be completely unexpected, I suppose."

Mr. Bennet, a good fifteen years older than his late wife, did not know just how to respond. He was feeling more and more confounded and insulted by his babbling guest who continued on without waiting for a response.

"Indeed, I do not know why I did not contact you as soon as I heard of your loss." Mr. Collins gave another wink.

"But"—Mr. Bennet paused once more, even more perplexed—"did you *not*? I mean…here you are now. And it only occurred two days ago, after all."

Mr. Collins gave a start. "But…I was under the impression the tragic loss took place a month ago."

"A month? She had only been north a little more than two weeks."

"*She? North?* My dear Mr. Bennet, of whom are you speaking?"

"My wife, of course! Of whom are *you* speaking?"

"Why, the reverend Mr. Dudley who passed away a month or more ago. My dear wife informs me that you have not yet filled the position, so I hurried here to assure you of my willingness to step in."

"I see. So you did *not* come here today to condole with me upon the passing of Mrs. Bennet?" Mr. Bennet said slowly.

He watched as Mr. Collins finally seemed fully aware of the situation and began to stammer in embarrassment.

"Mrs. Bennet? She has…died?" He fumbled in his coat for a handkerchief and mopped a damp brow. "How on earth…that is…no—I had no idea of your loss! My dear Mr. Bennet, I never would have broached the subject of the open position at Longbourn parish had I known. Please forgive me my rudeness—to discuss business affairs at such a time. I am utterly mortified. It sprang entirely from ignorance of your situation, I assure you. I am quite grieved to hear of Mrs. Bennet's sudden death—excessively grieved, indeed. How on earth did this tragedy occur?" He bowed his head, then mopped his face again.

Finally able to comprehend his cousin's bizarre behavior, Mr. Bennet sucked in a slow breath. "That is perfectly all right, Mr. Collins. I can see from whence the confusion arose. It did cross my mind that Sir William had notified you of the accident, which accounted for your swift arrival. But, of course, that would be quite remarkable since word of her death only reached *me* yesterday. My wife had a fall while visiting our daughter Lydia. The funeral is set for three days from now after Lydia, Lizzy, Jane, and their families arrive."

"You are too kind to speak of forgiveness, but no, my manners were reprehensible. How can I possibly make it up to you, my dear, dear Mr. Bennet?"

His host sighed. "Do not be hard on yourself, sir. Be assured that I accept your apology." "Thank you. I am so grateful." Mr. Collins's face brightened. "Oh—but I can still be of assistance. Since the living here is vacant, I shall be more than happy to step up and conduct Mrs. Bennet's funeral service. It will also give you a good idea of the kind of stirring sermon I am capable of when I am rector here and assure you of the good sense of hiring me."

Mr. Bennet tried to hide a smile. "I do not have the pleasure of understanding you, Mr. Collins—*hire* you? Do you mean to say you would quit Hunsford? You would leave the patronage of the great Lady Catherine de Bourgh? I thought you were well situated there. Has something gone amiss?" He watched, amused, as his cousin's face turned a blotchy red from embarrassment.

"Well...as I said, I heard there is a vacancy here. And my dear Charlotte is expecting our first child; she wishes to be closer to her mother and father. So, even though the living at Longbourn is less than I am accustomed to, we thought—that is, it seemed the best course of action to offer..."

"I see. However, I fear I must disappoint you. The position has recently been filled." Mr. Bennet rose, put his hand on Mr. Collins's arm to guide him out of the chair, and began to steer him from the library towards the front door. "You are, of course, most welcome to attend the service along with your in-laws, the Lucases. However, your services in the pulpit will not be needed. Mr. Yarby will be more than capable, I have no doubt."

A painfully desperate look washed over Mr. Collins's face. "But... that is...is it absolutely finalized, Mr. Bennet? I was so hoping to start anew with my family here—"

"Quite settled." Mr. Bennet nodded as he opened the front door. "Well! I have much to deal with at this time; I am sure you understand. Thank you for calling, Mr. Collins—good day."

With a final pat on the back, Mr. Bennet shoved his guest out of Longbourn, closing the door firmly behind him.

THAT AFTERNOON, MARY WAS RESTING IN HER ROOM WHEN SHE heard a soft knock at the door.

"Come in." Expecting Mrs. Hill, or perhaps even her father, she was surprised and pleased to see Mrs. Withers enter her room. Mary quickly scooted off her bed where she had been curled up, tried to smooth her now rumpled dress, and put on her spectacles.

"Oh! I did not expect you, Mrs. Withers. Why did Hill not come for me?"

"Forgive me the intrusion, Miss Bennet, but my brother and I were visiting with your father and sister. When I did not see you, I asked Hill whether I could just slip up to check on you. The parlor is quite full of people just now, come to offer their sympathies."

"Yes, word has reached most people in the village by now. I...I suppose I should go down to meet our guests. It would only be proper."

"Kitty and your father are managing."

Anguish washed over Mary as she spoke bitterly. "Naturally. I am not needed. Why should anyone wish to speak to me, after all?"

Mrs. Withers crossed quickly to Mary and took her hands in her own.

"Oh, that was not my meaning at all! Pray forgive me for distressing you." She guided Mary to sit beside her on the bed. "I only meant you should go down when you feel up to it. I am certain your presence is greatly missed."

Mary shook her head sadly. "And I am every bit as certain no one has even noticed my absence. You are too new to the area to know yet, but I am the unseen Bennet sister."

Mary fumbled in her dress pocket for a handkerchief, wiped her eyes, and blew her nose. "Forgive me; I am quite ashamed of my outburst. The sharing of my emotions is ill-timed just now. My thoughts should be on Papa, Kitty, and the others—not on myself."

"You may be assured of my discretion. As for your comments...well, doubtless it is the tremendous stress you feel. Certainly, once you are past the shock of it all, happier memories will surface to comfort you."

Mary gave her a wry look. "Your optimism is duly noted." She made an exasperated noise and shook herself. "Enough! I must go and do my duty as my father's daughter. Shall we go together?" She began to move towards the door when Mrs. Withers gently put a hand out and stopped her.

"Will...will you allow me to assist you with your hair before we leave, Miss Bennet? It is a bit mussed from lying down. You wish to look your best, I am sure."

Mary gave her companion a long look. "As if anyone would notice. Besides, does not the holy book warn against vanity? Our focus should be on higher things."

Mrs. Withers simply smiled, steered Mary to the dressing table, and made her sit. Before Mary could say another word, the widow had undone her hair and was combing out the tangles. As she brushed and arranged Mary's tresses, she kept up a quiet conversation.

"While undue vanity *is* a sin, I believe there is nothing wrong with trying to look our best while in this world. After all, does not our Lord wish all his creatures to be at their best? Why did he make flowers so lovely if they were not to be admired? I see no reason not to make the most of our physical gifts. No one would ever call me a great beauty, but I still do what I can with what the good Lord gifted me." After pulling back most of Mary's hair and securing it a bit loosely, she took the remainder and began to braid two thin side plaits and pin them in loops that framed Mary's narrow face.

"Oh—I do not wear it that way," Mary protested.

"But it will flatter your face—just watch."

Too tired to argue, Mary let her continue. When Mrs. Withers was done, Mary studied her reflection. She had always just pulled her hair back somewhat severely from her face, never making the most of its natural wavy tendencies. But now she saw how this new style softened her features. Heavens! It made her look—well, if not handsome exactly—at least a little less plain.

"Oh my," she whispered, leaning forward to see every detail in the mirror. "I look quite different..."

Mrs. Withers beamed. "You see? I did not have time to do anything very elaborate, but I think it quite pretty. Does that not give you a bit more courage to face the world?"

Mary blinked back tears, reached up, and clutched her friend's hand. "It does. Thank you."

Together, they descended the stairs and entered the formal parlor. If anyone noticed Mary's new appearance, the only one to comment was Kitty, who stared at her briefly before blurting out, "Good heavens, what have you done with your hair?"

Unable to think of a reply, Mary felt a surge of relief when Mrs. Withers, standing nearby, came to her rescue again.

"Is it not lovely? Your sister had truly been hiding her beautiful hair like a light under a bushel as it says in the Bible—but no longer."

Stunned by all the attention, Mary allowed Mrs. Withers to take her by the arm and walk her towards a group of visitors.

"Do be so kind as to introduce me to your guests, Miss Bennet," Mrs. Withers said in a low voice. "I am so eager to meet all who are a part of Robert's new parish."

The mention of the handsome rector gave Mary a brief start. Had *he* noticed how well she looked? She quickly gazed across the room where Mr. Yarby was speaking with her father. The rector glanced up and smiled before returning to his conversation. The briefest of looks—but Mary felt her heart swell. Then she found herself introducing Mrs. Withers to her aunt and uncle Phillips.

THAT EVENING, AS SHE PREPARED FOR BED, MARY WAS RELUCTANT to comb out her hair. She studied it again carefully, hopeful that she could somewhat replicate it in the morning. Or she might ask Sarah, the underhousemaid, for help. Sarah often had acted as a lady's maid to Mrs. Bennet, so she could certainly manage the new style, Mary thought. It had always been her desire to avoid vanity and eschew any great consideration to her looks, but now…she felt somewhat differently about it.

Mary braided her hair into one long plait, changed into her night-clothes, and said her nightly prayers. Would it be conceited to ask the Lord to have Mr. Yarby pay her a bit of attention? She concluded it probably would be.

But she added it to her prayers just the same.

Chapter 5

The next two days were a blur for the entire Bennet family. Friends and acquaintances came and went, offering condolences and eating liberally of the trays of treats Mrs. Hill and Sarah refreshed near continuously. Jane arrived with her husband, Charles Bingley, although they left their three children behind with the nursemaid. Lydia had also left her twin sons at home with her husband, George Wickham.

"Wicky was simply too busy with work to get away, Papa, but he sends his most sincere condolences."

Mr. Bennet, who had merely nodded, had been privately grateful for that son-in-law's absence. "I wish to speak to you at some point, Lydia, about the details of the fall your mother took."

Lydia had burst into tears. "Oh, Papa, I cannot speak of it even now! All I can tell you is she took a misstep and tumbled down the stairs. I saw the whole thing…it was dreadful!" Her weeping had escalated into full-fledged wailing, and as if on cue, Mrs. Hill had appeared to drag Lydia off to the kitchen for a strong cup of tea.

The last to arrive were Lizzy and Fitzwilliam Darcy in their finest carriage; it was drawn by four horses bearing black ostrich feathers in the headpiece of their bridles and attended by two footmen. Mindful of the crowded conditions at her childhood home with the presence of Jane, Lydia, and the Gardiners, Lizzy had reserved a suite of rooms in Meryton's finest inn, much to the disappointment of Jane who told her she had hoped for some intimate discussions with her favorite sister. However, Lizzy assured her they would be at Longbourn House most of the time.

"Besides, we just saw each other quite recently," she said in a low voice. "Fitzwilliam and I just need some peace. And you know as well as I that, with Lydia here, peace may be decidedly lacking at Longbourn."

Mr. Bennet gave his second daughter a long, heartfelt embrace. He could see that the hurried trip from Pemberley had been somewhat arduous, and after a brief chat, he sent them away.

"Go along to your inn and return tonight for supper," he told the couple. "We have it all well in hand. You need your rest."

"Well, if you are certain, Papa, thank you."

She and Darcy quickly greeted the other family members and departed.

AFTER DINING, THE FAMILY GATHERED ONCE MORE IN THE PARLOR. It was a somber group, made more so by the black clothing everyone now wore. Even Lydia, who always loved to be the center of attention, was subdued. She and Kitty quietly played piquet at a side table. No one spoke. What was there to say, after all? Yet the silence only seemed to emphasize the absence of Mrs. Bennet. She could always be depended upon to keep a lively—if sometimes a bit inane—conversation going in the evenings.

Jane and Lizzy sat side by side on the best settee, holding hands while their husbands stood by the fireplace, hands identically clasped behind their backs and similarly unable to think of anything to contribute.

Mary held her Bible, several ribbons marking appropriate passages she was ready to read as a comfort to her family. Her offer to do so, however, had been roundly rejected, much to her dismay. So she, too, sat quietly. The ticking of the clock was the only sound in the room as everyone considered their grief over the loss of Mrs. Bennet.

A knock at the door brought an almost audible exhalation of relief from the room, and Mrs. Hill showed Mr. Yarby into the room. The rector went straight to Mr. Bennet and asked how he was faring.

Mr. Bennet nodded slowly. "Thank you, Mr. Yarby, I am fairly well. It helps to have my daughters with me. You have not met all of them, and they are eager to make your acquaintance."

Mr. Bennet made the rounds, introducing his other children and their spouses. Then he motioned Mr. Yarby to take a seat. As it happened, the only available place was next to Mary on the other settee. Mary clutched her Bible more tightly as he settled in beside her, hoping nobody noticed her sudden nerves.

Mr. Yarby cleared his throat before speaking. "Mr. Bennet, I am sensitive to your request that your dear departed wife not be laid out in your home prior to her burial."

Lydia failed to smother a hysterical sob and ran from the room, crying, "I could not bear it!" Kitty rose to follow, but catching a glance from her father, sat again, her focus respectfully on the new rector.

After a moment, Mr. Yarby began again. "All the arrangements are in order. Following a short prayer and hymn, we shall process from the church to the graveyard. The rest of the liturgy will be conducted graveside. Is that as you wish?"

"Yes, Mrs. Bennet would not have wanted a big fuss."

Mary caught a brief but amused glance exchanged by the Darcys. She knew what her sister was thinking: a big fuss was exactly what Mrs. Bennet would have chosen. She started to say so, but her father interrupted.

"No. A simple burial would be best."

"Then, with your permission, sir, following the prayers but prior to lowering the casket, I should like to say a few words about Mrs. Bennet. It is a new thing many rectors are doing these days—sharing a few anecdotes about the deceased. Often it brings a sense of peace to those left behind, as it can be pleasant to end on some happy memories. However, since I am new here, I did not have the pleasure of knowing her. I thought you might all share a few thoughts to help me."

There was a long pause as the family waited for Mr. Bennet to speak. When he did not, Mary said piously, "She always enjoyed Sunday church service."

"Mostly to dress up in her best and get the latest gossip," added Lizzy with a small grin.

Mary was shocked at this comment and grateful when Jane jumped in.

"That may be true, Lizzy, but she did care very much about our estate tenants. Why, I can remember helping her put together Christmas baskets for them from my earliest years."

Lizzy, Kitty, and Mary nodded in agreement.

"She…" Kitty began. "That is, Mama also greatly enjoyed socializing. She was quite proud of the number of families she and Papa dined with—four and twenty!"

"Even if she had to nearly drag Papa from his study to do so," said Jane in a loving voice. There were soft chuckles all around.

"And balls and assemblies were the highlight of her year," added Lizzy. "Even after she gave up dancing herself."

"She was devoted to her girls," Mr. Bennet finally said in a husky voice.

"Devoted to finding us all husbands, you mean," said Kitty. "Mary, you and I must depend upon our older sisters for a match now." She snorted. "Not that you ever show any signs of interest in the opposite sex."

Mary blushed furiously and lowered her eyes. *So like Kitty to say something thoughtless like that!* She opened her mouth to respond, but to her surprise, Mr. Yarby reached over, patted her hand gently, and spoke.

"Two such lovely girls from as fine a family as this will have no problem securing eligible matches. I have no doubt."

Mary turned her face to Mr. Yarby in gratitude. His kind words lifted her heart. In the corner of her eye, she caught Kitty also staring at the new rector with a queer little smile.

It struck Mary that her sister's face was just like a cat who had spied a dish of cream.

FIVE DAYS PASSED IN WHAT SEEMED A HEARTBEAT, AND ELIZABETH now sat with her father in his study.

"Papa, I hate to leave you so soon," she said softly. "But Fitzwilliam is determined we shall leave on the morrow. Every day we delay makes the journey that much harder on me, and he fears for our unborn child."

"Pay it no heed, Lizzy, I am still somewhat amazed and grateful that you made the difficult journey at all."

"Well, of course I wished to be here—we both did. You could come back with us if you like. It might be good to have a change of scene after such a…difficult time. And we would love to have you."

"Thank you, but not just yet, my dear. Longbourn would seem every bit as empty coming back after time with you as it does now. Besides, I cannot abandon Kitty and Mary completely. And I have much to do to help Mr. Yarby and his sister settle in." He gave her a wan smile. "But know that I do not make this decision lightly or without significant regret; you know how much I enjoy your husband's fine library."

Lizzy nodded. "I also offered to take Kitty back with us, but to my surprise, she said no. I thought she would jump at the chance to spend time at Pemberley; she always loved to do so in the past. But she told me she would rather stay here at Longbourn for now."

Mr. Bennet smiled. "Could it be my second youngest is growing a sense of responsibility? One can only hope. She asked me whether

Mr. Yarby and his sister could be invited to dine with us tonight. I told her yes, and she fairly ran from my study to go invite them."

"Well, he does appear to be better company than poor Mr. Dudley ever was. But perhaps it signals a noble reason? Perhaps Kitty is taking an interest in doing some good works for Meryton's less fortunate."

Mr. Bennet chuckled. "Even I cannot raise my hopes quite that far, my dear."

Chapter 6

Mary sat in her room after dinner, fuming—her sister Kitty the source of her ire. Throughout the evening, Kitty had flirted shamelessly with Mr. Yarby. At least, that is how it appeared to Mary. But now she reflected on the possibility that she was overreacting and tried to give her sister the benefit of any doubt.

As the reverend Mr. Dudley often said, "It behooves us all to think most carefully before pronouncing an adverse judgment upon our neighbor." Perhaps Kitty was just being friendly. Oh, but the smiles Kitty sent his way. And the smiles returned to her!

On one hand, Mary felt anger over the attention her sister paid Mr. Yarby and jealousy as he seemed to welcome her comments. On the other hand, Mary found it implausible that Kitty would truly ever wish to set her cap for a rector. Being a preacher's wife would certainly not give Kitty the lifestyle to which she aspired. She was far too interested in fine clothing, ribbons, and dancing at assemblies. Try as she might, Mary could not imagine Kitty making the rounds of the parish families, offering solace and comfort when needed, much less making do with the same gowns year after year. Mary knew precisely how much the living at Longbourn paid, and it was not a handsome sum.

I could be happy with it, though. I have never wished to spend my pocket money on ribbons, lace, and new bonnets. Buying books to educate myself is a far better use of my shillings.

Mary gasped softly. Of course! That is how she would win over Mr. Yarby—with her mind. Her thoughts flew back to Mr. Collins's arrival at Longbourn that first time. He had made it clear that, in order to make up to Mrs. Bennet that he would one day be the cause of their eviction, he was agreeable to selecting a wife from among the five Bennet sisters. His first choice had been Jane, of course, as the eldest—and the most beautiful; he was mindful of the necessary respect to choose her. However, Mama had firmly but gently quashed that idea, telling Mr. Collins that Jane was likely soon to be engaged.

Then his eyes had fallen on Lizzy, another beauty, but whose personality, Mary knew, would never have been in harmony with that of Mr. Collins. In addition, Mary recalled that Lizzy had developed an attraction to George Wickham, and he had seemed to respond in kind. But as nothing was official between them, Mr. Collins had begun his dogged pursuit of Lizzy to be his wife, monopolizing her in lengthy conversations. Mary also recalled how Jane—in order to discourage Mr. Collins from interfering with the budding romance between Lizzy and Mr. Wickham—had devised a plan to help. She had asked Mary to pretend to be confused over a passage in *Fordyce's Sermons* to distract Mr. Collins from Lizzy's side and entice him to help Mary.

Little did Jane know that I agreed to do that not to help Lizzy, but to help myself. I was alone among my sisters who found Mr. Collins a good potential match, and I even now recall his admiring look towards me after our discussion. But then he went and proposed to Lizzy anyway, only to have her reject him so soundly that he flew into the arms of Charlotte Lucas without even a thought to me!

But this may yet be the way to Mr. Yarby's heart. I shall go to him and ask for his opinion on one or two scripture passages. Then he will know, as Mrs. Withers so kindly put it, that I am not a "flibbertigibbet" but a serious young woman who would quite clearly be his perfect romantic match. After all, I am two-and-twenty—the very same age Jane was when she accepted Mr. Bingley.

Feeling much happier now that she had a plan, Mary began to ready herself for bed.

MR. AND MRS. COLLINS ARRIVED HOME, WEARY IN MIND AND BODY from the long journey back to Hunsford Parsonage. Charlotte was especially tired as she had rushed to Meryton to attend Mrs. Bennet's funeral as soon as her husband sent word of it. Although she would have liked to stay at Lucas Lodge longer to have a good visit with her parents and her sister, Maria, Charlotte had to admit that Mr. Collins was right: they must return at once. The curate from a neighboring parish had been tasked with conducting the Sunday services while they were away. Young Mr. Manson had been most grateful to substitute, but Charlotte knew Mr. Collins was nervous about how Lady Catherine would react.

"I do hope Mr. Manson's first sermon was satisfactory," Charlotte said as the two entered the cottage. "I confess I did worry his inexperience might set Lady Catherine off on another tirade."

Her husband nodded. "My dear, that is precisely why I directed him not to attempt to write his own homily as I often do but, rather, to read one from my favorite book of printed sermons. It cannot have been too horrible if he followed my instructions."

The two were greeted by their maid, Betsy, who, after welcoming them home, handed them an envelope.

"I was instructed to give this to you directly, Mr. Collins, the moment you returned." She bobbed her head and left the room.

Turning it over, Mr. Collins saw the wax seal bore the imprint of de Bourgh.

"From Lady Catherine? What could this be?" he muttered as he broke the seal. He quickly scanned the page filled with her ladyship's familiar, spidery handwriting.

"Oh no. Oh no!" he exclaimed.

"My dear, what is it?" Charlotte asked.

He passed her the pages, then stumbled to a chair and sat heavily, his head in his hands.

"We are dismissed!" he cried. "Banished! How could she? How shall I bear the humiliation of losing her patronage? Oh, the scandal!"

Charlotte carefully read the pages, hoping her husband had somehow misread or misunderstood. But it was clear that he was correct: they were being sent away from Hunsford.

Mr. Collins,

For some time now, I have found myself ill at ease with your handling of Hunsford Parish. Your sermons are flat and uninspired, and I have observed many a dreary face in the congregation depart the church week after week. Clearly, you are not lifting any of the parish members towards a higher awareness of God.

On the other hand, this most recent Sunday, the curate, Mr. Manson, gave a spectacular and stirring sermon—one that members in the community still speak of and continues to ring in my memory. So erudite and enlightening.

In addition, you have failed in one of your more important duties of the parish—managing the maintenance of the roads. Last week, a wheel of my second-favorite carriage fell into a large hole in the road, breaking the axle. I was lucky not to have been killed. I have spoken to the local surveyors of our highways and learned that you have paid scant attention to this duty over the past two years—no doubt, the reason for the dreadful conditions that led to my accident.

Such negligence and dereliction of duty cannot stand. I have spoken to the bishop, and he agrees that you are to be released from your post as rector of Hunsford at once. The curate, Mr. Manson, will assume your role beginning this Sunday.

I shall make my third-best carriage available to you and your wife to transport you and your personal belongings to wherever you wish to go—within limits, of course. Please vacate the parish cottage by Tuesday next.

Enclosed is a cheque to assist you and Mrs. Collins in the coming days.

Thank you for your service.

Lady Catherine de Bourgh

There was one additional page—the letter from the bishop with the official notification of Mr. Collins's dismissal. *No hope then*, thought Charlotte. A wave of anxiety and sorrow washed over her. To have to leave her lovely home where she had been so happy these past few years! Where might they end up? How could Mr. Collins even find another living, much less one as well-off as Lady Catherine's? If she were perfectly honest with herself, Charlotte would have to admit that the security Mr. Collins offered her at Hunsford was the primary reason she wed him. *Now what?*

Charlotte pulled out the cheque. Thirty pounds. More generous than she would have expected from the old skinflint. She tucked it into her pocket and turned to her still-moaning husband. Dismayed as she was, Charlotte forced herself to swallow her grief and assume an optimistic attitude.

"Let us eat something and go to bed, dearest. Tomorrow things will look brighter."

"But where are we to go?"

"Well...back to Meryton, of course," she replied. "We shall stay with my parents for the time being."

"And then...?" Mr. Collins heaved himself to his feet.

Charlotte gave him a kiss on the cheek and attempted a smile. "We shall see what the good Lord sends to us."

DESPITE GRIEVING HIS WIFE (AND HE WAS SOMEWHAT SURPRISED to find that, despite her annoying ways, he truly *did* miss her presence), Mr. Bennet did not forget his promise to refurbish the parsonage at Longbourn. Eight days after the funeral, he presented himself at the cottage to speak with his new rector. However, he found only Mrs. Withers present. She invited him into the front parlor.

"My brother has returned to Dorset to see to all the details of moving our possessions," she said as she took her seat. "I offered to do it, but he insisted it would be too much for me, so off he went. In truth, I suspect he wanted to handle the packing of his library himself."

"He enjoys reading?" asked Mr. Bennet.

"Indeed, we both do. Although I hope your opinion of me will not fall when I confess that I enjoy popular novels as well as more serious works." Amelia smiled, and again Mr. Bennet was struck by how the small act improved her appearance. "In any event, I expect Robert back on Friday, or Saturday at the latest, so you need not worry about Sunday's service."

"I came to discuss the renovations of the parsonage with him, but perhaps it is best that you are here instead," Mr. Bennet said. "Such things usually fall under the guidance of the female sex, after all."

"Yes. Robert told me of your generous offer. It is so kind. I have taken the liberty to write up a few suggestions. I shall show them to you, but only if you promise not to think me too impertinent."

"Not at all. You seem to be a lady who knows her own mind and moves ahead accordingly, for which I can have no criticism. May I see your list?"

Amelia pulled a piece of paper from her pocket, smoothed it, and handed it to him.

"I keep it with me at all times so that, when I see something to add, I have it handy. I hope it is not too extravagant. Items could certainly be cut, be assured; it is just an initial assessment. Did you...have a budget in mind?"

Mr. Bennet perused the paper. He quickly saw that her keen eye had seen many of the same issues he had discovered when he first showed the parsonage to Mr. Yarby.

"My budget is somewhat flexible, although I was certainly hoping to make improvements for less than thirty pounds. This all seems very much in order." He looked again. "Oh, but you did not write down new curtains or paper for the walls for this room. Do you not think them very dated and dingy? Mr. Dudley was a pipe smoker, and I can see that has left its mark."

"I *did* note it, Mr. Bennet, but I felt that change might be too much of an extravagance at this time. Fresh upholstery for the furniture and a new rug in here will be costly enough. We can easily manage with what is here."

Mr. Bennet shook his head, and chuckled. "No, I believe the redone chair and settee with the new rug will only make the sad condition of the walls and draperies that much more apparent. You should go into Meryton and pick out the paper pattern and fabric you like. Have them send the bill to me. Then we shall hire the workmen necessary."

"You are too kind. And may I just say how very grateful I am to you for giving Robert the living? To have an entire house for ourselves? It is a dream come true! In Dorset, we rented somewhat cramped rooms above a shop in town; curates, as you know, are not provided any housing, and it was all we could afford. We shall both be so happy here at Longbourn."

"Will you miss your friends in Dorset?"

He watched as she considered her answer. "I shall. But if you will forgive me a tiny brag, I believe I am one of those fortunate people who can be content in almost any situation. After all, one is only as happy as one makes up one's *mind* to be."

"I am glad to hear it. But, could new paper for the walls not make one even happier?"

Amelia gave a musical laugh. "Indeed, it would, Mr. Bennet. Indeed, it would."

MR. AND MRS. COLLINS SPOKE BUT LITTLE ON THEIR JOURNEY back to Meryton. They had hastily packed what they would need most immediately and arranged for the rest to be shipped. In truth, there was not that much to deal with, seeing as how the Hunsford Parsonage came fully furnished. Therefore, they took their clothing and personal effects as well as books and wedding gifts that they could call their own.

Mr. Collins had attempted one last time to speak to Lady Catherine, but he was refused entry to Rosings Park. He had to content himself with writing a letter to his former patron, thanking her for all she had done for him over the years. He did not fool himself into thinking a gracious farewell missive would change her mind, but he was smart enough to realize that showing Lady Catherine his true disappointment and anger would only serve to harden her heart against him when it came to any reference she might later be inclined to write. A good recommendation would be invaluable to finding a new living.

Therefore, his mood was quite dejected as they left Hunsford. Charlotte did her best to raise his spirits even as she disguised her own sorrow, reminding him that the Lord would provide for them.

"Besides," she added, "it may well be that you will find yourself a landed gentleman quite soon. Mrs. Bennet has died, and it is not unlikely that her husband may follow quickly. I have oft heard of someone succumbing to despair and dying soon after losing their life partner. Not that I would wish it, mind you, but it is a possibility that you will inherit sooner rather than later. After all, did not Mr. Bennet turn fifty-eight just last year?"

But Mr. Collins could only give a wan smile. "It seems too much to hope for. In the meantime, how am I to earn a living?" he asked, mournfully.

"Something will occur for us," Charlotte replied in what she hoped was a confident tone. "I have written to Eliza, telling her of our troubles."

"Charlotte! How could you share my humiliation with her—and by association, Mr. Darcy?"

Charlotte calmly patted his hand. "Be at ease, dear heart. I wrote her because she and Mr. Darcy are people of great importance in Derbyshire and have many connections. It may well be they know of an opening and could put your name forward. A letter penned by Mr. Darcy from Pemberley would certainly be taken note of by any recipient. I have great confidence we shall be settled in a new parish quite soon."

She sat back and turned her attention to the passing landscape, trying to lessen the anxiety in her own chest.

"Oh dear."

"What's that, Lizzy?" Mr. Darcy asked his wife at lunch.

Darcy's sister, Georgiana, was dining with friends, so they were alone. Their butler, Barton, had delivered a just-arrived letter that Lizzy saw with delight was from a longtime friend.

"Oh, it is this letter from Charlotte," she said, perusing it a second time to be certain she had read it accurately.

"Bad news?"

She gave him a wry smile. "That depends on your point of view. It seems Lady Catherine has dismissed Mr. Collins from Hunsford Parsonage."

"Why on earth would she do that? I cannot imagine she would find a more—how did you put it to me once?—a more 'grateful object' of her largess than Mr. Collins."

"Charlotte does not write the exact reason behind Lady Catherine's actions, only to say he somehow fell out of favor. They are heading to Meryton."

"To take on the duties at Longbourn?"

"No—at least, I do not think so. Papa had promised the living to Mr. Yarby just before we learned of Mama's death. And then Yarby handled everything so well at the service. I cannot imagine Papa would turn him out in favor of Mr. Collins of all people."

"Well, that is a relief. It was hard enough to hear him drone his sermons whenever I visited Lady Catherine before we married. It would be punishment indeed to have to endure him at your father's church."

"Yes, but Charlotte begs us for assistance. She is hoping we may know of another living to which we could recommend Mr. Collins. Having a home of her own is so important to Charlotte. I know she must be worried about their future. Oh! Is not Lord Wellsford's parish vacant at present?"

"My dear, Lord Wellsford is a longtime family friend. I could not risk losing his affection by saddling him with Mr. Collins!"

"But Charlotte is with child. How will her husband provide for his family if we do not help?"

Mr. Darcy rose. "I shall tell you what I *will* do, my dear. I shall write a few notes to more *distant* acquaintances of mine about any openings they may know of. Perhaps we shall be in luck and an opening will appear in the westernmost tip of Cornwall." He winked, leaned over to kiss his wife's cheek, and exited the room.

Chapter 7

Mary sat upstairs in her bedchamber, poring over her well-worn Bible. She might have been more comfortable in the family sitting room downstairs, but she wanted complete privacy for her study. If her plan should be discovered—even suspected—by Kitty, all would be lost. Kitty would likely ridicule her, perhaps in front of Mr. Yarby and his sister! She could never bear that sort of humiliation. No—best to keep her strategy to win the rector's heart a closely held secret.

Mary searched for a passage that Mr. Yarby might reasonably believe confounded her. But there was a problem: she had shamefully displayed her knowledge of the good book during the rector's visit after the funeral. She had glowed with pride when he praised her after their discussion of Proverbs. Now, she wished she had kept silent and not exhibited so.

She thought about the rector's most recent sermon; perhaps there was something in that for her to question. But no—it was a simple, well-presented homily and left nothing for her to grasp as confusing or in need of explanation.

She sighed and leafed through the book of John when her eyes fell on verse seven: *"If ye abide in me, and my words abide in you, ye shall ask what ye will, and it shall be done unto you."*

This has possibilities, she mused. Mary carefully put her bookmark in the page and closed the Bible. The more she thought about it, the better it seemed. But when should she go to see Mr. Yarby? The timing must be just right.

A knock at her bedroom door interrupted her thoughts.

"Come in."

The door opened, and Sarah, the underhousemaid, poked her head in. "Beggin' your pardon, miss, but Mrs. Withers is downstairs and asked to see you."

"Tell her I shall be down directly." After Sarah left, Mary checked herself in the mirror, wishing she had put on a nicer dress—even if she was still wearing black. But her hair was the same flattering style Mrs. Withers had done before, so Mary thought she did not appear too plain. She proceeded downstairs.

"Mrs. Withers, what a nice surprise," Mary said as she reached the entry hall where her friend waited.

"Good morning, Miss Bennet. I hope my unexpected visit is no inconvenience."

"No, I was just in my room reading the Bible." Mary attempted not to sound excessively pious. It would not hurt for Mrs. Withers to mention that fact to her brother, surely.

"Well, I was just going to walk into Meryton to examine samples of fabric and paper for the parsonage upgrades your father is kindly paying for, and I thought, perhaps, if you were not too busy, you might accompany me. Your opinion would be most helpful. But if you would rather study..."

Mary felt a jolt of happiness. "Oh—no, I would love to go! Let me collect my shawl and reticule. Perhaps we could stop at the bookshop as well? There is a new book of sermons by Charles Simeon of Trinity Church in Cambridge that might be available."

"I am certain we could find time. Excellent!"

"Oh, good morning, Mrs. Withers. I thought I heard your voice."

The two ladies turned to see Mr. Bennet standing in the door of his book room.

"Are you come for a visit regarding the renovations? Mary, go to the kitchen and order us tea; there's a good girl."

Mary stood stock still, unable to devise a reply. Once again, she watched as Mrs. Withers smoothly took charge of the conversation.

"In truth, I am come to beg your daughter's assistance, Mr. Bennet. She has agreed to accompany me to Meryton to choose fabric and wall paper for the parsonage. We were just about to depart."

Mary glimpsed a perplexed expression on her father's face as he blinked once or twice. "Mary?" he asked. "I am sorry; did you say you wish *her* opinion?"

"Indeed, I do! I look forward to both her thoughts and lively conversation on our walk."

"*Lively* conversation, you say? Mary?" Mr. Bennet asked. "I am all astonishment."

Mary felt her face burn. Of course her father was surprised at the invitation; how often did anyone ask her anywhere? To her surprise, Mrs. Withers pulled her arm and tucked it possessively into her own. Mary caught a firm gaze in her friend's eyes as she stared at Mr. Bennet.

Humiliated, Mary lowered her eyes and mumbled, "If it is all right with you, Papa."

Mr. Bennet replied in a kinder voice. "Of course it is, my dear girl, perfectly fine. How lovely that Mrs. Withers has sought you out. Do enjoy yourselves, ladies." He turned and went into the study, shutting the door behind him.

Her humiliation only somewhat eased, Mary muttered to her friend that she would get her things and then they could leave for the village.

AS THEY STROLLED TOWARDS MERYTON, THE TWO LADIES CHAT-ted about nothing of consequence for a time. Then, Mrs. Withers stopped and put her hand on Mary's arm.

"Pray forgive my impertinence, Miss Bennet—and you need not reply if it is too painful—but how are you faring? Over the loss of your mother, I mean."

Mary took a deep breath before answering. "As well as can be expected, I suppose. In some ways, it still does not seem firmly fixed into my mind that she is gone. I keep expecting to hear her voice down the hall, or I look into her bedroom as I walk past and feel surprised not to see her lying there with one of her headaches.

"I miss her; yet, I must confess I am confused about my feelings. I have spent many hours since her passing trying to recall a specific kindness she ever showed me, or a compliment, or an encouraging word. Perhaps when I was very young, she might have thought me a delight—that is, after I returned from my foster mother—weaned and walking." Mary lifted a somber face to her new friend. "But for the life of me, I cannot recall any affection from Mama. From Jane and Lizzy, yes—they played with me for a time. But never Mama. Please do not think me disrespectful when I say that her criticisms come foremost to my mind when I think of my mother—criticism of my singing, my technique at the pianoforte, my plain looks. I wonder whether my very presence annoyed her. So, now that she is gone, I find myself grieving not the actual *loss* of Mama but the death of hope that I should ever find favor with her."

"I am so sorry to hear it, Miss Bennet. I hope—no, I *know* with time, your pain will ease. And your father—how is he?" The two began to walk again.

"As you saw, he keeps to his study much of the time. Of course, he

53

did so *before* Mama's death too. But I have noticed he has begun to take long walks in the afternoon, which he never did before. I have offered to accompany him, but he says he prefers the solitude."

"I see. And…where does he go on these rambles?"

"Through the wild area of our park—not far from the place we walked the first day we met. And from there along the fields of our tenants, I suppose."

"Your mother's death has left a great void for him, I am sure."

"Yes, but for me as well, it turns out," Mary said soberly. "As the eldest at home now, Papa has asked me to assume many of my mother's duties. It is now I who consult with Hill on the day's menu and I who must remind our maid to again dust the parlor after a first, careless attempt. And soon it will be time for me to supervise the making of jams and preserves from the fruit of our orchards. I am learning there was much Mama did of which I was blissfully unaware with my nose stuck in a book."

"I am sure your father must be grateful and proud of you for helping."

Mary gave a short laugh. "If he is, he keeps his opinion to himself for the most part—unless he does not like the dinner I ordered. I most definitely hear from him if *that* is the case."

The two walked on mostly in silence until they reached Meryton, where they began their quest for supplies. Mary was flattered that Mrs. Withers asked for her opinion on all the paper and fabric samples, even as she noted the way her friend cleverly promoted patterns clearly to her own taste.

"The rug I have chosen is in medium blue and cream tones, so I believe this fabric will go perfectly with that for the chairs, don't you agree, Mary?"

Mary gave a short gasp; Mrs. Withers had addressed her by her first name! She had not dreamt that their newfound friendship would presume such a step of intimacy.

As if knowing her thoughts, Mrs. Withers turned a kind face to

Mary. "I hope you will forgive me for using your Christian name so early in our acquaintance. But I truly feel we are kindred spirits, and our friendship is such that I should like to use first names between us. Unless that is not acceptable to you—you need only tell me. I shall not take offense."

Mary swallowed and firmly nodded. "No. I...I would very much like such familiarity." She smiled. "Indeed, I count you as a dear friend now...Amelia."

Amelia gave a satisfied nod and reached over to pick up two more paper samples. "Very good. Now...which of these do you prefer? I think the one with the birds most attractive, don't you?"

Mary, feeling a warm glow of happiness inside, nodded in agreement.

Chapter 8

"Charlotte! Welcome home, my dearest girl." Lady Lucas's husky voice called to her daughter as an elegant carriage arrived at the sweep in front of Lucas Lodge. Her younger daughter, Maria, bounced up and down on her toes in clear anticipation of seeing her elder sister.

Charlotte fairly bounded into her mother's waiting arms, then gave Maria a hug.

"It is so good to be back, Mother," she said warmly. "Thank you for taking us in on such short notice."

Mr. Collins, who had been directing the servants to unload the luggage, joined them. "Indeed, we are quite beholden to you, Lady Lucas. Your beneficent ways will be much appreciated and never forgotten, I assure you. We hope we shall not be too much of an inconvenience to you. I expect to be settled in a new situation quite soon, be assured. Oh yes, quite soon. My previous employment under the patronage of Lady Catherine de Bourgh will no doubt have great influence for any future applications."

"You are always quite welcome in our home, Mr. Collins," Lady Lucas replied evenly. "Whether it be a few weeks or…longer. We have plenty of room and look forward to a happy visit with you. Come! Let us go inside. Please direct your coachmen to the stables. I assume they will spend the night?"

"Yes, although we can return them immediately if you like," Mr. Collins said stiffly. "Although it is only her *third*-best carriage, Lady Catherine will surely wish it back promptly."

"But the horses need a rest, my dear," Charlotte said in a firm voice, then added with a pointed look, "Lady Catherine would be *most* displeased if they were returned to her in poor condition, would she not?"

Her tone knocked Mr. Collins out of his pique, and he nodded sullenly.

"Good!" Lady Lucas said brightly. She turned to the driver. "Our man will show you where you will stay tonight." Then she took Charlotte's arm and swept her into the house. "How are you feeling, dear? The first few months can be rocky for an expectant mother—as I well remember."

FOLLOWING REFRESHING CUPS OF TEA WITH FRESHLY BAKED currant cake, Charlotte continued to sit with her mother, although Mr. Collins, upon learning that Sir William was in London and not expected back for another week, announced he would go up to their guest room to settle in. His wife and mother-in-law nodded, barely pausing in their conversation to reply. Lady Lucas's other children were excused to go outside and play.

"Now, my dear," Lady Lucas began, when everyone had left, "we are all alone, and you can unburden yourself to me with no one to overhear. This is such shocking news you share. We have all been so proud of your husband's position at Hunsford. How did your husband come to be in the basket and lose the patronage of Lady Catherine?"

Charlotte gave a long exhalation before replying. "I fear my longtime association with Eliza is to blame."

"How so? What can *she* have to do with it?"

"Lady Catherine still hopes that Mr. Darcy will end his marriage to her and marry Miss de Bourgh. It is absurd, of course. By all accounts, he and Eliza are quite happy and she *is* pregnant with their second child. He would never set her aside that I can see. But for some reason, Lady Catherine has turned her disappointment into anger towards my poor William."

Lady Lucas shook her head. "But in most cases, only the bishop has the power to end a living. And there must be sufficient cause."

"Indeed, and she wrote that his lack of attention to the parish roads was cause enough. Frankly, such motivation for dismissing him seems a trifling excuse at best. But we all know how much power Lady Catherine wields. Perhaps a timely donation to the bishopric was all she needed for her wishes to be fulfilled."

"Well, no matter her motives, the result is the same. The most important thing now is for us to cut any malicious gossip firmly in the bud. Your husband's reputation is sullied, but so is ours by association. Therefore, we shall say that you are having a difficult pregnancy and that your husband brought you home so that you could be under my care. We shan't even speak of his dismissal but simply let people think he is taking a leave of absence. Such things are not unheard of; many a rector has left things in the hands of a curate for lengthy periods. With luck, word of Lady Catherine's actions will not reach Meryton for many months. And by then, he may well have a new position and you will be happily settled." She nodded and took a sip of her tea. "I know it is early days, but what are his prospects, do you think?"

"I have written to Eliza, asking her assistance in finding William a position. His new living might not come from such an illustrious patron, but that matters not. I also have suggested to my husband that he write to his former professors at Oxford. That university endows many livings, and perhaps one is vacant. A good word from a professor might secure it for him. Oh, Mama, I am so saddened to lose our home, but what counts most to me is that my husband put this disappointment behind him as soon as possible. William has a tendency towards a morose nature, you know."

"Becoming a parent will shake him out of that, to be sure!" Lady Lucas said briskly. "Fatherhood is quite a life-altering event. It turned your father into much more of a homebody than I ever would have guessed possible."

Charlotte nodded soberly. "I hope so. Although, we both know William is not very like Papa." She drank the dregs of her cold tea and asked as casually as possible, "How is Mr. Bennet doing? Since the death of his poor wife, I mean."

"Oh, I believe he misses her very much, much as he tries to hide it. At present, I hear he is much taken with renovations on the parsonage for the new rector, Mr. Yarby."

Charlotte rolled her eyes. "A position poor William and I were both hoping was still vacant so he could assume it and we could return to Meryton permanently."

"Poor timing—no doubt about it. But nothing to be done now."

"I don't suppose there is any chance of the congregants disliking Mr. Yarby enough to force Mr. Bennet to make a change?"

Lady Lucas laughed. "Put that thought away right now, my dear. Mr. Yarby is a gifted orator, and he has quite livened up services with his newfangled ideas."

"What do you mean?"

"Well, you know how dear Mr. Dudley often spoke of hellfire and damnation."

"As does William. He says it is important that people know a righteous and fearsome God awaits them when they stand before His throne."

"Yes…well, Mr. Yarby's sermons are much more…positive in tone. That is, he speaks of salvation of all souls through the Christ, and that we are not doomed to inevitable, eternal damnation. He often writes original sermons too instead of just reading the old familiar ones from books, and I must say they are quite compelling. Mr. Yarby preaches that we can all find a closer relationship with our Lord and Savior and use him as an example of how to live and treat our fellow man. It is quite refreshing to hear such things spoken from the pulpit. Your father is already a great admirer of Mr. Yarby, and we have had him and his sister, Mrs. Withers—she keeps house for him, you know—to dinner twice."

Charlotte swallowed her disappointment. "I see. And Mr. Bennet approves as well?"

"It appears so. At least, I have no reason to think he regrets his choice."

"Oh. And…Mr. Bennet's health—it continues to be well?"

"Indeed, I have seen no sign of illness or infirmity in him at—oh, Charlotte! Do not tell me you are *wishing* such things for him? That your husband may inherit early and have no need of a new position?"

"No! Not…really. It is just that the thought did cross my mind that many a husband or wife has pined themselves into an early grave after losing their spouse. And with Mr. Bennet having no sons and William set to be the next owner of Longbourn, I just…" Charlotte shook her head in exasperation. "No, you are quite right, Mama. I should not have such wicked thoughts. Forgive me."

"All will come around in the right way eventually, my dear; do not fret. Who knows how long until that day, but Mr. Collins will be the gentleman of Longbourn eventually. In the meantime, let us think optimistically that your husband will be settled in a new living very soon. And if not, well—I am quite eager to meet my first grandchild, you know!"

"Well, you have months and months to wait, Mama. I pray we shall be settled in a new parish by the time the baby comes."

Lady Lucas smiled. "A lot can happen in many months' time. No doubt about it."

MARY HESITATED BEFORE GENTLY KNOCKING ON THE DOOR OF her father's library. When he called to enter, she did so, but stood only a step or two inside the door.

"Papa, may I interrupt you for a moment?"

"What is it, my dear? More improvements for the parsonage that you and Mrs. Withers desire?"

Mary inexplicably felt herself blush. "No. I believe that is all well in hand. I did enjoy helping Amelia choose the fabric for the curtains, and I think you will approve of our choices when you see them."

"'Amelia' is it now?" Mr. Bennet raised his eyebrows. "Are you on such familiar terms as to use first names?"

"She is…that is…we are becoming good friends, Papa." Mary had just a hint of defensiveness in her voice. She watched her father study her a moment before smiling kindly.

"Well, I am glad to hear you are friends. It is important that Mrs. Withers feel at home here in Meryton. You are no doubt the first of many close acquaintances she will soon enjoy. And do not be too sad if, in time, her availability to you should diminish once her circle of acquaintances expands. She seems such lively company that one can hardly expect her to just stay friends with you or our family after all. I think she will be much in demand socially in due time."

Mary could only nod, crushed at his implication.

He thinks Amelia only pretends to like me because she is so new here. But we are bosom friends, I am certain.

"Well, well…off you go then, Mary, I have my accounts to work on." Mr. Bennet turned back to the ledger on his desk.

"But, Papa—I have not yet spoken to you of what I came to say."

"Oh. All right then, get on with it. What is on your mind?"

"Mr. and Mrs. Collins have been back in the neighborhood a full week now; they are staying at Lucas Lodge, you know. I was thinking we should invite them to dinner. Mama certainly would have done so by now."

Mr. Bennet gave a wry smile. "Are you certain? Your mother never quite forgave Charlotte for marrying Mr. Collins so quickly after Lizzy rejected his proposal, ending any chance of securing Longbourn for her—and perhaps you and Kitty when I die."

"Yes, but he is family after all—our cousin," said Mary, stubbornly. "I think it quite right to have them over. And Mama will not be troubled by his presence now of course."

Her blunt statement generated a smile from her father. "Very well." He consulted his desk calendar. "Invite them for dinner Tuesday next. And be sure to include Sir William and Lady Lucas so there will be someone with a bit of intelligent conversation in him with whom I can have sensible discourse."

Mary nodded and left the room to pen an invitation. When she finished, she decided to deliver it herself rather than send a servant. The June day was warm and lovely, and she felt a walk would do her good.

Rather than go along the main road, Mary took a side way that cut past the parsonage, telling herself that it was the shortest route, even as she knew her true motive was to perhaps run into Mr. Yarby or his sister. As she approached the cottage, she slowed her pace but saw no signs of either occupant. Disappointed, she walked on until she heard a voice call out.

"Miss Bennet—is that you?"

She spun around to see Mr. Yarby, smiling broadly and striding towards her.

"Are you out to enjoy the fresh air? Do you care for some company? I am bound for Meryton to be fitted for a new coat. My sister says my old one is too shabby for my new position here and insists I make an improvement. What do you say—shall we walk together?"

"That...that would be fine." To her horror, Mary felt her color rise. *Oh, please let him not notice or comment!*

"It cannot be thought inappropriate in any way or cause for gossip for us to be seen together. After all, I am your pastor-confessor."

Mary nodded mutely.

Oh, but I so wish you were more. How splendid to even think of the townspeople of Meryton conjecturing on the possibility of an intimate friendship between us.

"I should be glad of your company, Mr. Yarby," she said, more calmly than she felt. "I am walking to Lucas Lodge to deliver a dinner invitation."

They began to walk, Mary now utterly tongue-tied.

Finally, Mr. Yarby spoke. "How are you getting on, Miss Bennet? You must miss your mother dreadfully."

"I am quite well, Mr. Yarby, thank you. We are all adjusting to her loss and doing what we must to get on with our lives. There is no alternative after all."

"Indeed. May I say how glad I am that you and Amelia are becoming friends? I hope her society has been of some comfort or distraction to you over your loss. And she speaks quite highly of you."

Mary gave him a quick look. Was he making sport of her? But no, she saw no signs of humor on his face; he did not appear to be teasing. Realizing he was waiting for a response, she forced herself to smile.

"Oh, indeed! Your sister is quite the best friend I have ever had. I am so glad you came to take the living here."

He smiled at her comment, but then he stopped, and she saw his countenance become earnest.

"Forgive me if I am being impudent, Miss Bennet, but I did overhear some…idle talk in the village. Now that your cousin Mr. Collins has returned, there is speculation your father might ask me to resign… that he may give the living to him. I wish you to know that, should that occur, Amelia and I would not hold the least resentment. Family is family after all."

Mary could not help herself and gave a loud laugh. She quickly covered her mouth with a gloved hand to silence the outburst.

"Pray, have no fear of that ever happening, sir. Mr. Collins may be our cousin and the heir to Longbourn, but I believe I can safely say my father would leave off attending church entirely and declare himself a pagan before he would willingly put Mr. Collins in the pulpit."

Yarby lowered his head. "Now, I am heartily ashamed of myself for even bringing it up. You must think me a conniving fool. Please—do not speak to anyone of this conversation, I beg you." He looked up, and Mary could see the embarrassment in his eyes.

She studied his handsome face and felt her knees weaken. It took every bit of self control not to lay her hand upon his arm in consolation. But she could not be so familiar with him; instead, she took a deep breath.

"Be assured I shall keep our discussion completely private," she said soberly. "Mr. Collins will someday put us out of our home, but I cannot live my life in fear of Father's death. Papa may—no, he *shall* live many, many more years, I am certain."

"And by then, both you and your younger sister will be happily married and settled in your own homes no doubt."

Mary swallowed hard before replying in a weak voice. "Perhaps, Mr. Yarby. If it be God's will."

THE TWO CAME TO THE LANE THAT SPLIT OFF TO LUCAS LODGE where they parted amicably and went their separate ways. Mary delivered the invitation for dinner but declined an offer of tea from Lady Lucas. Instead, she decided to continue on into Meryton. Her father had just given his daughters their share of the yearly interest from Mrs. Bennet's inheritance. In all, it was £160 in interest per annum (which her mother had always squandered), so Mary's share was a hefty thirty-two pounds all to herself! Never before had she personally possessed such a sum of money to do with as she pleased.

She had brought some of it with her and had thought to spend it at the bookstore; instead, she found herself entering the dressmaker's shop. After looking over the bolts of cotton, silk, and wool, she chose a rich, silk fabric of deep maroon and spoke to Mrs. Davies about the design, asking for something a bit lower cut in the neckline than she usually chose. She saw the dressmaker nod sagely but noted a twinkle in the older woman's face. Heavens—was she perhaps gleaning an unspoken hint about Mary's intentions? The shopkeeper agreed to the style and suggested a lovely lace that would, as she put it, "enhance the smaller bosom." Mary felt herself blush but nodded in agreement.

The dress would be ready in ten days, Mrs. Davies assured her although Mary knew she would not be able to wear it until her and Kitty's mourning period was over—in late November. Nothing could be worn before then but black. What an ordeal; Mary thought the color made her look like a hideous crow. How could she look attractive and catch Mr. Yarby's eye while dressed so? It was annoying to have to wait six months, but Mary excelled at patience.

Leaving the shop, she began to imagine Mr. Yarby's compliments when she wore her lovely, new maroon gown, and as she walked home, she found a smile on her face and a lighter step than she could recall having in some time.

Chapter 9

Following luncheon, Mr. Bennet returned to his library, but only briefly. Going over the estate accounts held no appeal for him on such a fine summer day. The warm breeze coming through the open window enticed him to put down his ledger, grab his coat, and go out the back of the house for a brisk walk as had become his custom in the weeks since his wife's death. Initially, his strolls were a way to cope with his grief after her accident, but lately he had felt invigorated after his time out of doors and had decided to keep up the habit. He noticed he no longer fell asleep over a book in the afternoons, and unless he was mistaken, his trousers felt looser in the waist.

Ambling with no particular destination, Mr. Bennet, to his surprise, found himself in the church graveyard. He walked to his wife's grave and noted the wilted flowers there. He studied the new headstone, so clean and pristine compared to the many dirty and moss-covered stones nearby. Along with his wife's name, and birth and death dates, were the words:

Beloved Wife and Mother
She Has Soared Away to a Better Land.

That last line had been Kitty and Mary's touch. Considering how his wife had died—not soaring at all, but falling *down* the stairs—Mr. Bennet had thought the quote inappropriate, but he did not have the heart to argue against it. All he could think now was that Mrs. Bennet would have rolled her eyes at the sentimentality of the wording. He could almost hear her voice: *"A better land, indeed—I was quite content living in* this *land, thank you very much!"*

As he stood now, he felt a deep pang of remorse for some of the unkind jokes he had made at his wife's expense. She had been an easy target for his wit, being highly emotional and not of an intellectual nature; indeed, had he ever seen her willingly pick up a book? But he particularly regretted a time when Mrs. Bennet was once again bemoaning the fact that she would live to see Charlotte take her place at Longbourn. He had cruelly replied that they should be more optimistic; perhaps he might be the survivor. He shook his head in remorse.

And amazingly, here I am, the widower now. Inconceivable! At fifteen years her senior, it never seriously occurred to me that she would pass first. We both assumed I should go before her, which is why she was so determined to find good matches for our girls. Well, credit where credit is due, she did fairly well—three of the five gone off now. Kitty is likely to find a husband soon. I may take Lizzy up on her offer to give her a Season in London. But Mary—my poor plain Mary. I must be certain to make provisions for her. Not enough for a fortune hunter, to be sure, but something to give her a bit of independence. Although dear Lizzy did mention once that she and Mr. Darcy would be glad to take her in after I go. She would make a good help in the nursery for the children, or perhaps be their governess one day.

"Never worry, my dear, Mary will not be left on her own if I have anything to say about it," he spoke aloud.

"I beg your pardon," a voice replied.

Mr. Bennet spun around. Mrs. Withers was approaching, holding a bouquet of cut roses tied with a bit of twine. She made a small curtsey.

"Forgive me if I intrude on your solitary reverie, Mr. Bennet. I came to put these fresh flowers on your wife's grave—that is, if you don't object. I noticed just yesterday how shriveled the others were and thought to—" She broke off and shook her head. "Oh, but I should not presume. It is not my place. Please understand: I merely wished to brighten the grave a bit. Wilted flowers always…sadden me."

"Not at all. You are very kind, Mrs. Withers, and quite welcome to do so. I should have brought some flowers from our own garden but did not actually intend to walk here, you see. I found myself in the cemetery quite by accident." He leaned down, plucked the shriveled blooms from the grave and tossed them aside. Then he took the bouquet from Mrs. Withers and set it down gently. "That does look better—thank you."

"I wish I had had the chance to meet her," Mrs. Withers murmured. "Shall I leave you now?"

"I was going to continue my walk actually. If you would care for a stroll, I should be glad of your company." He saw her eyes brighten at the invitation.

"With pleasure," she replied.

The two walked out of the graveyard in a comfortable, easy silence.

MR. YARBY SAT IN HIS STUDY, PUTTING THE FINISHING TOUCHES on next Sunday's sermon. It was a good one, he felt, and likely to generate some thoughtful responses from his congregation. As much as he enjoyed speaking from the pulpit, he received even more pleasure from conversing with his congregants as they filed out after service. The many positive comments and smiles were encouraging. He knew it was unusual for a rector to write his own sermons, but clearly, it was working out well.

I was truthfully quite nervous to take on this position, but everything seems to confirm that it is the right place. Thank you, Lord, for bringing Amelia and me here to Longbourn.

A light tapping on the window broke his concentration, and he looked up to see a plumpish, grave face peering in at him. Good heavens—it was Mr. Collins! Mr. Yarby jumped up and went to the window, opening it to speak to the man.

"Good afternoon, Mr. Collins—what a surprise. How may I help you?"

"I was just taking a pleasant walk and, realizing I was near Longbourn parish, I thought to see whether you were in; I was hoping to have a short chat."

"Of course. Do come round to the door," Yarby replied.

Mr. Collins nodded and walked to the front entry where Yarby met him.

"Please make yourself comfortable in the parlor while I find Mrs. Pulson to see about some tea. I shan't be a moment."

Mr. Collins took the most comfortable seat and studied the furnishings of the parsonage. He had visited the reverend Mr. Dudley here only once, when he first came to meet the Bennets, although he did not like to dwell upon that trip. The painful memory of his cousin Elizabeth's stinging rejection of his marriage proposal still rankled. He saw a bit smugly that, aside from a new rug, next to nothing had been done to improve the parlor. Mr. Bennet was either too stingy or too unaware of the need to upgrade the furnishings.

The door opened and in walked Mr. Yarby, bearing the tea tray himself. Mr. Collins's mouth fell open. Did they not even have a maid? He saw Yarby smile.

"My sister, Mrs. Withers, would be serving us, but she seems to have gone for a walk. Aside from our cook we keep but one other servant in the kitchen, Ellen, but her hands are up to her elbows in sudsy water at the moment. I told her not to worry; I would serve you myself." He set the tray down and began to arrange the cups.

"We kept four servants at my old parsonage," said Mr. Collins, smugly. "But I suppose the living here is not as grand." He saw the rector took no offense at his comment.

"It is a huge step up from my salary as a curate, I assure you," Yarby said, laughing. "Amelia and I are more than content with our situation." He poured the tea and handed his guest a cup. "Sugar?"

Mr. Collins put two heaping teaspoons in his cup and stirred it noisily. "Tell me, do you plan to hire a curate? It would put you out only another forty or fifty pounds per annum."

"Oh no, we have no such plans at this time. If I were to take on another parish nearby, then, yes, I should need a curate to give the sermons at one while I speak at another, but I am unaware of any openings at present to which I could present myself as a candidate." He took a sip of his own tea before continuing. "Besides, are *you* not looking for a new living? With your wife expecting your first child, I can only imagine you would be well pleased to find a position near her family here in Meryton. If I knew of an opening, I should certainly defer to you before taking on another congregation myself."

Mr. Collins stared coldly at his host. "You seem to be up on all the village gossip, I see."

Mr. Yarby stammered an apology. "Forgive me, sir, I did not mean to offend. Miss Bennet and I walked together into Meryton the other week, and she did mention your...situation. No details, of course, just that you had departed Hunsford Parish. I did not mean to speak out of turn, and be assured I shall keep my ears open for any suitable living for a man of your vast experience."

Mr. Collins gave a tight smile. "Indeed, we rectors are all dependent upon the mercy of others, are we not? But I have high connections, be assured. Mr. Bennet's two oldest daughters are married to wealthy and influential men, you know. I have no doubt but Mrs. Collins and

I shall find a very advantageous situation quite soon."

"I shall add you to my prayers, naturally."

"Naturally." Mr. Collins took another sip of tea. "Your cottage is in great need of freshening if you will forgive my saying so. Mr. Bennet is likely unwilling to put out the necessary coin, but if you are still here when *I* assume Longbourn as my own—I am sure you know I am the heir presumptive—you may be assured of my paying as much as twenty pounds to bring some new life into these dingy rooms."

"You are so kind, but in fact, Mr. Bennet is being most generous with us. New fabrics and wall papers have already been ordered. I told him he need not bother, but he insisted. My sister is taking tremendous enjoyment in overseeing the improvements. No, Mr. Bennet has been a most accommodating patron, believe me. We dine with him and his daughters once or twice a week, and Amelia has become close friends with Miss Bennet."

Mr. Collins scowled. "Indeed. How lovely for you." He cleared his throat. "You are not wed, correct?"

"Yes. Not only have I not yet fallen in love, but I realized it would not be prudent to marry on a curate's salary."

"It would behoove you to find a suitable young woman and start a family as soon as possible, now that you have your own parish," Mr. Collins said, in an unctuous voice. "It sets a good example to your congregants to have their parish priest happily married."

"Well, I should like to find the right woman and be truly in love with her, not just marry for convenience or appearance's sake." Yarby shifted a bit in his seat. "That is—one should be certain it is a good match in every respect, don't you agree? That takes time."

"Oh, happiness in marriage is more a matter of chance than anything else, I believe. Why, my Charlotte and I knew each other but a day or two before I decided she was the one. Let me assure you we are quite content with each other. And, as you mentioned, she is going to make me a father—another important example to set in your parish."

He smiled proudly, awaiting the expected congratulations. But Yarby only nodded.

"Indeed," Yarby finally said, "I am fond of children and hope to become a father myself."

Bland conversation continued while both men had now finished their tea. Mr. Collins had a vague notion that he had already over-stayed his welcome, but he was not eager to depart. He reached over and took the last piece of seed cake.

"Now, I had some thoughts on your last two talks from the pulpit I wish to share with you," he said, and between bites began to drone on disapprovingly about the shocking nature of Yarby's uplifting sermons.

So enraptured was he by his own voice, Mr. Collins failed to notice Yarby's small sigh or that the new rector was only listening with half an ear.

Chapter 10

"Mrs. Withers is here, sir."

Mr. Bennet happily set aside his work for the unplanned visitor. "Thank you, Hill. Please send her right in." He smiled and rose as the lady entered. "Good day to you, Mrs. Withers. Have you come to see Mary? I believe she is out just now, calling on neighbors."

"Forgive me for intruding on your work, Mr. Bennet, I came to see you. I shan't take but a minute of your time."

"Not at all, I was just doing some estate work. You make a most pleasant distraction, I assure you. Please have a seat." He motioned to the chair next to the window opposite his desk. Amelia sat with her reticule perched on her lap. "Would you care for some tea?" he asked.

"Oh no, I don't wish to be any trouble."

"No trouble at all!" Mr. Bennet went to the bell cord and gave it a firm yank. When Mrs. Hill arrived, he ordered tea.

"Shall I set up in the parlor, sir?" she asked.

"Would you prefer that, Mrs. Withers?" Mr. Bennet asked his guest.

"Here is fine. I feel so at ease in this cozy room—it must be all the books."

Mrs. Hill nodded and departed.

Mr. Bennet moved from behind his desk to the chair next to Mrs. Withers. "Would you care to borrow anything from my library? I should be most happy to oblige. Though the collection is not very extensive, I am quite proud of it. I would rather spend money on books than almost anything, I believe."

"In that, you are very like your daughter Mary," Amelia said. "A bookstore is always her first choice on any visit to Meryton."

Mr. Bennet's eyebrows lifted. "Oh—I suppose we do have that in common. I never much thought about it, to own the truth."

"Have you never offered her a book to read and then discussed it with her later? I believe she would be very flattered."

Mr. Bennet was a bit flummoxed at the thought. "No. No, I have not done so. The thought never—" He broke off and shook his head. "May I make a small confession, Mrs. Withers? I fear I have not been the most attentive of fathers to my daughters. The only one who showed much wit was Elizabeth. The rest I rather lumped together as silly girls without any great intellect. Mrs. Bennet oft accused me of always giving Lizzy the preference, and I confess she was right. But even Lizzy aside, I let my wife deal with the girls for the most part. How could I have missed what a great reader Mary is? I feel heartily ashamed of myself for my lack of fatherly interest and affection."

Mrs. Hill arrived with the tea, and conversation halted for a time as she served. Once they were alone, they drank silently before Mrs. Withers ventured, "Regrets are a funny thing, Mr. Bennet. Sometimes they come and you know there is nothing you can do to change the situation; the opportunity has passed, and you must live with that knowledge. But other times—" She paused, seeming to choose her words carefully. "Other times, there *is* yet the chance to take a different path."

She sipped her tea, waiting for him to respond, but he could think of nothing to say. After a moment, she continued, "It is surely not too late for you to give Mary the attention you neglected to give before. And, if I may be so bold, it may help her to blossom a bit."

"Do you truly think so?" His expression conveyed his doubt.

"I do. Life can be hard for a middle child. I saw it oft in families in our last parish. Parents seem to leave them on their own, for good or ill. I myself am a middle child. I escaped the neglect others do because I was the only girl and, therefore, was singled out for attention in that way."

"I did not realize you and Mr. Yarby have another sibling. You have never mentioned him."

"Have I not? Yes, our eldest brother is Phillip, a solicitor in London. We hope he will come for a visit soon. Oh! That reminds me of my purpose in interrupting your day. The improvements are finished, and Robert and I wish to have all of the Bennets over for dinner this Thursday—four o'clock. Does that suit?"

"It does. I can speak for the girls, we have no fixed engagements."

"Wonderful. Now, let us find a book for you to give to Mary." She set her tea cup down, rose, and moved to the bookcase where she began to scan the titles. "Have you many novels? I am trying to encourage your daughter to read fewer books of a serious and weighty nature."

Mr. Bennet moved to join her. "I agree; not to reflect poorly on your brother's profession, but I believe choosing something that is not of a religious bent would be a positive change for her. Ah! Perhaps this—"

Mr. Bennet reached for a book at the same moment Mrs. Withers spied it and also moved to take it. Their hands met and lingered just a bit longer than necessary. Then Mr. Bennet dropped his hand and gave a nervous laugh.

"Pray excuse me, Mrs. Withers, I did not mean—"

"No, I should not have…that is, it is your library after all."

There was an awkward pause, their eyes holding a gaze warily, before

Mr. Bennet turned back to the books and cleared his throat.

"Well, we clearly both had the same idea. This novel is not one of those dreadful gothic tales so popular with young ladies, but a sound, moral story, although I do not believe Mary has ever examined it. Have you read it?" He pulled it out and showed it to her. "*Belinda* by Maria Edgeworth."

Mrs. Withers nodded, but he noted she did not move to take the book from his hands. "Oh yes, a very good choice. I believe she will enjoy it."

"And...do you see anything *you* would care to borrow?" he said hesitantly. Mr. Bennet was reluctant to see her go quite so soon. He never could discuss books with his wife. This was so...pleasant.

Mrs. Withers turned to study the shelves silently. Her eyes lit up at one title and she pulled it out. "Oh, this one, with your permission. I am so fond of poetry."

"William Blake," he said approvingly. "You enjoy poetry of a more romantic nature, Mrs. Withers?" His eyes now sought hers with more assurance. Why had he not noticed before how fine her hazel eyes were? A stray lock of her hair had come loose and it took all his will and concentration not to reach up and tuck it back in place. They stood silently for another long pause before replying.

"Indeed. I feel I am an incurable...romantic, Mr. Bennet," she murmured.

"Ah," was the only reply he could manage.

"Amelia!" Mary's voice broke in. "How nice you have come to visit. I am sorry I was not here when you arrived. I hope Papa is not boring you with estate affairs. Do you wish for some tea?" She moved into the room and saw the remains on the table. "Oh, I see Papa has anticipated me."

Amelia smiled and moved to stand next to Mary. "Yes, he was kind enough to offer me refreshments although I only came here to invite you all to dinner now that the parsonage improvements are finished."

"How delightful. Papa, did you accept?"

"Yes, Mary. We are expected this Thursday."

"Well, I must be going," Amelia said. "I have taken far too much of your time as it is. Robert and I look forward to dining with you in our beautifully refurbished home."

"May I walk with you back to the parsonage?" asked Mary. "Then we can catch up; we have not seen each other in many days."

"That would be lovely." Amelia turned to Mr. Bennet and inclined her head, but not quite meeting his eyes, he noticed. "Thank you again for the loan of the poetry book, sir." She picked up her reticule, tucked her arm through Mary's and practically pulled her from the study.

"Good afternoon, Mrs. Withers," called Mr. Bennet after them.

When he was alone, he returned to his desk and collapsed in his chair. His mind was spinning. What was happening? How could he be having feelings for another woman so soon? Why, he had only been a widower a little over two months! The better part of a year of his mourning remained; he could not be so forward. He must find a way to check his behavior. It would not do to go mooning about and have it noticed by anyone. He felt a surge of envy for Mary—already on a first name basis with Mrs. Withers.

"Amelia," he said softly to himself.

"Beg pardon, sir?"

A voice gave him a start, and he jerked his head to see Mrs. Hill waiting at the door. He stared at her blankly.

"I have come to clear the tea things," she said.

"Yes, yes, of course. Go right ahead. Thank you, Hill." Mr. Bennet busied himself with his ledger and tried to keep his thoughts on what was now in front of him instead of the lady who had recently departed.

Chapter 11

One month later, Mr. Bennet dispatched Mrs. Hill to bring Mary and Kitty to his study. They came at once, wondering whether they had done something to displease their father. Were they to be reprimanded? Mary was especially curious. Lately, her father had been unusually kind and seemed somewhat interested in her. He had given her two books to read and then had asked her to sit and discuss them with him! While she was unsure of his reason for taking the trouble, it was not unpleasant to be so singled out. However, she was only partway through the latest text he had loaned her, so it could not be that. She and Kitty stood patiently until he finally cleared his throat and spoke.

"Girls, I am in need of your assistance. It has now been three months since your mother died, and I believe the time has come for us to deal with some of her possessions. I have already given a couple of day dresses to Mrs. Hill as they were about the same size. If it would please either of you to take one or two of her fancier gowns and have them cut down or reworked for you, I shall gladly pay for the alterations."

Mary protested. "But, Papa, we cannot wear anything but black until the New Year—or at least mid-December—and even though our deep mourning period ends then, we should still show respect by dressing somberly."

Her sister rolled her eyes. "You may wish to dress in such a manner, but believe me: when our six months is up, I plan to be a veritable peacock!"

"But poor Papa must continue his mourning until nearly next June. Should we not show him support?"

Kitty opened her mouth to retort, but Mr. Bennet interrupted. "Do not fret, Mary. It would cheer me considerably to see both of you in brighter colors in another three months, even as I continue on in black and grey. I was not suggesting you wear your mother's reworked gowns yet. Just...please go through her wardrobe and do what you think best with them."

"Lydia might like a few things," Kitty said thoughtfully. "She wrote me just last week, complaining of not having any money to spend on new gowns for the upcoming assemblies."

"That is a fine idea, Kitty. Choose one or two to send to her, and I shall include the funds to alter them." He pulled open a side drawer of his desk and brought out a smallish, wooden jewelry case. Mary gasped, recognizing it as the one from her mother's dressing room.

"Now," Mr. Bennet continued, "your mother did not have much jewelry, but it does no one any good sitting in this box. I have already chosen two small pieces to send to Jane and Lizzy; they already have been gifted with far finer stuff from their husbands, so they will want your mother's jewelry only for sentiment's sake." He lifted the lid and pulled out a short necklace of small garnets spaced along a delicate gold chain. "What of this? It is one of your mother's finer pieces. Do either of you wish to have it?"

"I should like it, Papa," Mary blurted before Kitty could respond.

It would go perfectly with her new gown, now hidden upstairs in her closet, waiting for the six-month mourning period to end.

"Very well." He handed it to her then chose a cross of four topaz stones dangling from a gold chain. "This was another one of her better pieces. You should have this then, Kitty."

She took it, brushing a tear from her eye as she murmured her thanks.

"As for Lydia. I greatly fear anything of great value I send to her will soon be pawned by either her or her worthless husband. What do you say to this?" He held up a small but pretty cameo brooch. "It is not a costly piece, which is why your mother seldom wore it. It was an engagement gift from me, actually."

Kitty and Mary exchanged a glance, then nodded their approval. The rest of the pieces were easily divided between the girls—three apiece—with little disagreement over them. At last, one bracelet remained. Mr. Bennet caressed the thick, gold hoop with delicate engraved scrollwork, and a smile came over his face.

"I had nearly forgotten about this. I gave it to your mother after she gave birth to Jane. I don't know why she stopped wearing it."

"Likely it would not fit anymore, Papa," Mary said matter-of-factly. "Her wrists and hands became plump as she aged." The look on her father's face made her realize the bluntness of her statement, but he did not chastise her.

"You may be right. Well, since you each have three pieces and this one is too nice to risk sending to Lydia, what shall I do with it?"

"Keep it in the jewelry case, Papa, until you decide what to do with it." Mary said, "In the meantime, Kitty and I can share it if we like. I don't care that much for bracelets anyway. They interfere with my playing the piano."

"A sound idea. What say you, Kitty?"

"I agree."

"And perhaps you will think of someone to gift it to later," Mary added.

Later in her bedroom, Mary reflected that there was an odd

expression on her father's face when she said that—a queer little smile—as if he already had a prospect in mind.

TWO WEEKS LATER, MARY PROCEEDED WITH EAGER DETERMINATION towards the parsonage, her Bible clutched firmly in her hands. The late August sun beat down on her, and she felt a sheen of perspiration as she hurried to her destination. Thank heavens for the short walk and for her bonnet! She wanted to look her best; she was finally ready to begin a plan to improve her acquaintance with Mr. Yarby by discussing certain passages of scripture. While she had persuaded her father to invite the parson and Amelia to dinner several times over the past few months, Mary never felt she garnered the rector's attention. She would try, but when he turned his intense, dark eyes on her, her color would rise, causing her to retreat in confusion. Then she would be forced to watch her sister step in and act as hostess. Kitty was so much more comfortable with easy banter. How did she do it? Mary would spend most of the evening speaking with her father and Amelia, only to realize later that she had barely exchanged a half dozen sentences with the object of her desire—all the more reason to meet with him privately. Certainly, she would be able to converse more readily with him when they were alone.

Today being Monday, she knew Mr. Yarby would be at home, and although she did not wish to monopolize his free day, she could not chance dropping in on another weekday when he might be making parish visits.

As she turned the corner to the parsonage, she spied a figure in black coming towards her. It was Kitty! What could she be doing there? When Mary called out and waved, she saw a somewhat startled expression on her sister's face. Kitty then tucked something under her arm.

"Where have you been all morning?" Mary asked when the two reached each other.

Kitty tossed her head. "What do you care? Just because you manage the menus and a few other things Mama did, that does not make you mistress over me!" She pushed past and hurried away, much to Mary's puzzlement.

How very odd. And what was she hiding under her arm?

She shrugged and, concluding it was likely new ribbons or such her sister had bought as a treat for herself in Meryton, continued to the parsonage where she knocked on the door, nearly trembling in anticipation of spending time with Mr. Yarby.

The maid, Ellen, showed Mary to the small study. Better and better, Mary thought—less chance of being disturbed by anyone there than if they were in the parlor.

"Miss Bennet, what a surprise," the clergyman said, rising from behind his desk. "I was just—that is, what can I do for you?"

"I have a question about something in the Bible that I cannot quite decipher. I was hoping you might help me understand." Mary was suddenly nervous and heard her voice quaver a bit. Heavens, this would never do. He must see her as a strong, intelligent woman and prospective partner, not a blithering ninny. She cleared her throat. "I do not wish to disturb your work, however. If this an inconvenient time, I can come back later…"

Mr. Yarby smiled. "It is no imposition. It is certainly nice to know that the Bennets are interested in the holy book. Please, sit." He gestured to the uncomfortable-looking chair across from his desk. Disappointed that they could not sit next to each other on the small cushioned window seat, Mary took the chair and scooted it as close as she could to the desk.

"Now. What has you so perplexed, Miss Bennet?" Mr. Yarby asked as he settled back into his own chair.

"It is this line from the book of John," she said as she fumbled with her Bible, opening it to the page she had marked with an old ribbon. "Chapter fifteen, verse seven: *If ye abide in me, and my words abide in you, ye shall ask what ye will, and it shall be done unto you.*"

"And what confuses you about that?"

"Well...it is just that it makes it seem as if anything we desire can be ours for the having. Our Heavenly Father is not just going around granting wishes, is he?"

Mr. Yarby smiled and picked up his own Bible, quickly finding the book of John.

"We must first remember, Miss Bennet, the context in which our Lord is speaking. Recall that earlier, Jesus calls himself the true vine, but warns that our Father is keeper of that vine. And any branch that does not bear fruit is cut away, that the other branches may produce more fruit. And then he says just as a vine cannot bear fruit of itself, neither can we, except we abide in Him. We must keep God's commandments, and also the new commandment Jesus gives us in verse twelve, which is to love one another as he loves us."

"But if we do so, we are guaranteed to get whatever we want? Riches or a fine house?"

"Jesus has told us He will intercede on our behalf to God Almighty, so yes, everything we wish for could be ours."

Mary frowned, pondering this. "*Could* be? Since everyone does not have a fine carriage or home and great wealth, does that mean they are not devout enough? Or that they are sinners?"

"You may have hit upon the very thing there. Again, that passage you quote says Jesus exhorts us to have His words abide in us. But that is so much more than simply being able to quote them. Sadly, many of us are sinners—and I don't mean in a great way. We are not all thieves, deceitful liars, or murderers. But most of us are sinners in small ways—not turning the other cheek, holding resentments, or gossiping perhaps. We might fail to offer comfort to those that need it most or be too concerned for material rather than spiritual matters. In these small ways, perhaps, we hurt our God and then do not receive the things we ask for."

"Forgive me for sounding rude, but sometimes wealthy people are dreadful, are they not? Of course, I do not know that many, but one hears tales of how greedy and cruel the rich can be, always wanting their own way. And yet they have *everything* while most people have very little. Why should God reward them and not a poor beggar?"

Mr. Yarby laughed gently. "That is a question scholars have been trying to answer for many, many centuries, Miss Bennet. I can only tell you this: a true believer of Christ, full of passion for him and his words, shall have no will that is *not* in harmony with the Divine will. Then, faith is possible in the fulfillment of his own desire, and prayer becomes a pledge of that answer. Do you see?"

"Hebrews chapter eleven, verse one." Mary quoted from memory, *"Now faith is the substance of things hoped for, the evidence of things not seen."*

She saw a broad smile spread across Mr. Yarby's face. "Exactly. We cannot go around expecting God to grant our every wish like some magical being in a fairy tale. But it is faith, Miss Bennet; *faith* is what brings us to accord with God's will for us."

"You make it sound so logical and understandable, Mr. Yarby," Mary said. "Thank you so much. May I...may I call again if I have other questions?"

"Of course, Miss Bennet. You are one of my spiritual flock here, and I must tend to you as I would to any of my parish."

Wishing she could somehow continue the conversation, but realizing she had no more questions, Mary nodded and rose. He stood as well and smiled. Was there anything in particular in that smile for her? She could only hope. Mary curtseyed and left.

AS SHE WALKED HOME, MARY REFLECTED ON HER FIRST PRIVATE encounter with Mr. Yarby. She was slightly disappointed to be referred to as just one more of his "flock." And she was equally dismayed that no offer of tea was issued; that would have been a good opportunity for more informal conversation. Still, she decided it was a good start. Surely, more time discussing the holy book would bring them closer. And one day, she had no doubt that he would begin to realize Mary would be the perfect wife for him. It was only a matter of time.

Chapter 12

It was now October. Shawls were brought out and worn with regularity around the Bennet household so as to keep warm without having to use too much costly wood for heating. However, the cooler weather did not stop Mr. Bennet from taking his daily walks, frequently in the company of Mrs. Withers. He doubted any tongues were wagging in town about their tours although he continued to suggest paths that would steer clear of Meryton or areas more populated. The hills and meadows seemed to give them plenty of areas to explore and enjoy in solitude.

That month the Bennets were also anxiously awaiting word from Pemberley on Elizabeth's safe delivery of her second child. When the letter did arrive, it did not bring happy news. It was a horrifically long labor, Darcy wrote, and Lizzy bled so much she nearly died. She was still confined to her bed. The baby—a girl—seemed sickly and of a poor constitution. They had named her Lavinia Jane, and prayed she would rally. Darcy asked the Bennets to add their prayers for Lizzy and the child as well.

The day after receiving the news from Pemberley, Mr. Bennet called Mary into his library. She brought along the most recent book they were discussing, but he waved it aside and asked her to sit.

"Mary, I have decided I shall send you to Pemberley. Your sister is not well following her difficult childbirth, and I believe having you there will help."

"Papa, I shall do as you ask, of course, but I cannot see that I shall be of much use. Surely they have servants and nursemaids and such who are more suited to the tasks at hand."

"Your role will be more of spiritual, uplifting support than actual caregiving, my dear. In his letter, Darcy says she is 'quite low in spirits' and in need of cheering up."

"Is Jane unable to attend her? They are much closer than Lizzy and I ever were."

"Jane is not able to be with Lizzy at this time. She and her children have caught very bad colds and it would not be prudent to send her now. Go and pack your things, for you will leave tomorrow. Think of it as an opportunity to become closer to your older sister. And," he added with a smile, "do not discount the joys of the Pemberley library. It is the envy of many counties."

Mary nodded obediently and exited, calling for Sarah to assist her in packing.

THE TRUNKS WERE NEARLY FILLED—AFTER ALL, WHEN YOU ARE still in mourning, what did it really matter what you wore, Mary thought—when Kitty poked her head in the bedroom.

"Papa just told me you are going to Pemberley—lucky you."

"Am I?" Mary replied as she dismissed Sarah with a nod. "I think you would have been a better choice. You enjoy all the socializing of Pemberley. Who knows? Perhaps you could meet some dashing young lord from the county and gain a husband."

Kitty snorted as she strolled in. "Yes, and dressed in black I would be *such* a fetching catch. I cannot wait to be done with deep mourning and at least be able to wear violet or something. Two more months." She plopped down in a chair and arched an eyebrow at her sister. "Besides, who is to say I shan't find somebody local?"

Mary blinked in surprise and pushed her spectacles up on her nose. "Is there someone—that is, have you met someone of interest around Meryton? There are just the same old people we all know. Oh! Is it Digby Morrison? I believe he has always admired you."

Kitty burst out laughing. "I would prefer to remain single my entire life than marry that picksome old thing! Besides, Maria Lucas has her eyes set on him and is welcome to him. No. There is nobody…in particular, but who knows? Things can always change in a heartbeat, you know." She got up and walked to the door, then turned with what Mary thought was an impish expression. "I shall miss you though. With just Papa and me here, it will be so quiet. Give Lizzy my love. And who knows—perhaps *you* will be the one to catch the eye of a handsome lord in Derbyshire." With a laugh, she flounced out.

Mary closed the lid on her trunk. She knew she had to go; it would not do to disobey her father. But she might be gone for weeks—a month or more! That would mean so much time away from Mr. Yarby. She had contrived to come up with Bible passages that needed his explanations at least once a week, and she felt that it had been time well spent. The two were more and more comfortable with each other, Mary felt. While she had to admit there was nothing overt in Mr. Yarby's behavior to make her believe he was falling in love with her, and he *was* still formal in all his addresses to her, it was only a matter of time, she was certain, before he would declare himself.

I hate to be gone just now, but perhaps he will miss me. As the old saying goes, absence makes the heart grow fonder. Annoying as it is to leave, it might actually work in my favor.

THREE DAYS LATER, MARY ARRIVED AT PEMBERLEY. MR. HILL HAD accompanied her, but he was a man of such a taciturn nature that, even when he was not sleeping, there was next to no conversation to make the tedious journey seem faster. Mary reflected she might as well have traveled alone after all—improper though that would have been. Mr. Hill would stay the night at Pemberley and return at once to Longbourn.

The housekeeper, Mrs. Reynolds, was the sole person to greet Mary. She apologized for Mr. Darcy and his sister being absent from Pemberley at present. She then led Mary down the hall, but stopped at an unexpected door. Before she could open it, however, Mary cleared her throat, stopping her.

"Pardon me, Mrs. Reynolds, but shan't I be staying in the bedchamber where I usually stay when we all come at Christmas?" Mary said. "I normally get the west-facing room with the green wall paper, farther down the hall." She gestured lamely. "This room is always taken by my sister Jane and Mr. Bingley."

Mrs. Reynolds firmly shook her head. "Oh no, miss—you are to have the Rose Room on this visit. Mrs. Darcy was quite insistent upon that!" She flung open the door, and nodded for Mary to enter. "I shall send your trunks up directly." With a final smile and nod, she bustled down the hall, leaving Mary to explore her new accommodations.

It was a large and well-appointed bedchamber with three separate sitting areas, all furnished with one or two upholstered chairs or a settee—one in the corner to the right of the entry, one at the fireplace, and yet another near the windows. *More than anyone could ever really need,* Mary thought. *Rather a waste of furniture, to own it.* However, she had to admit it was all beautiful. There was also an elegant desk that was set by the windows. She walked over and stroked the beautiful burl oak and noted there was an ink stand, freshly sharpened pens and plenty of paper already set out—such generosity!

I shall make use of this desk to write Amelia very often. It could not hurt to have her share my letters with her brother and therefore keep me in his mind.

There was a knock at the door, and upon her calling "enter," two footmen carried in her trunks, followed by a maid who curtseyed, introduced herself as Julia, and said that she would act as lady's maid. She informed Mary that she would unpack if the lady would like to stretch her legs around the estate for a while.

"I should like to see my sister if possible," Mary said, keeping her duty in mind.

"Mrs. Darcy is asleep at present, miss," came the reply. "She should be awake for tea and a bite to eat around four; that has been her routine of late."

"I understand Mr. Darcy is not at home?" Mary was a bit miffed not to be greeted by him when she arrived.

"He had urgent tenant issues to deal with on the far end of the estate. Took young master Thomas with him too. I don't expect we shall see him until dinner."

Mary nodded, donned her pelisse, and went down the stairs. She was tempted to visit the library, but she knew that, if she did, she would soon curl up with a book, and it did seem like a better idea to stretch her legs after all the hours of sitting in the carriage.

AFTER AN HOUR OR SO, MARY RETURNED TO THE HOUSE, THOR-oughly chilled. She hurried upstairs to sit by the fire in her room. One thing about her brother-in-law, he was not one to skimp on the wood for heating!

As she moved towards her room, she heard a plaintive wailing from down the hall. The new baby? Mary walked to the nursery and cautiously opened the door to see a nursemaid walking back and forth, holding a tiny bundle from which the screams emanated. When the nursemaid turned around, she gave a little start to see Mary, then dropped a small curtsey.

"G'day, miss. Are you the sister, then?" she asked.

"Yes, I am Mary Bennet. And you are…?"

"Beatrice, ma'am. Pleased to meet you. Sorry for the noise, but this'un fusses night and day. The wet nurse just fed her, so it's not that she's hungry."

"May I see my niece?" Mary moved closer, and Beatrice turned the bundle towards her. A squalling, red face peeked out of the blankets. Never one to feel much interest in babies before, Mary surprised herself by reaching out and taking the babe from Beatrice's arms. She jostled her niece and made soft shushing sounds as she walked around the nursery. To her amazement, little Lavinia stopped screaming and stared up at the strange face with intensity.

"Hello, Miss Lavinia Jane Darcy," Mary said. "Very pleased to meet you. I am your aunt Mary."

"Gracious me, I can hardly believe it," exclaimed Beatrice. "I thought she'd never stop screaming. You have a touch, you do for sure, miss."

"I doubt it," Mary said practically. "More likely she just cried herself out." She peered closer and reached out one finger, smiling as baby latched onto it firmly. Noting a comfortable chair by the window, Mary walked over and sat, still rocking her niece. She smiled as she watched Lavinia's eyes slowly droop and close.

I barely remember Kitty and Lydia as babies, since they were sent away until weaned. And why were we all sent to a wet nurse? Did Mama not enjoy holding us? Goodness, I quite like the feel of this.

Mary was quite content to hold her sleeping niece until Julia arrived to suggest that Mary change for dinner.

"Oh. I quite lost track of time and forgot about visiting my sister—is she available for a short visit now?"

But Julia shook her head, saying Mrs. Darcy was indisposed. Mary reluctantly gave the baby back to Beatrice and went to her room.

Chapter 13

M r. Collins was in a foul mood. Months of living with his in-laws had brought him to the sad conclusion that the optimism with which he had entered into his current arrangement as only a short break before moving to his next parish was not to be realized. He took a long walk across the fields one afternoon to think about how he might improve his situation.

Charlotte enjoys time with her parents and siblings, and I know it is a comfort to be near them while she awaits the birth of our child, although I have seen how she and her mother often huddle together for whispered conversations that always stop when I enter the room. No doubt, the two are complaining about my inability to secure a new location. I am doing my best, after all! Does she think I am happy with the way things are? I have no space of my own! I cannot share Sir William's library. Our own bedchamber is quite small, and every other room in the house seems to be filled with people at all times!

Adding to his unhappy disposition, was a recent letter from

Mr. Darcy informing Mr. Collins that, sadly, there were no livings available in Derbyshire and, further, that Mr. Darcy knew of no other potential positions.

"I wish you all the best, and be assured I shall certainly put your name forward should any suitable position come to my attention," Darcy had written. All the proper words, but Mr. Collins could perceive no real offer of help in them.

Although he had no evidence, Mr. Collins was persuaded that Mr. Darcy's inability to help was due to the influence of Lady Catherine. Could she have instructed her nephew not to assist him? He had had such hopes of help from Pemberley. Mrs. Darcy was his wife's dearest friend, after all. Why had she not been able to do more?

"Bosh!" he exclaimed, abruptly striking a bush hard with his cane, causing the leaves to fly off. "She has poisoned his mind and heart against me, no doubt. What am I to do? What kind of a man cannot support his own family? Oh, the humiliation!"

He stood, fuming for a moment, and was about to turn back towards Lucas Lodge when he spied a couple crossing a nearby field. He squinted, trying to discern their identities. A man and a woman, that much was clear. And they were heading his way. For some reason, Mr. Collins felt an impulse to hide himself in a grove of trees off the main path. From there, he observed the couple strolling together, and snatches of a clearly comfortable conversation and laughter floated on the wind towards him. Still, he could not identify them.

The two reached the end of the field at the stile, and the gentleman—for it seemed apparent that it *was* a gentleman, Mr. Collins thought—gave his hand to assist the lady up and over the fence. The man then followed, jumping down beside her, laughing when he nearly lost his balance. Mr. Collins heard the lady join in with the merriment. Then the gentleman held his arm out, and she took it, but they did not continue walking at first. Mr. Collins's mouth fell open as he watched the gentleman reach over to remove a bit of leaf from the lady's bonnet near her face. He showed it to her, and she laughed again and took his hand, pressing it to her cheek.

The two turned towards the still-hidden Mr. Collins, and he gasped as their identities became clear to him.

Mr. Bennet and Mrs. Withers! Such intimate behavior between them. And him still in full mourning. Shocking! Well, well, well.

He continued to stay hidden as the couple walked up the path towards Longbourn, their hands just brushing each other as they strolled. When they were gone, he left the grove of trees, a small smile of satisfaction upon his face.

This might well be the answer to my securing a new position.

MARY WAS MORE THAN READY TO GO DOWN TO DINNER PRECISELY at six thirty. She was used to dining earlier at Longbourn in the autumn—around four o'clock. Consequently, she was famished. However, she knew it was fashionable to dine later.

Especially when one has the means for enough candles to light the dining room, as my brother does.

She had dressed in her nicest black gown and taken pains with her hair, thanks to her maid, Julia, who had proved quite adept at styling. Still, as she had looked at her pale image in the mirror, she had frowned. Black was so unflattering to her.

Not much longer until our mourning period is done. Then I wish never to wear black again.

She pushed her glasses up securely on her nose and, with a final nod, went downstairs. As she entered the impressive dining room, brightly lit with candles on every table and sideboard as she had expected, she saw Mr. Darcy and his younger sister, Georgiana, standing together, conversing softly.

The young lady, seeing Mary, smiled brightly and crossed over to take both her hands.

"Welcome, Mary. My brother and I are so dreadfully sorry not to have been here when you arrived. What must you think of us? But he had sudden business to attend to on the estate, and I returned too late this afternoon from taking foodstuffs to an ailing tenant to greet you. I hope you have not been too bored."

Mr. Darcy joined them, bowing his head in greeting. "We are pleased to have you, Mary. I was just speaking with Lizzy, and she looks forward to your visiting her tomorrow." He frowned a moment before continuing. "Today was…not a very good day for my wife. She had but little energy for conversing and slept much of the time. But I assure you she is glad—as we all are—that you have come."

Mary tried to think of a proper response. Why did the words never come easily to her when she was around Mr. Darcy?

"I am…happy to be here. Yes, indeed, please be assured of it," she said. "I hope that I may be of use as I believe that is the most vital thing in life—to be useful."

She saw the siblings exchange a startled glance. Then Mr. Darcy gestured to the table and invited her to take a seat. She was seated on his right, and Georgiana sat across from her. Mr. Darcy took his chair at the head of the table and nodded to the staff to begin serving.

So much food! Mary was unused to so many courses for a family meal. Generally, they served but two courses at Longbourn unless there was company. She recalled with pride the five courses she had meticulously ordered when Mr. Yarby and Amelia came to dine the other week. But that meal was nothing to the bounty she saw before her now. Mary enjoyed the leek soup and the venison, which was then followed by roast capons. She began to eat as little as possible as plate after plate was served, but by the time the second fish dish was plated and after no fewer than four platters of vegetables had been offered, she had to wave away any more portions.

"Do you not care for fish?" Georgiana asked politely.

"I do enjoy it; however, I am unused to such abundance at dinner. You must understand: I practice mortification when it comes to food.

I believe in concentrating less on the material things before me and, therefore, keeping my mind open to dwell on more spiritual matters." Seeing the stunned expressions on her hosts' faces, she quickly added, "Everything *is* quite delicious, however. I thank you."

She saw Mr. Darcy try unsuccessfully to hide a smile as he took a large swallow of wine. "Of course, even our Lord was not above enjoying a good meal, true? And did he not turn water into wine for his guests? While you are correct, Mary, that overindulgence is never a good thing, I do hope you will not deny yourself the many pleasures that Pemberley has to offer."

Mary blinked a moment, trying to come up with a reply. "Yes. My father urged me to explore your library, if that is agreeable to you."

"Completely."

There was a long pause before Mary turned her attention to his sister.

"Georgiana, your housekeeper, Mrs. Reynolds, mentioned to me that you were recently visiting your aunt at Rosings Park. Did you have an enjoyable time?"

"Yes, thank you, my visit was quite pleasant. I enjoy my cousin's company very much. Like me, Anne is on the quieter side, and we spent many hours reading in the warmth of the greenhouse. Lady Catherine does not care to sit in there, you see, so we had a good deal of privacy. I had planned to stay longer, but then, of course, your sister had such a trying time with her delivery, so I returned sooner than expected. But I know I am welcome to return to Rosings Park at any time."

"I remember hearing Lizzy speak quite a bit about that great estate after her first visit with Mr. and Mrs. Collins at Hunsford rectory. They, of course, are no longer at the parish."

"Yes, I am aware that Mr. Collins has left. My aunt is quite enamored of his replacement."

"What is your opinion of the new rector, if I may ask?"

"A very high one," Georgiana replied, smiling. "I do not wish to be critical, but I never found Mr. Collins all that...inspiring."

"Mr. Collins thinks himself quite a wit," Mr. Darcy broke in, grinning, "but he is only *half* right."

"Fitzwilliam! You are being unkind! He is our guest's relation, after all." But Mary noticed Georgiana was unable to keep a small smile off her face.

"I take no offense; please be easy on that account. Mr. Collins will someday have Longbourn," she said thoughtfully. "I only hope that he will be worthy of it. I suppose he will give up preaching once that day comes and be content with managing the estate and living a gentleman's life. Charlotte is a good person, and I feel certain she will tend to the house carefully. Although, I must admit it is hard for me to imagine her—or anyone— in my mother's position."

"You will always have a home here, Mary," Mr. Darcy said. "You need not worry about being without a place once your father passes."

"Which, of course, we all hope will be many, many years away," added Georgiana earnestly.

Mary felt their pity. She looked down at her plate to gain control of her emotions.

They think me completely unmarriageable. They have already put me on the shelf. But I am but twenty-two! Georgiana is twenty, and nobody assumes she will remain unwed. Of course, she is quite pretty and has a handsome dowry. But still...

She took a sip of wine before trusting her voice to speak. "Yes, thank you both. Father is in good health, and will likely live for some time. And, one never knows what the future may bring. I could surprise everyone and marry after all. Then I would have no need of being... taken in."

"Oh no! Mary, we did not mean to imply—that is..." Georgiana stammered.

Mary watched as Georgiana, unable to finish her thought, cast a desperate glance towards her brother who quickly filled the silence.

"Life is full of unexpected things, as you say, Mary. Why, there was a time when your sister could no more imagine herself being married to me than finding herself on the moon—such was her dislike of me!"

Both Mary and Georgiana laughed, smoothing over the moment of discomfort. Mr. Darcy then went on to entertain them with amusing stories of the nearly botched courtship.

Chapter 14

The reverend Mr. Yarby took his time removing his vestments following Sunday's service. He was loath to return to his home as he was expecting a visitor—and not one for whom he had much fondness.

He was still puzzled over the short, terse note that had been delivered to him earlier in the week. Mr. Collins had written that he must speak with him that very Sunday on a "matter most urgent." What could he mean?

When Mr. Collins arrived, Ellen ushered him into the small library where he took his seat across from Mr. Yarby. No tea was offered as Yarby was hoping the duration of the visit would be short, and he did not wish to prolong it with cordialities he did not wholeheartedly feel. Amelia had given him a rather surprised look when he told her specifically not to order tea or invite Mr. Collins to stay for supper, but she only nodded in agreement.

Now, Yarby took a deep breath and began. "Your message appeared very businesslike, Mr. Collins, so I urge you to bring forth your matter at once. What is most urgent that you required this meeting?"

Mr. Collins declined to answer directly, asking instead, "Is your sister, Mrs. Withers, around the parsonage at present?"

"No. She is taking a walk, I believe. Despite the chilly autumn weather, she has become most devoted to her regular perambulations."

"And…does she walk alone today?"

Why does Mr. Collins's voice sound so smug? Yarby wondered. He gave a tight smile. "I have no idea and I cannot see what bearing it may have on anything you have to discuss. Please get to the point if you will, Mr. Collins, I have work to do." Mr. Yarby knew he was being a bit testy, but his guest was truly beginning to vex him.

"In fact, good sir, the company your sister keeps is precisely the reason I am here." Mr. Collins replied.

Utterly confused, Yarby waited a moment for further explanation. When none was forthcoming, he was forced to ask, "Whom do you mean, Mr. Collins? I know she has become good friends with Mary Bennet. But I cannot see how that is an issue of any possible controversy."

"It *is* a Bennet to whom I refer, Mr. Yarby, although not the Bennet you may be thinking of." Yarby saw a smile spread across Mr. Collins's doughy, but animated, face. "I see I must explain. Well. I happened to be strolling around the countryside the other day and saw your sister also enjoying the out-of-doors—with *Mr.* Bennet as her companion. As I observed them, it became clear to me they now have a very… *intimate* relationship."

Mr. Yarby was so stunned, he could make no response. Leaning back in his chair and folding his hands across his ample stomach, Mr. Collins gave a satisfied chuckle.

"You are unaware of their friendship; I can tell from your countenance," he continued. "Of course, they are both widowed at this point, so that is not shocking, although because Mrs. Withers is your sister, any such connection to your current employer is certain to raise eyebrows. But what is unacceptable by any definition of decorum is the quickness with which this relationship has…flourished. Mr. Bennet is still in full mourning. And for him to be traipsing around the neighborhood with her—so ostentatiously, so *indiscreetly*—will certainly damage both her and your reputations."

Yarby struggled for a response to this shocking news. "I…I did not know—are you quite certain it was them?"

"Indeed. I watched them for some time. Thinking themselves alone, they did not attempt to hide their affection. At one point, she even lifted his hand to her cheek! To her *cheek*, sir!"

Yarby tried to think of a way to end this distasteful conversation. He stood. "Well. I shall speak to my sister and ask that she be more careful. Thank you for bringing this to my attention."

"I fear that will not be sufficient, Mr. Yarby."

There was a long pause as a wave of dread washed over the rector. He slowly returned to his seat.

"No?" he asked softly. "What else is there?"

"Naturally, you will chastise your sister and insist that she check her behavior, but the matter cannot be so easily hushed up."

"I fail to understand your meaning." Mr. Yarby did, in fact, begin to see where this was leading, but he was hoping against hope that he was mistaken.

"I dislike having to resort to this, but I think, in order to assure yourself that word of this scandalous relationship does not escape into town, we must come to…an agreement."

Mr. Yarby let out a long breath. It was as he feared: Mr. Collins was blackmailing him. But for what?

"If you…that is…I cannot pay you for your silence if that is your meaning."

There was a pause as Mr. Collins stared at him with a satisfied little smile on his face.

Mr. Yarby felt his temper begin to rise. "And if you expect me to vacate the position so that you may take it, be assured that I would then report your attempted extortion to Mr. Bennet myself!"

Mr. Collins gave a dry chuckle. "Now, now…things need not escalate to such an extent. Mr. Bennet has hired you, and only he or the bishop can fire you. And sadly, although I am his cousin, there is no guarantee that, should you depart, I would be given the living."

"Then what are you asking?"

Mr. Collins crossed his legs and leaned forward, speaking in a low, urgent voice. "Despite all efforts, I have been unable to secure a position in a new parish. I feel I must bring in something to support my family. Living at the mercy of Sir William Lucas has been quite difficult for me. So. What I am proposing is this: you will take me on as your 'curate'—really more an equal partner than curate—but call it what you will. You can say you feel the need of a more experienced hand to guide you in your first parish. You will pay me sixty pounds a year and allow me two sermons a month as my own. In exchange, on the sad day when Mr. Bennet passes and I become the owner of Longbourn, I shall keep you on. In addition, I shall keep the secret of your sister's attachment to Mr. Bennet. But if you refuse my terms, all your sister has done will be revealed. Dare you risk the scorn of your flock or the wrath of your bishop? Most likely, you will be dismissed on moral grounds. But even if you survive, I assure you that when *I* take charge of Longbourn estate, I will not only dismiss you, but I will so tarnish your reputation that you will essentially never work as a clergyman again." He sat back, clearly waiting for a response.

Mr. Yarby's head was whirling. His position at Longbourn parish—so secure, so happy—was all at tremendous risk. If he refused Mr. Collins's demands, Amelia's reputation—and by association, his own—would be badly damaged. If he agreed and took on Mr. Collins, he would not only have to survive on little more than he was paid when he was a curate but also work closely with a man whose very presence irritated him beyond measure. But what could he do? Perhaps he could send

Amelia away for a time. No, that would never work. Where could she go, at any rate? Their older brother did not own a home but took rooms in a respectable lodging house, so Amelia could not join him there. And they had no other family. Plus, there would be no guarantee that Mr. Collins would not sully her reputation just for spite.

He took a shaky breath and let it out slowly.

"Very well. I agree to your terms."

Chapter 15

"It is good to see you, Mary; thank you for coming," Elizabeth said in a subdued voice. Propped up in bed, she appeared wan and her cheeks a bit sunken, Mary thought.

"You are pale," Mary said. She crossed the room, bringing a chair with her to sit next to the bed, still studying her sister. "And far too thin. Are you eating enough?" she demanded, bluntly.

Elizabeth smiled. "I am just now beginning to get my appetite back. No doubt, if Mama were still with us, she would be down in the kitchen, ordering beef bone broth to be made at once."

Mary half rose from her chair. "I can do that—do you wish me to do that for you?" she asked earnestly.

Elizabeth laughed softly and motioned Mary to return to her seat. "No. I never cared for it personally. Our cook is excellent. I only fear I am injuring her feelings by sending back too many uneaten trays." Mary watched her sister close her eyes briefly and sigh, as if speaking so many sentences had tired her. Then Lizzy opened her eyes again and gave a small smile. "I truly am glad you have come to Pemberley. Tell me all the news of Meryton and Longbourn."

"Things are very much as they always were, I suppose," Mary said, then fell silent.

After a pause, Lizzy said with mock severity, "You shall have to do better than that, Mary, if you are to see me become well again. I am quite in need of some good gossip! Tell me, do you see much of Charlotte and Mr. Collins?"

Mary blushed at the gentle rebuke and gave a tiny laugh. "More than Papa would like, I am certain. I have invited them to dine with us three times, and of course, the Lucas family has had us to dinner at least as often. Charlotte is showing her pregnancy quite a bit now; she is due to give birth in late December, you know. She called on me at Longbourn before I set off and asked me to give you her best wishes for your recovery. In truth, I think she is quite fearful of giving birth herself. Hearing of your…difficulties may have made her nervous."

"Childbirth is fraught with peril for all women, sadly," Elizabeth said softly. "However, she is healthy if a bit older for a first time mother. I am sure all will be well. Let us just hope the baby favors her more than her husband." She winked at Mary.

"Lizzy—you are quite wicked! You must truly be feeling better." Mary smiled warmly. Had she ever had such an intimate conversation with her older sister? She could not recall.

After gossiping for another quarter of an hour, during which Mary detailed her growing friendship with Amelia Withers, Elizabeth's eyes began to droop.

"Perhaps I should leave you now to rest?" Mary asked hesitantly. "I can return and read to you if you like."

"That would be nice," murmured Elizabeth. "They will bring Lavinia to me this afternoon after the wet nurse feeds her. Then you can meet your niece."

"I have already met her," Mary replied proudly. "I think her quite pleasing."

Elizabeth gave a small smile. "Do you? Please do not mention this to Fitzwilliam, but I fear our daughter is not, well…very attractive. Thomas was such a beautiful baby, whereas Lavinia seems to have such a pinched little face: her chin is a bit too pointed, and I cannot call her eyes exactly lovely. However, I am sure I am needlessly worrying. She will, no doubt, begin to blossom soon. Her arrival into the world was hard on her as well."

Mary stared at her sister, one of the two great beauties of her family. She took a deep breath. "Lizzy—would you love her any less if she were *not* a beauty?" she asked, trying to keep her voice calm.

"No, of course not, Mary—you misunderstand me. I love my daughter with all my heart. As I said, I am likely worrying without cause. But you must own life is more difficult for those who are unattractive."

Mary felt a jolt of anger. Was that comment directed at her? Was Lizzy making a reference to her plain looks? "Time will tell, Lizzy. Perhaps you are right and it was the difficult birth. She will most likely end up being quite a beauty. After all, you and Mr. Darcy are her parents, and nobody would call either of you plain."

Elizabeth rolled over in bed and shut her eyes.

"Yes, of course," she said in a drowsy voice. "And even if Lavinia should be plain, she will have dowry enough to guarantee she will not be left on the shelf."

Clenching her fists, Mary left Lizzy's room and walked rapidly downstairs. She replayed the conversation with her sister in her mind. Did Elizabeth really mean those things she said? No, she could not have. Surely, the comments only came from the strain of her long recovery after giving birth. After all, Lizzy was innately kind, and even though she had a renowned wit, she never used it in a mean-spirited or cruel manner. And yet…what she said about life being "more difficult for those who are unattractive" stung. Mary reached the music room and paused, then walked with deliberation to the pianoforte.

Although she knew it would only be polite to first ask permission from Georgiana to play it, Mary went straight to the beautiful instrument—a gift to her from Darcy for her fifteenth birthday, Georgiana had said—and sat on the bench covered in needlepoint depicting angels and flowers. After a moment, Mary chose a sonnet from her memory and began to play, gently at first, but soon she was pounding hard upon the keys, trying to release her anger.

When she finished, a familiar voice spoke.

"Gracious. I have never heard that particular piece played with such...vigor, Mary."

Mary's head snapped up to see Georgiana standing in the doorway. She dropped her hands in her lap and, avoiding eye contact, mumbled an apology.

"Forgive me, Miss Georgiana, I had a need to...release some slight irritation. I should have asked your permission before I touched your piano. I apologize."

Georgiana crossed the room and sat beside her on the bench. She placed her hand on one of Mary's.

"Do not be sorry. You are more than welcome to play while you are here. Your sister often plays it, and you are my sister too, so you must not think you require my permission."

When Mary did not reply, Georgiana stood and riffled through some sheets of music on a small table nearby. She chose one and set it before Mary.

"Have you seen this? It is a duet. I know both parts, but have not yet had anyone to play it with me. Would you...would you like to try?"

Mary felt tears prickle her eyes; gracious, why was she so emotional? She nodded and shifted down a bit on the bench. After scanning the score a moment, she adjusted her glasses and placed her hands on the keyboard to signal her readiness. Georgiana happily set hers in position, and giving a nod, the two began to play.

When they finished, Georgiana considered her sister-in-law.

"That was quite good, Mary; I am pleased to finally hear it as it should be played. Thank you."

"I made a few mistakes."

"Hardly even noticeable, to my mind. However"—Georgiana seemed to consider her words carefully before continuing—"it would be a small improvement if you put more emphasis on the melodic nature of your lines."

"But your lines have the melody for the most part," Mary protested.

"What I mean is, you seem to play each note and chord with the very same emphasis—the same pressure on the keys, if you will. I do not wish to criticize you, but I had an instructor who taught me that merely hitting the correct notes is not enough. One must sometimes caress the keys and other times strike more forcibly. I have found that, when you allow your emotions to enter into it in such a manner, that is when it truly becomes music."

Mary was silent, staring at the music.

"Oh, but I should not have spoken. Pray forgive me," Georgiana hurriedly said. "I did not wish to offend you, believe me."

"I do not take the least offense, be assured. I *want* to improve my technique. My father only paid for a very few years of formal instruction, you see, and since then I have been on my own, learning as I can." She turned an earnest face to Georgiana. "I appreciate your comments, truly. The things you just said I have never heard before, and now I understand why someone once referred to my piano work as *plodding*, rather than *playing*." Mary smiled. "Shall we try it again? I shall endeavor to take your instruction into account and then you can tell me whether you see improvement."

Georgiana nodded, and the two happily started once more.

"I CANNOT APOLOGIZE ENOUGH, ROBERT...CAN YOU EVER FORGIVE me?" Amelia spoke in a shaky voice after her brother informed her that her affection towards Mr. Bennet had been witnessed by Mr. Collins. The two sat behind the closed door of his study and kept their voices hushed to prevent any servants overhearing.

"It is not for me to forgive you, Amelia. You know I only wish you to be happy." Robert rose from his chair and knelt beside her, lowering his voice even more. "But tell me: Are you...I mean...*is* there an understanding between you and Mr. Bennet?"

"Not in so many words, no. Eugene—I mean, Mr. Bennet has never spoken of it, nor have I. And he has not been indiscreet or too forward; he has not compromised me. I truly can have no expectations in respect to his feelings at this point. But I must own that we *have* become closer during these walks. He is, as you know, a most amiable gentleman. Our conversations began with him pouring out his heart to me in the grief over losing his wife, and his regrets at not having been a better husband. Then our conversations slowly turned to other topics—books, music, philosophy, his family. I have tried to soften his views towards his daughters, particularly Mary. But again, no—there is no understanding in the formal sense, Robert." She saw a skeptical expression on his face.

"But there could be. You sound as if you would not reject his addresses." Yarby rose and returned to his desk chair.

Amelia threw her hands up, helplessly. "I cannot say! It is far too soon to predict what may occur between us. I can only apologize for being too unguarded in my actions towards Mr. Bennet, and I promise I will check any such behavior in the future." She lifted her eyes in appeal to her brother. "We had been enjoying such a lovely walk that day. He was in the finest spirits I had seen since the funeral, so I suppose I encouraged it a bit by teasing him. When he plucked the leaf off my bonnet, he had such an impish expression, I could not help but laugh. And then he laughed, and my heart filled so to see him thus, I…I took his hand and placed it to my cheek." She shook herself. "Oh! Of all people—to have that odious Mr. Collins see us!"

"And he could hardly wait to inform me of his discovery," Yarby said grimly.

"Will he stay quiet? Above all, I do not wish to see your reputation damaged. As for my own, I do not care. I am a widow without any expectations, so it matters little what people say about me. But I could not bear to see you slandered or your position here compromised."

Yarby took a deep breath and exhaled slowly before replying. "Mr. Collins and I have…come to an understanding, Amelia, but I have not told you the terms."

Amelia gasped. "*Terms?* Mr. Collins had demands?"

"I am to take him on as my 'curate' although he fancies himself as an equal rector. I must allow him two sermons a month to preach, and pay him a salary of sixty pounds. In exchange, he will keep silent."

Amelia began to weep. "It is all my fault. What a cost…such a price to pay! Why can we not tell Mr. Bennet? Perhaps there is something he can do."

"Absolutely not. We cannot involve him in any way. I fear Mr. Collins would make good on his threats if we did."

"But what are we to say when Mr. Collins is there in church and speaks from the pulpit? I confess that Mr. Bennet has told me more than once of his loathing of the man. He will surely question your taking him on."

"I have given it considerable thought. We shall say that I have a chronic illness that has flared up—gout, perhaps, or weak lungs. Therefore, I must bring a curate on to assist me. It is not uncommon for a rector to have one, as you know."

"Yes, but Robert, that occurs mostly when a rector has more than one parish to manage—you have but this alone."

"I know, which is why my poor health must be my stated reason. Then I shall say that, because Mr. Collins is so nearby, we considered him the perfect man for the job. That is, until he finds a full time parish for himself."

"Something for which I shall pray daily," Amelia replied grimly. She rose and dabbed her eyes with her handkerchief. "I suppose I must review our budget and see where economies can be made. If we are to give nearly half our salary to Mr. Collins, we shall have to retrench a bit. I think, if we let Frank go, we can save twenty pounds there. We can always hire someone for any jobs we cannot do ourselves." She walked to the door and turned a sad face to her brother.

"Again—I am so very, very sorry, Robert. Will you…will you write Mr. Collins now?"

Robert nodded silently and took out a sheet of paper.

IN THEIR BEDROOM IN LUCAS LODGE, A CONVERSATION WAS ALSO being held between Mr. Collins and his wife.

"But, William—a curate position? Is that not a step backwards?" Charlotte asked. "Why would you accept it?"

"It will be only temporary, my dear, I am sure," Mr. Collins replied. "I am eager to be busy again. Idleness is not my way, as you well know. Yarby has promised me two sermons of my own per month. Plus, the money will help."

"We have next to no expenses now, living with Mother and Father. Although, I do long to manage our own home again."

"Precisely. But with sixty pounds to call our own, we may consider moving out of Lucas Lodge." Charlotte began to object, but he held up his hand to silence her. "I am extremely fond of your family, of course, but I have no place to call my own. I shall need a place to do my work now that I am to be curate—well, with my experience, it will be more of an advisory rector position, truly—and there simply is not anywhere in this house for me to have peace and quiet."

He saw Charlotte press her lips firmly together a moment before replying, "But sixty pounds is so little! And where would we go? Do you see us living in rented rooms above a public house in Meryton for Heaven's sake, William? Noisy, furnished shoddily, and no doubt damp—that cannot be good for our future child. Like you, I long for a place to call our own, but rented rooms will not do."

"You can spend a goodly amount of each day here, of course, my dear, but I must have my own place. And I would expect my wife to be there with me."

Charlotte stood. "No. Rent rooms for yourself and spend all of your day in them if you please. Then you may return to Lucas Lodge each evening. But I shall not budge from here for the sake of your vanity alone."

Mr. Collins considered her proposition a moment before nodding. Easier to agree with Charlotte for now and persuade her to move out once he finds a place.

"Very well, I shall do just as you wish. I am sure it will all be temporary on any account. A permanent living is certain to come up soon."

"Or, as we discussed before, Mr. Bennet may expire for sorrow over his late wife."

A queer little smile come over Mr. Collins's face. "Oh, I do not think we can count on that, my dear. I am afraid his mood has quite altered of late. Indeed, the boot is quite on the other leg now."

He walked over, kissed his wife, and proceeded downstairs.

"I shall be in Meryton exploring possible rooms for rent. You can expect me back by supper."

Chapter 16

The following day, Mary had to force herself to visit her sister. She was still vexed with Elizabeth's comments about beauty. But knowing her duty to her father, she knocked gently, then opened the door to see whether Elizabeth was awake.

As soon as she stepped into the room, Elizabeth, sitting up in bed, reached out with both hands to her. Mary caught the glimmer of tears shining in her sister's eyes.

"Mary, I am so glad you have come to see me today. I must speak with you. I have not slept but a wink last night, and I fear tonight will be no different if I do not settle things between us."

"Oh?" Mary was so surprised, she could think of nothing else to say. She crossed the room and sat beside the bed to give Elizabeth her full attention.

"Mary, I wish to apologize for my thoughtless and hateful comments yesterday. Not only was I far too harsh about my own, dear daughter, but I greatly fear you might feel I was also speaking of you in some way. I was not—please be assured of that. I can only account for my language by saying I was feeling weak and unwell yesterday, and I let my mood get the better of my manners. Please excuse me. You have come all this way just to cheer me up, and now if I have hurt your feelings to the point where you wish to leave and return to Longbourn, I shall be so angry with myself. Please say you will forgive me, *please*."

Mary blinked a moment, taking in this remarkable apology. "Of course, I forgive you, Lizzy. After all, the Bible exhorts us to forgive our trespasses, as we forgive those who trespass against us."

Elizabeth nodded. "But do speak from your heart please, Mary—not the Bible. Do you accept my apology?"

Mary could see remorse in her sister's eyes—and a hint of fear as well. She felt her own resentment melt away.

"Yes, Lizzy, I fully accept your apology. Let there be no impediment to our sisterly bond."

Elizabeth exhaled and smiled. "Thank you, Mary. Now—if you will ring the bell for tea, I have a treat for us." She reached under the covers and pulled out two letters. She held them up, with an excited expression. "These two letters arrived today, and I have saved them to read with you. One is from Jane, and one is from Charlotte. Let us savor their news and gossip and have a happy afternoon together."

Mary returned Elizabeth's smile. She could not think of a better way to spend the next couple of hours.

For two days, Mr. Bennet had gone to his and Amelia's usual meeting place for their afternoon walk and found no one waiting for him. He had tarried for a quarter hour both times, hopeful that she would appear, only to be disappointed and continue his walk alone.

On the third day, finding himself unmet yet again, he turned from his usual path and went to the rectory. Perhaps she was ill. He knocked on the door and asked to see Mrs. Withers. He was shown to the parlor, and after a few minutes, Amelia entered, a subdued expression on her face. She remained near the door, making no effort to come closer.

"Good afternoon, Mr. Bennet," she greeted him as she dropped a polite curtsey. "I hope you are well this day."

He stood. "I am, thank you. It is *you* I have come to inquire about. You have not met me for our walk for three days now. I feared you were ailing."

Amelia glanced behind her and shut the door, then motioned Mr. Bennet to sit, taking a place on the settee across from him, leaning in to speak softly.

"I am well—be assured. I have not been able to walk of late because I feel our rambles are putting you in a somewhat compromising position."

"How so?"

Amelia took a deep breath before replying. "Remember the recent walk we took when you plucked a leaf from my bonnet and I impulsively brought your hand to my cheek?"

"I do. Why do you bring this up? If you are worried that I considered your action inappropriate, be at ease. It felt both natural and comfortable."

"Indeed, it was for me as well. But you see—someone witnessed that act and has made mention of it to Robert."

"How dare someone spy upon me! Who was it?"

"It matters not who it is. But for the sake of our reputations, we must reduce our time together in public. And we must be more circumspect in our behavior towards one another at all times so that, if we are seen, no one will suspect we are anything other than…indifferent acquaintances who happen to be walking together."

Mr. Bennet pressed his lips together a moment then rose, crossed over, and sat beside Amelia, taking her hand. She did not pull back but did not look at him. He spoke in a low voice, gazing at her intently. "But we *are* more than indifferent acquaintances, are we not?"

When she remained silent, he softly stroked her hand. "I do not think I am misinterpreting your feelings for me. I confess, my own inclination towards you has led me to hope for a time—very soon—when we may be quite close...Amelia."

Hearing him speak her given name brought tears to her eyes. She lifted her face to his, but still could not speak.

"Am I wrong to speak of this?" Mr. Bennet asked, anxiety in his voice. "Am I being a presumptuous old man? If you do not return my feelings, you have only to say so, and I shall be silent on the issue from here on."

She gave a gentle smile and placed a hand on one of his. "I *do* return your feelings...Eugene. I never anticipated it, nor sought it, but I do care for you a great deal." Her face turned serious. "But you are still in mourning! It would be a scandal for us to make any pronouncement at this time."

He nodded. "I am aware of that. And while I do not care three straws for society's good opinion of me, out of deference and respect to my late wife's memory, we cannot make our... understanding known—yet." He drew her hand to his lips and kissed it gently. "Dearest Amelia. I shall count the days until the mourning period ends."

"As shall I," Amelia replied breathlessly.

"And dash it all—I *still* wish to walk with you! The exercise is quite beneficial to me, I find. We shall simply take more care where we walk and be mindful of our comportment when together. But I simply cannot be content only seeing you at our dining table once or twice a month, or at church. Will you continue to meet me for our strolls—at least three times a week? Are you agreeable to that?"

Knowing she should say no for her brother's sake, Amelia instead replied, "Oh yes. Very agreeable, my dear Eugene."

TWO DAYS LATER, MR. BENNET AND THE RECTOR SAT IN THE parsonage's study. Yarby had sent a note to his employer, asking to discuss something of importance. When he related his decision for Mr. Collins to work at the parish, Mr. Bennet blurted his astonishment.

"I simply do not understand it, Mr. Yarby—of all people to bring on as curate—Mr. Collins! I suppose if your health is in need of assistance that is one thing, but I wish you had consulted me beforehand. I should have severely counseled you to find another candidate—*any* other candidate, for that matter," he ended in a mutter.

Mr. Yarby shifted uncomfortably in his chair. He knew he could not confess the real reason Mr. Collins was sharing the pulpit now, and he hated exceedingly to lie to his employer as he considered how to reply.

"It will be temporary at best, I am certain. I shall be my old self soon and able to handle things on my own. I am…quite grateful to Mr. Collins for stepping in."

"Frankly, I am surprised my pompous cousin would even take on the curacy—a demotion of sorts as it is."

Mr. Yarby fiddled with a letter opener on his desk. He found it hard to look Mr. Bennet in the eyes. "Oh…no. He was…most gracious. And I am certain he will be accepted by the congregation. All will be well, Mr. Bennet, have no fear."

"But this will be a financial burden to you, will it not? I wish I could afford to supplement what you will pay Mr. Collins to lessen the impact on you, but I allow I am unable to."

Yarby raised solemn eyes to Mr. Bennet. "I would not permit you to do so, sir. The…reasons for taking on Mr. Collins are mine, and I alone must bear the cost. My sister is quite good with a budget. We shall be fine."

Later, as Mr. Bennet reflected upon the rector's words, they had all the appearance of sincerity, yet they rang hollow to his ear. He made a note to himself to ask Amelia about it when they next walked.

However, he found Amelia every bit as reluctant to discuss the matter as her brother. Several times during their stroll, he pressed her for the real reason her brother had hired Mr. Collins, but she would only demur and say he "knows best, no doubt."

At last, Mr. Bennet had no choice but to drop the subject. But his instinct told him there was something else at play. And he determined he would do his best to somehow get to the bottom of it.

November 5

Dear Amelia,

I hope this letter finds both you and Mr. Yarby well. Thank you for your last letter, and for writing that my father and sister are both enjoying good health. I appreciate your visiting them—the house must seem so empty now, and I am certain you keep them from dwelling upon it.

I feel quite settled now at Pemberley and have a routine that is not too taxing. I spend mornings with my sister Lizzy, sometimes accompanied by Mr. Darcy's younger sister, Georgiana. Together, we have exhorted Lizzy to leave her sick bed and begin walking a bit—first around her room, then up and down the hallways, and finally to come downstairs and sit in the morning room for brief periods. Her color is better, and she seems to have more stamina. Her husband's relief is palpable. I never believed I had the least skill in nursing, but perhaps I am wrong and can claim some minor talent in this regard.

In the afternoons, Georgiana and I go for walks around the grounds of Pemberley if the weather is fine, or I read if not. We often play the pianoforte too. Sometimes we perform together, sometimes separately, but she has been kind enough to coach me on some of the finer points of my playing, and I hope when we next see each other, you will notice, perhaps, some not insignificant improvement in my performance. She has also helped me with my dancing. How kind she has been to spend so much effort on me. In truth, she has shown more sisterly affection than most of the Bennet sisters! I do not wish to write unkind things about my family, but you know me too well for me to try and dissemble in my discourse.

After tea, I return to my sister's room when they bring the baby to her for a visit. Lavinia Jane, although still small, is also improving in health, and I believe fears of her not thriving have been put to rest. She seems to have taken to me quite well, and I find I adore holding her— another revelation to me.

Despite all the kindness shown to me, and the marvelous library at Pemberley, I long to return to Longbourn, my family and, of course, your society. As rapidly as Lizzy is improving, I expect I may depart for home in early December if the roads are not too bad. Everyone here wishes me to remain for Christmas, but I would much prefer to be at home since Papa wrote he is not planning on traveling with Kitty to Pemberley as we always have in the past. I fear he thinks such company would be too taxing on Lizzy. So it will be a quiet Christmas at Longbourn. I look forward to it and to hearing Mr. Yarby's first Christmas sermon.

With kindest regards,

Your friend,
Mary Bennet

Chapter 17

Ten days before Christmas, Mary arrived back at Longbourn, having been transported by one of Darcy's best carriages with two footmen in attendance for security. She was a bit surprised at the welling of emotion that overtook her as the carriage turned into the sweep and she saw her home. Her father, Kitty, and Mrs. Hill came out to greet her, despite the chilly, overcast day.

"I am glad you are come home, Mary," said Mr. Bennet, kissing her on the cheek. "It will seem a bit more like Christmas with both my daughters here."

"Oh, but Lydia, Wickham, and the boys are coming too, Papa," Kitty chimed in. "Do not forget that."

"As if I could."

"It is good to be home," Mary said as they entered the house. "I bring Christmas presents for you all from Lizzy and Mr. Darcy, although I confess I did most of the shopping for her as she was still not feeling strong enough. She did accompany me into the village but waited in the carriage and gave me instructions on what to purchase—even my own gift." She laughed. "So 'twill be no surprise when I open mine!"

Mary saw Father nod approvingly. "I believe Pemberley has been good for you, Mary. You appear quite content. You must give us all the news over tea—all that you did not share in your letters, that is."

"Oh, but we have little time for that, Papa; the Christmas assembly is tonight!" Kitty exclaimed. Mary noticed for the first time that her sister was now out of mourning black and wore a deep purple dress with accents of green. "I was so afraid you might miss it, but you came back just in time. Of course, I know you dislike dancing in general, but just to mingle with people and not be dressed in full mourning, that is worth celebrating, is it not? What will you wear? Your dark green dress with the gold stripes?"

"No…" Mary thought of the new, beautiful maroon dress in the back of her closet. "I have another dress in mind."

THAT EVENING, MARY INSTRUCTED SARAH TO TAKE PARTICULAR pains with styling her hair. At Pemberley, Georgiana had helped her devise a new look that Mary thought quite attractive, and she was determined to have the Bennet's underhousemaid recreate it. When it was finally as she liked, Mary enlisted Sarah's help to put on her new gown, relieved to see it was every bit as beautiful as she remembered. She resisted the urge to tug the neckline up, telling herself that the ecru lace gave her modesty enough while still flattering her smaller bosom. Her corset had but little to push up, she reflected sadly, but as she studied herself in the mirror, she decided she was more than presentable. She could only hope Mr. Yarby might also think so. As the daughter of his employer, she was confident of getting one dance, but—oh!—she hoped for so much more!

Mary opened her small jewelry box and lifted out the dainty garnet necklace that had belonged to her mother. She fastened the clasp behind her neck and smiled to see how perfectly it rested just below her collarbone—the gold chain and gems glinting as they caught the candlelight. With a hopeful heart, she grabbed her best shawl and went downstairs to join her family.

THE ASSEMBLY HALL WAS CROWDED, NOISY, AND WARM AS THE Bennets entered, and Mary thought she would likely soon discard her shawl. Kitty, seeing Maria Lucas, skipped away to join her friend, leaving Mary holding her father's arm while they stood, scanning the room.

Frankly, Mary was rather surprised her father chose to come to the gathering; he rarely had done so in the past. *But that was when Mama was still alive and could chaperone. I expect he feels it is his duty now.*

"Papa, thank you for bringing us, though I know you do not care much for balls and dancing." She leaned in close to be heard over the music. "I hope you shan't be too bored."

Mr. Bennet patted her arm. "Do not fret over me, my dear. I shall find some way to amuse myself."

Sir William Lucas came up to them, clapping his hands in delight. "I see you are back from Pemberley, Miss Bennet. Capital! Quite capital to have you attend tonight. You are looking very well, if I may say so. And I am certain many an eligible young man will be asking for the honor of a dance tonight, so pray do not refuse even though we know you consider dancing to be a touch frivolous!"

"Thank you, Sir William," she replied, evenly. "I confess I do not have such high hopes as you, but we shall see what the evening holds." Spying Amelia across the room, she excused herself and hurried over.

The two women embraced and stood together with their arms about each other's waists, watching the dancing.

"It is so good to have you back, Mary," Amelia said. "I appreciated the fine letters you wrote, but words on paper cannot compare to a true conversation with my friend. You left your sister well?"

"Lizzy is very nearly her old self, I am happy to report. It is a pity not to have Christmas with them all at Pemberley, but in truth, I am so glad to be home."

"Did I see your father enter with you?"

"Oh yes, he does not care for dancing, so I suppose he will spend most of his time in the card room. Perhaps we shall see him in the supper room later. Is…is your brother here?"

"Is someone speaking of me?" a familiar voice said behind the two ladies.

Mary spun around and felt her breath catch in her throat. "Oh! Mr. Yarby…I did not know whether you would be here." She curtseyed. "It is a pleasure to see you again." Oh, he was every bit as handsome as she remembered. Such kind eyes—and those dimples!

"It is equally good to see you back home, Miss Bennet. I know Amelia certainly pined for your company during your long absence, but I hope your time away resulted in a beneficial outcome to your sister's health."

Mary felt her face begin to flush—good heavens, what was wrong with her? She cleared her throat. "Oh, yes. I was just telling Amelia that Lizzy is doing quite well. The more her wicked wit displayed itself, the better I knew she was."

"Mary is quite fetching tonight, do you not think, Robert?" Amelia asked. "Now that she and Miss Kitty Bennet are out of full mourning, they can enjoy assemblies and dance as all young ladies should."

Oh, please ask me to dance—please! Mary silently begged.

"You look quite well indeed, Miss Bennet," said Yarby. "And if I may—"

"Mr. Yarby—the last set has ended. I believe this is our dance," a voice broke in.

Mary turned to see her sister Kitty smiling, her eyes firmly fixed on the rector. How on earth did she get an invitation to dance with Mr. Yarby so quickly? He must have promised it to her earlier in the week. Perhaps he is smitten with Kitty! Mary felt her confidence begin to ebb away.

"Indeed, it is, Miss Catherine. But first, I wished—"

But Kitty was already tugging at his sleeve. "Come, or we shall have a bad position in the line!"

With a small smile and an apologetic look back at his sister and Mary, Mr. Yarby allowed himself to be pulled onto the dance floor.

While the dance set commenced, Mary and Amelia chatted although Mary found it hard to concentrate on the conversation as she watched her sister and Mr. Yarby. Kitty was so light on her feet and seemed to be enjoying herself enormously. Much to her dismay, Mary saw that Mr. Yarby appeared equally engaged. Did he particularly care for her, or was this just the kindness he always showed her family? Mary was in agony as she watched them. The set seemed interminable, but at last it ended, and Mr. Yarby escorted Kitty off the floor, where another young man immediately engaged her for the next dance. Mary stared resolutely at the floor, wishing she could disappear into the crowd, but Amelia's arm was firmly linked in hers.

"Goodness, that was robust. I am quite glad my new shoes fit well." Yarby said as he rejoined them. "I believe this next dance is ours, Amelia."

Amelia turned to her companion. "Mary, would you do me the gracious favor of taking this set with my brother? I suddenly feel overheated and am quite thirsty and in need of refreshment; it is so very warm in here. You don't mind, do you, Robert?"

Mary saw a flustered expression on Yarby's face for a moment, although it quickly changed to his usual smile. Was he feeling forced to dance with her? She lowered her eyes to the floor and stood, mute.

"Not at all," she heard him say. "That is, if Miss Bennet is agreeable."

Mary nodded, fighting back tears. Likely, it would be her only dance all night with the rector and was due to a gift from Amelia—not even his own idea. She took his arm, and they walked onto the floor to take their positions.

Why should I have thought it would be any different than before? I am homely, awkward, and not at all a desirable partner. He was clearly uncomfortable with Amelia's request. I have his pity, not his affection. Well, at least I know the steps to all the latest dances, thanks to Georgiana, so I shan't make a complete fool of myself.

"YOU LOOK QUITE WELL TONIGHT, MISS BENNET," YARBY SAID AS they brushed past each other, took hands and turned. "Is that a new hairstyle? Amelia always exhorts me to notice such things, for she says ladies enjoy such comments. Am I correct?"

"It *is* a new style. You are all flattery, sir, I thank you." Mary could think of no other answer, but fortunately, the dance steps moved them apart for a time. When they reunited again, she changed the subject. "There was an assembly last month, was there not? Did you and Amelia attend? The subscription fee is not too steep, is it?"

"No, I think it quite reasonable. And to answer your question, we had planned to attend in November, but one of my parishioners became quite ill—indeed, we feared he might die—so I was at his bedside. Amelia could not attend alone, of course, so she stayed home."

"Papa might have been persuaded to take her—oh, but so soon after Mama died, that would have opened him to criticism, most likely."

She saw an odd, brief expression on Mr. Yarby's face, but he did not have time to speak before the two parted again, taking new partners for the next few lines before reuniting.

"Yes, and Amelia as well," Yarby continued. "I should hate to see her injured in such a public manner."

Mary gave him a serious gaze. "You are such a good and devoted brother, Mr. Yarby. You make me quite envious. I believe all we Bennet sisters would have benefited from having a brother such as yourself. And not just because we could have kept Longbourn in the Bennet family."

"You are generous to say so. I hope I am the kind of brother she deserves."

They continued to dance silently for a time before Mr. Yarby spoke again.

"Miss Bennet, I wonder whether I could ask you for some advice."

Mary felt her color rise again—how gracious of him to seek her opinion! He *must* think highly of her.

"Of course, how may I help?"

"I have been wracking my brain trying to think of a good Christmas gift for Amelia. I have purchased a book for her, but I should like to get her something…you know…"

"More feminine and suited for a lady's taste?" Mary asked with a small smile.

"Yes! Exactly. What would you suggest?"

"Well, I did notice her reticule is in need of replacing. The velvet is quite worn away in spots. I am sure you could find one that would suit in Meryton."

"The very thing! Thank you, Miss Bennet—that will do perfectly!"

THE TWO MOVED TOGETHER SO WELL, MARY WISHED THE DANCE set would never end, but at last Mr. Yarby escorted her from the floor. She looked around for Amelia but did not see her, so she found a chair and sat, waiting and hoping for another dance with Mr. Yarby. She studied the other single young ladies in the room, some younger than she, others a bit older. They all seemed in high spirits, gaily laughing and flirting. Mary wished she could flirt. It simply was not in her nature; such a false act to attract a man's attention was abhorrent to her in every way. And, she had to admit, she would not even know how to begin.

But could Robert fall in love with her if she did *not* flirt a little? How else could she let him know of her feelings for him? She could not simply declare her feelings to him in a blunt fashion. It would be terribly forward. And what if she did and he rejected her? She would die from embarrassment.

Oh, Mama, if you were here, I am certain you could give me some guidance. Tell me how to use my mind and words to win him over.

But as she watched the other young ladies, she reflected that Mrs. Bennet might not have been able to advise her on a strategy. It was not her intellect after all, but her mother's beauty and charm that had won over her father.

Neither of which I have in abundance...

Chapter 18

After leaving Mary and her brother to dance, Amelia went to the supper room. Of course, at the low subscription prices for these assemblies, a full meal was not served, but there were a couple platters of cheeses, some bread and sweet rolls, and hot tea, as well as a large punchbowl of negus. She would have preferred a cool beverage to the warm wine punch, but as it was the only other option, Amelia moved towards the table.

As she reached for the pewter handle of the ladle, her hand collided with another's. She jerked her hand back with a small gasp and heard a familiar chuckle.

"Forgive me, Amelia. It seems we are again wanting the same thing at the same time," Mr. Bennet said.

Amelia took a step back, and gave a small curtsey. "Good evening, Mr. Bennet," she said formally. Noting his confused countenance, she glanced around to see whether anyone was watching. Assured they were not being observed, she said in a lower voice, "Pray pardon the formality of my greeting. I only wish to keep from drawing attention to ourselves, of course." She turned away slightly and casually picked up a punch cup. "I am so happy to see you, Eugene."

"And I you," he said softly. "May I?" He took the cup from her hand and filled it with the warm mixture of port wine, water, and sugar, and handed it to her, then served himself. The two strolled to a corner of the room where they could observe others.

"You are not dancing?" Mr. Bennet asked.

"I had a set reserved with my brother, but I felt a bit faint from the heat and asked him to escort Mary onto the floor instead so I could get a drink."

"Mary? But she rarely dances."

"Really? She seemed content to do so. Oh dear, I hope I have not erred in asking her to step in for me."

"The only issue will be whether she knows the steps at all! Robert may have a challenge on his hand, but it will likely be fine. Do not overly concern yourself."

"And…are you of a mind to dance tonight, Eugene?" She kept her eyes on the others in the room as she asked, a serene, impersonal expression on her face as if they were not truly having a conversation.

In a similar fashion, Mr. Bennet looked placidly straight ahead. "I know very few of the newer dances, but if they play a tune for a good old country dance, I might be inclined to take to the floor. If…you would be my partner."

Amelia briefly cut her eyes over to see whether he was teasing, but he appeared in earnest.

"I should love it above all things, but…would that be wise? You have nearly six months more of mourning. People would talk."

"Let them. If I do not have some happiness in my life, I believe I shall not live the next six *weeks* altogether, Amelia. You are all I think of, day and night."

"And you are so often in my thoughts, I fear Robert thinks me quite addlepated these days. More often than I care to admit, he has to ask me something twice because I did not hear him the first time. My mind being more...pleasurably occupied."

A movement at the door caught Amelia's eye, and she sharply drew in her breath. Mr. Collins was entering the supper room. He immediately spied her and gave a nod along with what Amelia thought was a smirking smile. Struggling to remain calm, Amelia finished her drink and set the cup down on a nearby table. To anyone observing, there was nothing that would signify she and Mr. Bennet had anything more than a casual, genial relationship, but she knew Mr. Collins had deep suspicions. She should leave the assembly soon, perhaps tell Robert she was unwell. She turned to curtsey to her companion. Under her breath, she murmured, "I must decline any dances with you tonight. But soon, Eugene, soon."

She swept out of the room, leaving him gazing with longing after her.

KITTY PLOPPED DOWN ON A CHAIR NEXT TO HER SISTER.

"Oh, it is utterly stifling in here! Why do they not open any windows?"

"I feel quite comfortable," Mary replied. "But then, I have not been dancing nearly every set as you have."

Kitty sat up again, her eyes shining with excitement. "To own it, Mary, I do not think I have ever been more popular at an assembly! Without Jane and Lizzy to steal my thunder with their beauty, some gentlemen are noticing me for the first time, it seems. But you look quite well, Mary—your hairstyle is so becoming and Mama's necklace goes perfectly with your new dress."

Mary gave Kitty a sharp look—was she sincere? She appeared so.

"Thank you. Much good it does me though. I have only had the one dance with Mr. Yarby, and I am certain it was only because Amelia asked him to do so." As she spoke, her eyes followed the rector, still on the dance floor—now with a girl Mary knew only slightly. Agnes was her name, she recalled. Blonde, lithe, and exceedingly pretty, Agnes was sixteen and just come out into society. Did Yarby find the girl attractive? She could not tell. She prayed not.

Kitty frowned. "And yet I believe he thinks highly of you."

Mary turned her attention from the dance floor to her sister. "How so? Why do you say such a thing?"

"Because he told me so while we were dancing." Kitty rolled her eyes. "Quite rude to speak of another lady while dancing with me, in my opinion, but as it was only you—my sister—I suppose he did not think it would be impolite."

"What...did he say about me?"

"Oh, something about your having a fine mind. He admires that you like to read. I think he was trying to encourage me to read more, but there is no one in the family who cares for reading less than I. Except for Lydia, of course. Oh, I am so looking forward to Lydia being here with the twins! Do you think she will bring us both presents? Quite frankly, I don't expect much this year with Mama gone. How could Papa possibly know what to buy us? I can only hope Jane and Lizzy send nice gifts."

She prattled on about her eagerness for Christmas, but Mary did not hear a word she said.

He thinks I have a fine mind! My plan to win him with my intelligence is working. Now that I am back, I shall continue to bring my questions of scripture to him. And soon—soon he will no doubt figure out that he could not choose a better wife from among the ladies of Meryton than me.

Chapter 19

Mr. Bennet shifted in his pew, trying to focus his mind on Mr. Collins's droning sermon. He glanced around, noting he was not the only one who appeared bored with the interpretation of the familiar Bible passage the curate had chosen: the parable of the prodigal son. Mercifully, Mr. Collins was coming to the end of the story wherein the older son confronts his father over the celebration he throws for his newly returned younger brother.

"'And he answering said to his father, Lo, these many years do I serve thee, neither transgressed I at any time thy commandment: and yet thou never gavest me a kid, that I might make merry with my friends: But as soon as this thy son was come, which hath devoured thy living with *harlots*…'"

Did Mr. Collins seem to put particular emphasis on that word? It felt that way to Mr. Bennet.

"'…thou hast killed for him the fatted calf.'"

Mr. Collins paused and let his eyes travel over his congregants before continuing with the father's response.

Oh, get on with it, Mr. Bennet thought, shifting again in his seat. But Mr. Collins was clearly enjoying having all eyes upon him and making the most of the moment.

"'And he said unto him, son, thou art ever with me, and all that I have is thine. It was meet that we should make merry, and be glad: for this thy brother was dead, and is alive again; and was lost, and is found.'"

Mr. Collins paused again, tapping the Bible to let the story sink in before raising his head from the lectern.

"And what are we to learn from this story?" he asked the congregation. No one spoke, for they knew the speaker was not truly wanting an opinion. "Only this. That by disobeying your beloved family, you are rewarded. As you just heard, the younger son asks his father for his inheritance early—a scandalous, greedy act in itself—but then after he wastes his money on women of loose morals and unchaste living, he comes crawling home in disgrace. But instead of being punished, the son is given the fatted calf and the best robe! Indeed, it is clear that this is a parable of a lack of brotherly love. For had the younger son truly loved his older brother, he would not have sought to rise above his station. He would have been content laboring in the fields alongside him, and not have his life plunge into ruination. Let us all remember this when tempted by the devil to desire more than what the good Lord has already given us."

Mr. Collins soundly closed the Bible and with a final nod at the congregation, took his seat next to Mr. Yarby.

Yarby stood and went to the pulpit.

"Thank you. A most…enlightening interpretation, Mr. Collins." He cleared his throat before continuing, "I do love this parable. My favorite part is when the repentant son returns and his father, seeing him from a distance, runs to him and kisses him, calling him beloved—which was quite out of tradition for those times, as the father should naturally wait for the son to come to him in a show of respect.

"So, how are we to understand that? Well, I believe the true meaning here is that the father in this tale represents our own Heavenly Father. And what Jesus is telling us in this story is that when *we* take a single step towards God in repentance and ask forgiveness for anything, He will take one hundred steps towards us, embrace us with a loving heart, and assure us we are His own."

Yarby glanced over at Mr. Collins, who was now openly scowling. Yarby gave a weak laugh. "There you have it! Two interpretations of our time-honored parable this Sunday. I encourage you to think on them both. Let us open our hymnbooks now for the concluding anthem."

"I did not appreciate your contradicting me in church today, Mr. Yarby," Mr. Collins said testily.

His "curate" had followed Yarby after the service to the parsonage and right into the study, much to the rector's annoyance. Any hopes Yarby had had that Mr. Collins's now extremely pregnant wife would be a higher priority were apparently misplaced. Mr. Collins had helped Charlotte into the Lucas's carriage with her parents and then waited until Mr. Yarby started home, following him, silently fuming.

Yarby sighed and turned to face the man, trying to keep his temper in check.

"Perhaps if you had shared your thoughts with me before you gave your sermon, we could have avoided it. I would have steered you away from such a harsh theme. I do apologize if I injured your pride, Mr. Collins. But I simply did not think such an unusual interpretation of a story of love and forgiveness could go without answer. I wish to see my—*our* parishioners leave church uplifted in heart and spirit, not feeling poorly about themselves!" His comments were waved away by Mr. Collins with a dismissive hand.

"You are simply too young and inexperienced to know the truth,

Yarby—that most people are naturally bad with inclinations to laziness, greed, and deceit. It is only by reinforcing from the pulpit the dangers of eternal damnation that we can have a hope of keeping people on the straight and narrow path to righteousness!"

Mr. Yarby's mouth opened, but he was unable to reply. He finally managed to say, "We have fundamentally different philosophies of human nature, clearly."

"I accept your apology," Mr. Collins said. "But, do not worry overly about it. You are young, as I said, and will grow in knowledge—especially with me here to guide you. Now, about the Christmas services. I propose you handle Christmas Eve, and I shall give the one on Christmas Day."

"That will not do," Yarby said firmly. "In fact, I know Mr. Bennet is particularly looking forward to my speaking then. He mentioned it just this week again. Therefore, I shall give the Christmas Day sermon. I am the senior rector, after all." He knew he was treading on thin ice to say that, but he was beyond letting his fear dictate his speech.

Mr. Collins's eyes narrowed. "Need I remind you of our agreement, Mr. Yarby? It would not do to have the scandalous behavior of your sister with your employer become public knowledge."

Yarby's jaw clenched. How much longer must he endure this blackmail? But was it worth fighting over? He finally nodded his agreement and saw Mr. Collins give a smile of victory.

"I am glad you see it my way. I certainly hope when *I* am in charge of Longbourn and—do not forget—your employer, you will be more tractable to my requests." With a final sniff, he turned around and stomped from the room. The front door slammed moments later signaling his departure.

"Please, God—let that day be many, many years from now," Yarby muttered under his breath, then went to join Amelia for lunch.

Chapter 20

Mary was resting in her room, trying to overcome a fierce headache—so unlike her to be ailing, she thought with annoyance. And such bad timing. With just four days until Christmas, she knew she should be consulting with Mrs. Hill on the final details of the Christmas dinner, but her head was throbbing so! From her room she could hear Lydia downstairs, yelling at her sons, Gerald and Edward, and their wailing response. The upset they brought to the house was the source, no doubt, of her pain.

Seeing how rambunctious and unruly my nephews are makes me think I might not want children after all! Of course, they are not to blame. I have seen how Lydia manages them—giving into their every demand, or stuffing them with more sweets than could possibly be good for any child, then suddenly turning around and becoming the strict mother! There is no consistency in her parenting. The boys are only slightly better around their father. Pity he went hunting with Papa and cannot take them in hand now.

The noise from downstairs abated somewhat, but after a while, Mary, realizing she would not be able to nap after all, got up and resolved to look for some of her mother's special headache powders for relief. As she approached her mother's bedroom, she noticed the door was closed. Odd—she was certain it had been open when she came upstairs to lie down. She softly pushed the door open, entered the room, and took a sharp intake of breath at what she saw: Lydia, rummaging through their mother's jewelry case.

"What are you doing?" Mary asked, even as she likely knew the answer.

Lydia held up the gold bangle—the sole item in the jewelry box. "Papa sent me very little of Mama's jewelry. I was just curious to see what was left. I suppose you and Kitty have the lot."

Mary noted her sister did not even have the grace to look the least bit ashamed of being caught rifling through their mother's belongings. She crossed the room, snatched the gold bangle from her sister and tucked it securely in her pocket.

"Items were sent to Jane and Lizzy as well," she said, evenly. "It was all divided as Papa wished." She pressed her lips together before continuing, "To be frank, Lydia, we were all worried you would sell any of Mama's finer pieces, and none of us wished to see that happen. That was why you were given just the cameo brooch."

Lydia turned a fierce face on her sister. "So you cheated me out of my share of the inheritance! And what if I did wish to sell them? That would be my right, would it not?" She suddenly burst into tears, turned away, and sat on the bed. "I am desperate, Mary; we are so in debt! Nearly on the rocks, to be honest."

Mary felt both shock and a pang of sympathy. She sat next to her sister and took her hand. "What about your share of money from Mama's inheritance? I know Papa sent it to you."

"A paltry thirty-two pounds!"

"You will get it every year. And as for paltry, many people survive on as little," Mary pointed out.

"Oh, don't give me a sermon," Lydia snapped. "The money was helpful but gone in a flash. I said we have debts. And I have two growing boys to feed!"

"But I thought Wickham was doing so well in his business ventures. You wrote that he was."

Lydia fumbled for a handkerchief and blew her nose. "I may have... exaggerated slightly. I can't bear being thought of as the daughter who made such a bad marriage—especially after Jane and Lizzy's luck in marrying so well. Wickham's business is managing to bring in a modest income, to be sure, but my husband spends far too much of his profits at the gambling tables. Plus"—she broke off with another sob—"I believe he may have a mistress! We cannot afford a nursemaid, but Wickham finds money enough for some light-skirt. Be grateful you will never have a husband, Mary. They can be fun, but sometimes..."

Lydia pointed to the pocket in which Mary had secured the bracelet. "That might gain me five or maybe even ten pounds. Which I desperately need! If I do not pay the rent again next month we will soon be out in the street! *Please* let me have it, Mary. No one need know."

"I cannot," Mary replied firmly, peeved at Lydia's assumption she shall never marry. "Kitty and Papa both know it is the last item in Mama's jewelry case. If it were to suddenly vanish, they might blame a servant, like Sarah, and fire her without a reference. That would be neither fair nor just." Her expression softened. "But I promise I shall speak to Papa on your behalf."

Lydia turned a sulky face to her sister. "You always have to do the right thing, don't you? Well, I suppose that will have to suffice. Bear in mind when we are cast in the streets that it was all due to you!" Without another word, she flounced out of the room.

Mary continued to sit on the bed, fingering the heavy gold band in her pocket and wondering whether she had said the right thing to Lydia. Her musing was interrupted by a loud commotion from downstairs. Then Mary heard a scream, and someone calling her name. She raced from the room.

"Mary, come quick! Papa! Oh, Papa!" Kitty was screaming. Mary reached the bottom of the stairs to see her father being half-carried into the house by Wickham and Mr. Hill. Mr. Bennet's face was ashen, his eyes half closed.

Mary felt her knees weaken, and she clutched the railing for support. "What has happened?" she asked.

"An accident," Mr. Bennet muttered. "Wickham's gun discharged and hit me."

Kitty wailed even louder, and no one seemed to be taking charge of the dire situation. Mary drew on a strength she did not know she had. "Put him on the settee in the morning room," she ordered Mr. Hill. "Then run for the doctor—at once!" She turned to Mrs. Hill. "Is there hot water? Bring it, and Kitty—get the good linen rags we use for bandages. Go!"

Kitty flew up the stairs to obey. Lydia was cowering in a corner, holding both boys tight to her skirt, her eyes trained not on their injured father, but on her husband, who stood off to one side. Mary caught a glimpse of her countenance and was puzzled; she could not quite make it out—shock, perhaps?

Mary ran ahead of Wickham and Mr. Hill into the morning room, arranging the pillows at one end. The two men eased him onto the settee where Mary gently removed his coat. She could see dark blood had soaked her father's shirt on his left shoulder, but it did not seem like an excessive amount. Not life-threatening she hoped, but she was not a doctor. She helped him lie down, biting her lip in dismay as he cried out in pain. She had a fleeting thought of how annoyed her mother would be about the blood on the settee before remembering her mother was dead. And now this. Good Lord, was she to become an orphan tonight?

"Papa, we are sending for the doctor. Are you in much pain?"

She saw him grit his teeth. "A bit, yes. I suddenly have a sense of empathy for those grouse we shot earlier. But I believe I shall live." He smiled briefly before gasping in pain and clutching her hand.

Mary turned her attention to Wickham, still standing nearby. "How did this happen?"

"Oh…well, you see…it was like this. Your father was up on the stile about to cross into the next field. I was not far behind him when my gun just…discharged. It was an accident—I swear." Mary caught a brief expression of desperation on Wickham's face before it altered into his usual confident arrogance. "I confess, I have not been hunting much of late and seem to have forgotten some of the more elemental safety rules. Can you ever forgive me, sir?"

"Good thing I lost my balance at the top of the stile and veered to the right just as the gun went off—eh, Wickham?" Mr. Bennet asked between gasps. "Else I would have taken the shot full in the back."

Mary gasped, and her eyes cut over to Wickham as he gave a weak laugh and agreed. He seemed to have broken out in a sweat. Mary spotted a sheen on his upper lip. Odd.

"Oh, where is the doctor?" Mary fretted as Mrs. Hill and Kitty returned with the hot water and bandages.

TWO HOURS LATER, MARY AND KITTY WERE EFFUSIVELY THANKING the doctor, Mr. Mills, as he prepared to leave Longbourn. Wickham had taken Lydia and the boys out for a walk in order, he said, to reduce the chaos in the house by a small percentage.

"Your father is a lucky man," Mr. Mills said. "But he should fully recover in due time. I shall ask Mr. Jones, the apothecary, to send over some medication for pain. And I shall return in two days time to change the bandages and inspect the wounds. We do not want infection setting in. Merry Christmas to you both."

When he was gone, a teary-eyed Kitty turned to Mary. "I swear I would not give three straws whether I receive any presents this Christmas. I only want Papa to live."

Not one to be demonstrative, Mary found herself embracing her sister. "Which Mr. Mills believes he shall, Kitty. Have no fear, all will be well, I am certain of it. Why do you not see whether Papa needs anything just now?"

Kitty sniffed once and proceeded upstairs to their father's bedroom where he had been moved.

Mary turned to clean up the morning room, when a ring of the bell at the front door gave her a start. Since she was so close, she opened it to find Mr. Yarby.

"Miss Bennet, I am terribly sorry if I am imposing, and if I am, please tell me at once and send me home, but I happened to see Mr. Mills departing Longbourn just now and wished to know whether all was well here."

Mary stared into Yarby's face a moment before covering her mouth with her hands and crumpling into the tears she had kept at bay since seeing her father carried into the house.

Mr. Yarby hesitated a moment before stepping forward and enveloping Mary in his arms.

"Oh, Miss Bennet, please tell me—what has happened? Has someone taken seriously ill? How may I assist?" he asked as he guided her into the library. He sat her down and joined her, keeping one arm on her shoulder as he tried to calm her down.

Finally, Mary governed herself enough to be able to speak and related the story of the accidental shooting.

"This is dreadful!" said Mr. Yarby. "But what does the doctor say?"

"Papa will recover, he is certain." Mary pulled away, embarrassed by her outburst, and dabbed her eyes with her handkerchief. "Forgive my unseemly display of emotions. But you understand, the shock of seeing him so weakened...and all that blood. It quite overcame me, I am afraid."

"It would anyone, to be sure. But it seems to me that you handled things quite well, Mary. I would expect nothing less. You are so capable. Always so dependable."

"Am I?" she whispered, looking up at him. She had never been so close to the rector before—not even when they danced.

"You are. I am very, very proud of you," he said in a low voice. His head began to lean closer towards her. Mary held her breath and fixed her gaze on his. Oh, heavens! Was he going to kiss her—the moment she had dreamt of and longed for finally here? She tilted her chin ever so slightly up towards him.

"Mr. Yarby!" a voice exclaimed.

Startled, the two broke apart and turned to see Kitty at the door.

"I am so glad you have come. Has Mary told you everything? Please come into the parlor and lead us in prayer for Papa. The doctor says he will be fine, but your prayers would only add assurance to that, would they not? Please—come at once."

Mr. Yarby stood, then helped Mary up, and they followed Kitty to the parlor.

Chapter 21

I t was the day before Christmas. Mr. Bennet was recovering quite well according to Mr. Mills. There was no sign of infection; therefore, the doctor declared he would allow the patient to come downstairs for Christmas dinner as long as he did not overly exert himself. Church services, however, were ruled out as entirely too strenuous.

When word of the accident became known, friends and relations visited, but Mary put her foot down and refused them access to the sickroom. She, Kitty, and Lydia were astounded at the many gifts of food brought to Longbourn; even Mrs. Hill grumbled upon the lack of space in the larder for such bounty.

"What am I to do with all these jams and preserves?" she was heard to remark. "Do they think we don't put up our own?"

Mrs. Withers was especially disappointed not to be allowed to visit the patient, but since even Mary was unaware of the intimacy of her and Mr. Bennet's relationship, all she could do was bring over custards or soup and sit and make brief, polite conversation with Mary and her sisters. She was, of course, deeply relieved to hear that Mr. Bennet would survive, but how badly had he been hurt? She longed to speak to him alone. As rector, Mr. Yarby had been allowed a personal visit, and his report to her upon his return helped calm her mind a bit at least.

Mary had been most attentive to her father since the accident, spending many hours in his room, reading to him or sometimes just watching him sleep. But today, he seemed more alert and in less pain, so Mary asked whether they could have a conversation about an incident the day of the accident. When he nodded, she shut the door to his room and pulled a chair close to the bed to relate the tale of her finding Lydia rummaging through their mother's jewelry case.

"So, I believe you should take this bracelet, Papa, and keep it safe," Mary concluded. She held out the gold band, and he took it, shaking his head and exhaling slowly. She was struck by his expression. He had not shown such a sorrowful countenance since Mrs. Bennet died.

"Thank you, Mary. You handled not only that situation well, but I must also compliment you on the way you took charge in the chaos after the shooting. Things were in such a state, and you seemed to be the only one with your wits about you."

Mary could not help but feel pride in his rare compliment. "What will you do, Papa? I mean, about Lydia?"

"I shall give Lydia some money—yet again."

"It seems an endless cycle though, does it not?"

"Sadly, yes." Mr. Bennet leaned back against his pillows, wincing slightly. "And it also, perhaps, explains something about the accident."

Mary felt a chill come over her. "What is your meaning?" she whispered.

"That day—I have been replaying it in my mind ever since. Wickham and I had already bagged several birds. I was ready to head back, but Wickham wanted to continue and pushed us on to the far edge of the estate—the end of the large field north of us—you know the one that's rather hilly?" Mary nodded silently. "We came to a fence, and Wickham gestured for me to climb the stile first. I thought he was being polite. I went ahead but took a misstep at the top, which made me lurch to the right. I had to grab a post to keep from falling. Then I felt the sting of shot and tumbled off."

Mary forced herself to ask the question that had been uppermost on her mind since that dreadful afternoon. "On…*purpose*, do you think?"

"Every hunter knows the basics of safety when climbing or even walking with a gun, Mary; you must disengage the barrel so it cannot fire. Despite his protestations of forgetfulness"—Mr. Bennet leaned closer to his daughter—"I fear he was hoping to stage a fatal accident in order to get his hands on Lydia's inheritance early. I dismissed the thought before, thinking my general dislike of Wickham was the only reason I would conjecture such a thing. But now that you tell me he and Lydia are deeply in debt, it does create a sort of motive, I believe."

Mary's hands shot to her mouth, and tears sprang to her eyes. After a moment, she softly replied, "Papa, I must tell you: I happened to see Lydia's expression as you were brought in. She did not look at *you* at all but fixed her eyes firmly on Wickham's. And her expression—I can still see it in my mind—I could not decipher it at first, but now…now I believe it was one of accusation. She knew what her husband did was not an accident."

She took her father's hand. "I should like to always think the best of our fellow human beings—and especially of a member of our own family. But I fear I cannot comprehend any other possible explanation of the situation you just related. You must ask them to leave at once."

Mr. Bennet sighed. "I cannot do that. Just before Christmas? It would cause too much of a ruckus, and then Kitty and your aunt and uncle Phillips would demand to know the reason behind their sudden departure. No, I believe Wickham will be on his best behavior now that he has failed and likely knows I suspect him."

Mr. Bennet took the gold bracelet and put it the drawer of his bedside table. He gave his daughter a wry smile.

"I can tell you this much, however. It will be a cold day in hell before I ever go hunting with him again."

Chapter 22

Despite everything, the Bennets had a most happy Christmas. Kitty was good to her word and accepted all her gifts with grace, gratitude, and nary an envious glance at what others received. Lydia and Wickham were unusually quiet throughout the day and either spent their time conversing and playing whist with the Phillipses or taking the boys on long walks—despite the cold weather.

Mr. Bennet was getting stronger each day, and he had to be persuaded to retire from the festivities even though he said he felt "so well." Mary noted his cheerful demeanor and agreed it was the correct decision not to send Lydia and her family away before Christmas. However, now and then he caught her eye and raised an eyebrow, a way of signaling the secret they shared. It made her feel oddly happy to be close to her father in that way, even regarding such an unpleasant issue.

Happiest of all, perhaps, was Mr. Yarby, for Mr. Collins had sent word late on Christmas Eve that Charlotte had begun her labor. Mr. Collins regretfully said, therefore, that he did not expect he would be able to give the Christmas Day sermon after all. Yarby's talk was hastily written but well received, and following Christmas morning services, he and Amelia joined the Bennets for dinner: white soup, roast beef, venison, roast potatoes, and carrots. The crowning achievement was the Christmas pudding served flaming on a platter and decorated with freshly cut holly. Mrs. Hill was called in to take a bow in recognition of all her work.

Following the meal, everyone sang carols as Mary played the piano. She was thrilled when Amelia complimented the improvement of her technique in front of everyone. She truly thought she had never enjoyed a nicer Christmas, despite its being the first without her mother.

Later that Christmas Day, news arrived from Lucas Lodge that Charlotte had given birth to a boy who appeared to be healthy and strong. Mr. Collins was over the moon with happiness, knowing that, once he took possession of Longbourn, his heir would secure it for the Collins family for the next generation. It was, he told Charlotte, the best Christmas present he had ever received.

TWO DAYS LATER, MR. BENNET CALLED HIS YOUNGEST DAUGHTER into his library and handed her a cheque for thirty pounds.

"I trust this will more than get you out of your difficulty with the landlord, Lydia," he said. "I advise you to keep the rest of the money well hidden once you cash this at the bank so your husband does not waste it at gambling. Or—other items of pleasure."

He saw that Lydia had the good grace to look somewhat abashed.

"Thank you, Papa, you do not know how much this means to me." She tucked the paper into her pocket. "Wicky feels most terribly awful about the accident, you know. He would never wish to see you hurt—ever! I hope you believe that."

Mr. Bennet briefly considered pointing out his side of the event but realized there would be no use. It would likely just send Lydia off in a tearful storm and upset the household yet again. He gave a small smile.

"Yes, of course. Who could even imagine him capable of plotting such a thing? After all, your inheritance is not so grand that it would be worth dispatching me. A thousand pounds may seem like a lot but would not last all that long for your family. But, my dear, do you wish me to speak to him—about the gambling, I mean? I should be happy to."

Lydia shook her head. "Oh no, Papa. He has sworn he will give up the gambling tables and devote himself to our family. Thank you, but I believe all will be well." She smiled brightly and stood. "I am so glad you are feeling better. I can go back north with confidence now."

As Lydia left the library, Mrs. Hill appeared at the door.

"Mrs. Withers to see you, sir—only if you are up to it, she says."

"Please send her in."

"Good afternoon, Mr. Bennet," Amelia said formally as she entered and curtseyed, holding out a parcel. "If this is not an inconvenient time, I wished to return the book you so kindly lent me."

"Of course. I hope you enjoyed it, Mrs. Withers," he replied, just as formally.

Once Mrs. Hill closed the door and they were alone, Amelia set the book down and rushed to take Mr. Bennet's hands and kiss them.

"Oh, Eugene," she said softly. "I have longed to be alone with you so that I could truly express how much happiness and gratitude I have that you survived the shooting. Seeing you able to be at Christmas dinner was a relief, but even so, I need to know for certain you are completely well."

He drew her close in a long embrace, ignoring the sting of pain in his shoulder. "I am, thankfully. I must tell you, as I stumbled in pain back towards the house with Wickham half-carrying me, and felt the blood wet my shirt, my thoughts were only of you, dear Amelia—not the estate, not even my children, but only you. I can hardly account for it except to say that, to have discovered this magnificent new love at this point in my life, all I could think was: What if I do not survive to enjoy it?"

"But you *did* survive and will live many, many more years, I know it. And once we can make our feelings public and wed, I pledge to devote my entire life to your happiness."

"Oh? What of your own happiness?" He arched his eyebrows and pulled back to smile at her.

Tears came to her eyes, and she pulled his hands up again to kiss them. "My happiness is complete. Merely knowing you feel as I do, I can want for nothing."

Mr. Bennet gave a quick glance out the window to be certain no one was about. It was too cold for anyone to be out walking, but you never knew. Assured it was safe, he cupped his beloved's face in his hands and kissed her gently. Her arms stole gently around his neck, and she eagerly returned his kiss. He broke the embrace reluctantly.

"Sit, sit. I have something for you—a Christmas present I dared not give you when you and your brother were here for dinner." He gave a mischievous smile and went to his desk, opening a drawer and bringing out a roughly wrapped item. He returned to the settee and placed it in her hands.

"I must confess it is not new; it belonged to my former wife. She had not worn it in years. I think we both can agree it would cause too much gossip and suspicion if I went to the Meryton jeweler and bought anything. But I hope you will accept it and know and appreciate the love that stands behind it."

"It is beautiful," she whispered when she unwrapped the gold bracelet. She slid it over her slender hand and admired it on her wrist, glinting in the light. "I shall treasure it, Eugene. But…I did not anticipate we would exchange gifts this year. I have nothing for you." She smiled shyly. "Except my heart, which I give to you with all my love."

"A better present, my dear Amelia, I could not hope to imagine."

Chapter 23

The New Year arrived, and with it came a visitor eagerly anticipated at the parsonage. Amelia fairly bubbled over with delight
when Mary came for a visit.

"Mary, I cannot wait for you to meet our eldest brother, Phillip. I
think you and your family will find him quite diverting."

Privately, Mary thought no brother could possibly be of more interest
to her than Mr. Robert Yarby, but she smiled politely. "I think you
said he is a solicitor?"

"Yes—in London. But he has confided to Robert and me that he
has grown weary of the big city and wishes to relocate. And it is my
hope that, if Phillip fancies Meryton, he may in fact move here! That
would be so wonderful. It has been years since all three of us were
together in the same community."

"He may find it quite dull after the vibrant life of London," Mary
said.

"Yes, but town is also exceedingly expensive. His expenses nearly outweigh his income, so he hopes to find a place where he can build a flourishing career at much less cost."

"And will he move his family here as well?" Not that Mary particularly cared, but it seemed the polite thing to ask.

"Phillip is still not married—even now at thirty-six!"

"How unusual."

Amelia leaned in and lowered her voice. "I tell you this in confidence, Mary, because I know you are not one to not spread idle talk. Phillip's heart was severely wounded some years back. He was engaged to a charming young lady—Letitia was her name—from a prominent, wealthy family in town. We were so happy for him. We all thought it was true love, but her parents strongly objected to the match and broke it up."

"That is very sad. Why did they object?" Mary shunned gossip as a rule, but this story seemed quite interesting. Besides, this was about the Yarbys of whom she was so fond. It could not be harmful to hear it, she reasoned. And Amelia seemed most eager to share the story. The least she could do was politely listen.

"My brother was not wealthy enough for them. A mere solicitor? Unpardonable!" Amelia threw her hands up in mock horror. "Of course, we all knew he was not in the same class as her family, but we hoped love might prevail. However, her father was so dismissive. 'Not even a court attorney—just a clerk,' is how he put it. Phillip was not sufficiently grand for them, so they sent Letitia away to live with an aunt. After six months, she fell in love with someone else who owned a fine estate, and she became his wife! Poor Phillip was devastated. I fear it has quite put him off the idea of marriage now."

"But true love should survive such a separation, should it not?" Mary said seriously. "If her heart had truly been attached to your brother, a separation of six months—nay, even six years—should not matter."

Amelia laughed softly. "Six *years?* Oh, Mary, I fear my suggestion that you read more novels may have altered your frame of mind." She paused before continuing soberly. "I agree—had the attachment been strong enough, she might have been able to wait, but no doubt unable to communicate with Phillip, her heart was too easily turned to another. However, in the end, I blame the parents. You must agree that, if Letitia's parents had not interfered in the first place, she and Phillip might well be married now—and quite happily too!"

"A sad story indeed. Everyone deserves to have love, I believe. May I ask: Do you hope to marry again, Amelia?" Mary asked cautiously. "You are but thirty-three or so, are you not? You may well find romance again, although here in Meryton the selection might be said to be skimpier than in larger places. Oh, wait! Jonas the butcher is a widower and only forty-five. You should set your cap for him. You will never lack for meat in the house."

Amelia laughed and patted her friend's hand. "I would like to think I should marry for love, not for *beef*, Mary! If a new man comes into my life and…love should happen, that would be wonderful. But if no such thing occurs, I can be content as I am. After all, I have my brother, dear friends such as you, this charming cottage, and food and drink enough. I feel it would be greedy to ask for…more." As she ended this speech, Mary saw Amelia's eyes drift away and a small smile play on her lips as if lost in memory.

Mary observed her countenance silently.

Poor thing, she must be remembering the love she shared with her husband. Despite her protestations of contentment, I shall pray she finds a new husband who is worthy of her.

TWO DAYS LATER, PHILLIP YARBY ARRIVED FOR HIS STAY AT THE Longbourn rectory to the delight of Robert and Amelia. As soon as he was settled, the three walked to Longbourn House to pay their respects to Mr. Bennet and his daughters

The eldest brother proved to be quite a diverting conversationalist, as predicted by Amelia, and shared his lively thoughts with not just Mr. Bennet—as would be expected—but also paid attention to Mary and Kitty with great courtesy, asking for their opinions on different topics. He told stories of his work and clients in London that had them all laughing. At one point, Mary noticed Kitty stiffen a moment, then become a bit fidgety in her seat, though she could discern no cause for her sister's distress.

After more than half an hour, far longer than the usual "polite call," the Yarbys departed with a promise to have everyone to dinner soon. The minute Longbourn door closed and they were gone, Kitty grabbed Mary and dragged her upstairs to their mother's bedroom. She shut the door firmly behind them and turned to her sister.

"Did you *see* that? I can't believe it!" she exclaimed.

"What do you mean?" Mary replied. "I thought it a very fine visit. Mr. Yarby's brother seems quite an amiable gentleman, just at Amelia promised he would be. Much taller than our rector, and with the same nice, thick hair. I would call him handsome, would you not agree? Although he does not have the same dimples—" She broke off when Kitty grabbed her arm.

"No, not that, you goose! Did you not see what Mrs. Withers was wearing?" At Mary's blank stare she hissed, "Mama's gold bracelet! The one that was left over after we divided up her jewelry."

Mary could not keep her mouth from falling open. "What? Are you certain?"

"I saw it peek out from the sleeve of her spencer. I recognized it at once. There is no doubt about it and furthermore…" She moved quickly to the jewelry box on the dresser and flipped back the lid dramatically. "…see here? It is gone!"

"Oh, well, it is no longer in Mama's jewelry case because I removed it after I…well, I dislike speaking unkindly of our sister, but you should know that, over the holidays, I caught Lydia trying to pinch Mama's bracelet to sell. Apparently, she and Wickham are very much in debt. So, I took it from her and gave it to—" She halted her speech a moment as her mind raced.

"To Mrs. Withers, clearly," Kitty finished. "Well, you might have asked me first! We were supposed to share that bracelet, you know."

Mary waved a hand in agitation. "No, of course I did not give it to her. I would certainly discuss it with you first. I gave the bracelet to Papa for safekeeping. So, if Amelia has it, it is because—"

Kitty gasped. "*He* gave it to her? Why would he do such a thing?"

Mary tried to focus after this remarkable news. Suddenly, things began to fall into place—the times she called on the parsonage to visit Amelia only to learn she was taking a walk. Was her father not also taking walks about that same time? And suddenly, Mary realized that her father always seemed to become more lively around Amelia although, as a rule, he disliked company interrupting his daily routine. And then there was Amelia's dreamy look the other day when they were speaking of her falling in love again.

"Mary? Mary!" Kitty's voice called her back to herself. "What should we do? Pretend we just don't know about the missing bracelet?"

"Absolutely not. We must speak to Papa about it—at once."

Chapter 24

Once Mary persuaded Kitty to let her begin the conversation, they presented themselves at their father's library that very afternoon. Mr. Bennet looked up from his book with curiosity at his daughters.

"Well, well, what is all this then? Are you two off to Meryton on this chilly day? Or to visit your aunt Phillips? Try not to be too long; you know how I hate a late dinner."

"No, Papa, we are not going out. We have come to speak to you on a matter most...most urgent," Mary said.

His eyebrows rose. "Indeed? Very well, let us all take seats." He gestured to the settee and took the chair at the front of his desk to join them. "Now, what is troubling you? What is so important?"

For a moment, both Mary and Kitty were silent and exchanged nervous glances. Then Mary began: "Papa, during the Yarbys' visit just now it came to our attention...that is, Kitty noticed something, and we wish to clarify the situation. She may be mistaken, but she is certain...

or rather, she perhaps *believes* she saw something quite distressing."

"Oh? I thought it a very nice visit," Mr. Bennet said. "Mr. Phillip Yarby seems a pleasant enough fellow—much like his brother and sister. What did you see that distressed you so?"

Mary twisted her hands in her lap. "Well…Kitty is under the impression that she saw…or noticed—and she *could* be mistaken, after all, but—"

"Why was Mrs. Withers wearing Mama's gold bracelet?" blurted Kitty.

A long pause followed, during which Mr. Bennet's eyes turned to the floor, unable to look at his daughters.

"I see that you do not deny it nor question what Kitty says," Mary said quietly after the silence lingered. "That is confirmation indeed that what she believes she saw is true. Did you, Papa? Did you give Mama's bracelet to Amelia?"

Mr. Bennet slowly nodded his head. "I did," he replied softly. He seemed reluctant to speak further and still did not meet their gaze.

After another pause, Kitty spoke in a tearful voice: "But, Papa, why? Such a costly gift surely indicates a significant attachment. Just what *is* Mrs. Withers to you?"

"At this point, she is just my rector's sister, but soon"—he raised his head and spoke more firmly—"I hope she will become family and… my wife."

Mary drew a sharp intake of breath while Kitty gave a little shriek and began to weep.

Mr. Bennet continued. "I did not plan it nor intend for any of this to happen, my dear girls, but Amelia and I have…fallen quite deeply in love."

Kitty stamped her foot. "Mama has been gone barely over seven months! I cannot believe you would do such a thing!" She fumbled for a handkerchief, unable to control her emotions.

"You are still in full mourning, Papa," Mary said soberly. "It would not do to go flaunting your…relationship with Amelia around town."

Mr. Bennet gave a wry smile. "Count on you to always think of the practical aspects, Mary. But no, while we have taken walks together and had one or two pleasant conversations in public settings such as church and the Christmas assembly, we have made every effort to be discreet. No one...suspects."

Mary noticed his pause and thought it strange. "Until next May, when you are out of mourning."

"At which time we shall begin to allow ourselves to be seen together in a more familiar manner, yes." He reached out and patted the girls' hands. "As I said, I did not seek this, nor did I anticipate this ever happening, but Amelia has made me so happy these past months. I find myself quite a new man. I know you cannot accustom yourselves to all of this at once. But, Mary, you and Amelia are dear friends. You must not think that will change in any way once she and I are wed."

"She shall *not* be my mother! She shall *not*!" Kitty snatched her hands back and leapt to her feet, then ran out of the library, sobbing loudly. Moments later, Mary and Mr. Bennet heard the slamming of her bedroom door as it echoed down to them.

"Does Mr. Yarby know?" Mary asked after a moment. How could he keep that information from her during their scripture studies?

"He does. At least, Amelia has told me he is aware of our attachment. He and I have not discussed it yet for the very reason you mentioned, Mary: I am still in mourning for your dear mother."

"And Lydia, Jane, and Lizzy have no idea."

"They do not."

Mary took a deep breath. "I saw an odd expression on Amelia's face when we were discussing love recently. I thought at the time that she was remembering her first husband with sorrowful longing, but now I see it was likely *you* of whom she was thinking.

"I must say, Papa, I am quite taken aback at this news. However, to own the truth, I know that you and Mama were not always a good match; your temperaments seemed different. You enjoy intellectual pursuits; Mama did not, and she was considerably more social than you were. And yet, despite the amount of time you enjoy in solitude here in your library, I cannot think it is healthy to be alone. In Genesis, the Lord God said, 'It is not good that the man should be alone; I will make a helper fit for him.' Yes"—she nodded—"I believe Amelia would be a good companion for you, Papa. I mean, it is not as if she is as young as I am; she is nearly thirty-four and a respectable widow. Therefore, Amelia is quite a suitable wife for a man of your age."

Mr. Bennet smiled. "True. I cannot think, once we make our attachment known, that there will be any scandal or salacious gossip generated."

"I agree. The timing may be ill, but as long as you can keep your attachment well hidden until the summer, I cannot think it will damage anyone's reputation," Mary said thoughtfully.

"Thank you for your level-headed assessment. I am glad you are not as violently opposed as your sister seems to be at this moment."

"Kitty will come around in time." Mary rose and went to the library door, then turned to give her father a smile. "I suppose congratulations are in order." At his nod of thanks, she left and went upstairs to comfort her sister.

Chapter 25

Two weeks later, Kitty was at least on speaking terms again with her father, even as she still firmly disapproved of his finding new love so soon after the death of Mrs. Bennet. Life returned somewhat to normal, and after Mr. Bennet related to Amelia that his daughters knew of their attachments, they made even more of an effort to keep their distance in public places. Invitations to dine at Longbourn were reduced from the usual two times a week to just once, and on one occasion, when Phillip and Amelia stopped in for a visit, Mr. Bennet stayed firmly in his library and let Mary and Kitty entertain them. But behind all this, both he and Amelia were counting the weeks and days until they could make their affections known.

Mary had also briefly discussed the matter with Amelia, assuring her that their friendship need not alter from this news. "Indeed, I quite look forward to turning the household management over to you, Amelia, so that I may have more time for reading and practicing my music."

Now, on a sunny but brisk January day, Mary walked towards Lucas

Lodge to see the Collins's new baby. She had knit a small blanket as a gift, although she would be the first to admit it was being given more with obligation than with love. Still, Mary knew it was what her mother would have wanted her to do, and as the lady of Longbourn now, she was always conscious of her duty.

Lady Lucas warmly welcomed Mary and escorted her upstairs to see Charlotte, sharing her enthusiasm for being a grandmother along the way.

"It was a long labor," she confided, "and at one point, we feared things would not go well, but the little one finally made his appearance—a healthy boy *and* a Christmas baby! What a delight! My husband had to go to town this week, but he can hardly wait to return to his grandson, I am certain. He has become quite the doting grandpapa!" She knocked at her daughter's door and did not even wait for a reply before she opened the door, and announced Mary's arrival. Then with a quick, loving glance at the bassinet, she left to return downstairs.

"You look very well, Charlotte," Mary said, when they were alone. She moved to the bed and handed her the bundle she had brought. "I made this for the baby. Pray do not look too closely at my stitches. I fear knitting has never been the greatest of my accomplishments. But I did use some very fine quality wool and it will keep your son warm."

"Thank you, Mary, you are so kind," Charlotte replied, unwrapping it. "Oh! It is lovely and shall be of great use, I am sure."

Mary moved to the bassinet where the baby lay sleeping. "Goodness, what a head of hair for a newborn!" she exclaimed.

Charlotte laughed. "That is what everyone says. It would appear I have given birth to a miniature Mr. Collins."

"And what name have you chosen?"

"Since it is his first son, I deferred to my husband in this regard, and he has decided upon Alexander—with William as a second. Rather a grand name for such a small thing, but he will grow into it, I have no doubt."

"And, someday, be the master of Longbourn," Mary said softly.

She felt an inexplicable sorrow at the thought, followed by a pang of annoyance at her sentimental emotions. Gracious, what was wrong with her? It is not as if she had not spent most of her life knowing the estate was entailed away from the Bennet line because she had no brother; her mother had spoken of it often enough, goodness knows. With a firm nod, she turned away from the sleeping baby and took a chair facing Charlotte.

"May he be worthy of it," Charlotte said softly. She paused before continuing, "You know I have always been so fond of your family, Mary. Your sister Eliza and I were the best of friends growing up, and some of my happiest childhood times were spent at Longbourn with her and her sisters. Believe me, I intend to temper any inclination I might see of arrogance in Alexander. Just because Longbourn will fall to him one day, he shall not think himself better than others—you may depend upon it."

Mary gave Charlotte a studious look. "Well. That is good of you, Charlotte. Of course, such a transfer is not likely to occur for some time."

"God willing," Charlotte hastily added.

After another few minutes of polite, banal conversation, Mary took her leave. As she reached the front hallway, Mr. Collins entered Lucas Lodge and, seeing Mary, greeted her.

"Mary, how good of you to come visit on such a brisk day. I am just returned from my rented rooms in Meryton where I do my work for the parish. You have been to see Charlotte? What do you think of my son, eh? He is a handsome boy—now, admit it!"

"I have always been of the opinion that it is very hard to discern the true beauty of a newborn, Mr. Collins. To me they all look like little old men. However, I think I may state with confidence that there is every indication he will become pleasant looking in due time."

"And pray tell, how is your father? We were all so distressed to hear of the dreadful accident."

"He is very well, thank you. Quite himself, in fact. I assure you he expects to make a full recovery."

Mr. Collins gave an oily smile. "Yes...of course, he has something delightful to live for now, does he not?"

Mary blinked. "I...do not have the pleasure of understanding you, sir. Something to live for? What is your meaning?"

"Why, the charming Mrs. Withers, of course."

Mary caught her breath. "Oh—I did not know you were aware of their...affection for each other. How did you—"

"Well, I *am* curate and co-rector to her brother, am I not? And he has quite taken me into his confidence. Oh yes, completely. He views me as rather an...older brother, you see." He gave a bit of a chuckle that ended in a snort.

This was news to Mary. Why had Amelia not mentioned this development to her when they last spoke? "Oh" was all she could think to reply.

"So, when shall we be free to wish them joy?" Mr. Collins pressed her.

"Um...well, once Papa's mourning is over, I suppose they will make their intentions known to the general populace."

"So sweet. And, how old is Mrs. Withers, again?"

"Nearly thirty-four—why?"

"And your dear father is what—fifty-nine?"

Mary frowned. "This month, yes. To what end do these questions lead, Mr. Collins? What concern are their ages to you?"

"Nothing, nothing. I note just a bit of an age difference between the two, but it should not be insurmountable. True love should see that as no impediment, to be sure." He glanced at the clock standing in the hall. "Gracious, is that the time? I must bid you adieu, Cousin Mary. Do give your father my best wishes, and—perhaps do not mention that I am aware of his relationship with Mrs. Withers—in case he thinks I spoke out of turn in bringing it up. I should hate to offend him. Mr. Yarby took me into his confidence, you see."

"You may be assured of my discretion," Mary said earnestly. "Good day."

K. C. Cowan

AFTER MARY LEFT, MR. COLLINS WENT INTO HIS FATHER-IN-LAW'S
library to think.

*Thirty-three, eh? The same age as my dear Charlotte. And if she was
able to bear me a son, Mrs. Withers might well be able to do the same for
Mr. Bennet once they marry. Of course, Mr. Bennet has only managed
to produce girls, but I can't take a chance of losing Longbourn if he gets
a son. I must find a way to sever this relationship.*

He thought about spreading the gossip of Mr. Bennet and Mrs. Withers's early and improper relationship throughout Meryton, but he knew
that might not be enough to force Mr. Bennet to release Mrs. Withers
and fire Yarby. He had often seen how little his cousin cared for the
good opinion of others. Money allowed one to do that. And what did
it matter if the romance *was* a bit hasty? Once he married her and
installed her as the mistress of Longbourn…the speed of it would
likely soon be forgotten.

*No, I must find some other way. Perhaps I need to focus on my co-rector.
What do we know about Yarby anyway? Perhaps there is some scandalous
behavior that led his rector to encourage him to move on. Yes. Mr. Bennet
might well have been taken in by a deceitful parson, unaware of his true
character. Indeed, it is my obligation to Longbourn to source out any
disreputable behavior of Yarby's past. I shall write a letter at once to his
former rector in Dorset and see what may be learned that I could turn
to my advantage.*

Unwilling to walk back to his rented rooms in Meryton for this
task, Mr. Collins sat at Sir William's broad mahogany desk, pulled out
a sheet of paper, dipped a pen in the inkwell, and began to compose.

Chapter 26

Birthdays were not something ordinarily much celebrated in the Bennet household. A favorite dessert might be prepared, and note of the anniversary date made at dinner with a small gift or two. However, Mary felt it would be only proper and right to mark the occasion in a bigger way for her father this year in light of the fact that, had the shooting accident ended in a different result, he would not be celebrating a birthday at all.

Knowing her father would likely not want a big fuss made, she proposed a simple dinner party and suggested that he choose the guests. He immediately listed both the Yarby gentlemen, and Amelia as his desired attendees.

"Not the Phillipses?" Mary asked hopefully. The more people who attended, the more Mr. Bennet would have to circulate and therefore not be able to spend much time with Amelia in close conversation. "What of the Collinses, or at least Sir William and Lady Lucas?"

"No," her father replied. "I believe a smaller party will suit me quite well."

The sole invitation was duly written and hand delivered with a happy and grateful acceptance immediately issued.

THE DAY OF THE CELEBRATION ARRIVED, AND THROUGHOUT LONG-bourn House the aromas of roasting beef and parsnips mingled with the scent of the spice and fruit cake baked earlier that morning. Mary and Kitty made decorations of colorful paper streamers and hung them in the dining room, hoping their father would not think them too silly. As they worked, Kitty muttered that she would have preferred to have this celebration be "family only"; however, she allowed as how she was "resigned to it" and would do her best to be a gracious hostess.

That evening, Mary again wore her maroon dress with the garnet necklace and made Sarah rework her hair style twice until it was exactly the way she wished. Satisfied, Mary went downstairs where she found Kitty looking quite elegant, dressed in one of their mother's more beautiful gowns that had been cut down for her. Their father was wearing his finest attire as well. They all moved into the drawing room to await their guests.

The Yarby brothers and Mrs. Withers arrived on time and bearing gifts. Mr. Yarby's present was obvious from its wrapping: a bottle of spirits of some kind. However, Mary could not discern what was in the long, flat package Amelia carried. Acting as hostess, she took both offerings and added them to the gifts from Kitty and her that she had already set out, then invited her guests to take seats and tried to steer the conversation to safe and uncontroversial topics. Mr. Phillip Yarby sat next to Kitty, and he was as charming as before, paying her attentions that were solicitous without being too flirtatious.

Mary could not help but note that her father had sat, not in his favorite chair, but on one of the two settees, likely in the hopes Amelia would join him. But she had chosen to sit by her brother Robert on the opposite settee—a place Mary herself had hoped to claim. No matter, she would have him on her right at the table during dinner, she thought as she joined her father on the settee.

And once Amelia becomes mistress of Longbourn, she will take her place at the head of the table across from Papa, and I shall once more be relegated to a place somewhere in the middle.

FOLLOWING THE DINNER—DECLARED "UTTERLY DELICIOUS" BY all—the party moved back to the drawing room for dessert, tea, brandy, and the opening of gifts.

"I should have advised everyone in advance not to buy me presents," said Mr. Bennet. "It was not necessary; your attendance here at this little celebration is more than enough."

"Nonsense, Papa, you certainly deserve all you can get this year after what you went through in the accident," declared Kitty. "Even though, if we are going to be honest, you *did* receive a goodly number of Christmas presents." She giggled.

"It is true that most people make little mark of their natal day with a grand celebration and presents," Phillip Yarby noted. "But if such a meal as we just enjoyed might become a tradition, then I can only hope to receive an invitation every year to honor you, sir."

Mr. Bennet laughed. "Should you choose to move your business to Meryton, Mr. Yarby, I think I may safely say I should be willing to invite all of you to every birthday from here on." His eyes slid over to Amelia's briefly, and Mary could easily see their mutual admiration. She was still getting used to the idea, but she told herself her father deserved to be happy.

"Now!" Mr. Bennet continued, "I believe we should get this embarrassment of generosity over with. Kitty, dear, will you pass me your present?"

Her eyes dancing with excitement, Kitty jumped up and handed her father a wrapped package, noting that she would like the ribbon back, please, as it was one of her best. He opened it and exclaimed his delight at a pair of felt slippers.

"During your convalescence, I noticed your slippers were beginning to look shabby, Papa," she said, clearly proud of her choice. "Do you like the color?"

"Indeed, I do—it goes perfectly with my dressing gown. Thank you, my dear girl."

Next came a book on philosophy from Mary, which was gratefully acknowledged, then the bottle of fine brandy from Robert and Phillip Yarby.

Finally, there was just the package Amelia had brought. Mr. Bennet made a display of trying to guess its contents, with teasing glances at Amelia who, Mary noted, again did little to hide any affection on her countenance. Finally, he removed the wrapping to reveal a beautiful white shirt, and it was immediately apparent that Amelia had sewn it. Mary took a sharp intake of breath—such an intimate gift! A handmade shirt was something only a wife would sew for her husband, or perhaps a sister for a brother. She was stunned at the personal nature of the present, and a quick glance at her sister showed she was having a similar reaction.

"Well!" Mr. Bennet said a bit too heartily. "How thoughtful. I have been in need of a new shirt since the hunting accident, Amelia, and neither of my girls are quite clever enough with a needle to make me one. I thank you very much."

Kitty jumped to her feet. "If you needed a new shirt, Papa, you could order one from the seamstress in town. Or, I am certain Mary and I could have managed it, somehow!" She turned to Amelia, her face reflecting her anguish. "How...very *inappropriate* of you, Mrs. Withers. You are not his wife—yet!"

Amelia's face flushed red. "I am so sorry. I thought that, since everyone here tonight is aware of our intentions, it would not...offend. I beg your pardon, Miss Kitty, Mary, and yours too, Eugene, for my foolish behavior." She lowered her head and pressed a hand to her mouth, trying to keep her emotions in check.

Kitty's response was to cry, "I know you have an understanding, but…it is simply happening too fast!" and rush from the room, sobbing. Then everyone heard the front door slam. They sat in awkward silence a moment, trying to figure out how to navigate this breech of manners.

"Now, now—let us not get in an uproar and spoil this fine party," Mr. Bennet said to smooth over the upset. "Perhaps Amelia's gift is a bit premature, but as she said, you are all aware of our attachment. Come next summer, she will be my wife and mistress of Longbourn."

"Indeed, Papa," Mary said, "but Kitty is not quite reconciled to it yet. This whole thing is still just a bit raw for her, you see. Amelia, please do not berate yourself. Nobody outside of the family need even know of your gift, and therefore, there is no reason for shame."

There were murmurs of agreement all around at Mary's practical viewpoint, and Amelia sent her a grateful smile. After another moment, Mary asked, "Shall I go find Kitty and attempt to calm her?"

To Mary's surprise, Phillip Yarby stood. "Will you allow me to seek her out, Miss Bennet? At times like these, sometimes an impartial voice can deliver the greatest influence." At her nod, he strode from the drawing room, grabbed his coat from the entry, and went outside.

"AH, THERE YOU ARE, MISS CATHERINE," YARBY SAID WHEN HE AT last located her walking in the back garden. "Oh, but I see now that you came out here without your coat. Please, allow me to lend you mine." He did not even wait for her to accept but took off his heavy wool coat and wrapped her shivering body securely in it before guiding her to a stone bench by some large fir trees and gently helping her sit.

Kitty sniffed once or twice before remembering her manners. "Thank you, sir," she whispered. "I should not have behaved in such a manner. Is everyone most frightfully angry at me?"

"Not at all," he assured her. "My sister feels it is entirely her fault and is quite remorseful for upsetting you, believe me."

"I know she did not mean to disturb me. It is just as I said; this romance between her and Papa has all happened so very quickly. Mama did not always take my side in family matters—I was not her favorite—but somehow I feel I am now the only one trying to honor her memory." She brushed away another tear that had slipped down her cheek. "It is all too fast," she repeated softly.

"I can assure you, it came as sudden news to me as well. Indeed, Amelia had written not a word of her growing affection for your father in her letters. It was a great surprise when I learned of it that first day after we visited you here at Longbourn. However, after meeting your father, I soon realized, much to my relief, that I can brook no opposition to the match. And believe me, I am quite protective of my little sister!" Seeing a brief smile cross Kitty's face, he continued. "Of course the thought of your father replacing your mother in such haste is very distressing; it would be for anyone. But I am certain it does not mean he can easily cast aside the memory your mother. And I can assure you that Amelia does not seek to be a mother figure to you but, rather, more of a friend."

Kitty nodded and sniffed again.

He pulled his handkerchief from a pocket and handed it to her, waiting until she wiped her eyes and blew her nose before continuing. "And…truly, Miss Catherine, would it be the worst thing in the world for your father to find happiness again? It seems to me that love is so rare that, when it comes, you must grab it quickly with both hands, for circumstances can sometimes arise to cause a severing of that affection from which there can be no recovery. Trust me, I know."

"You…lost a love?" Kitty whispered, looking into his eyes for the first time.

"I did. I shall not bore you with the particulars, but I spent years agonizing over my lack of courage for not claiming that love more boldly. Instead, I counted on the lady's affections remaining steadfast throughout an enforced separation, only to learn our love was not strong enough to endure. She married another while I waited."

"Oh, how sad," Kitty whispered. "How tragically romantic."

"So, if I learned anything from that experience, it is this: when love comes, you must rejoice for it, even if the timing might be thought ill or inappropriate by some."

Kitty nodded slowly. "I *do* want Papa to be happy. What kind of daughter would I be if I did not? And your sister is very nice. Her friendship with Mary has been a blessing. Mrs. Withers will make my father very happy, I am certain." She covered her face with her hands. "Oh, I am an idiot! I have ruined Papa's party."

Phillip laughed softly. "Not at all," he said gently. "You do the memory of your mother credit with your love and loyalty to her. But would you have your father or you and your sister pine away for Mrs. Bennet forever? Life goes on, and so must we. It does no good to dwell in the past, even as we keep the happy memories of our lost ones in our hearts forever."

He stood. "Come, I am eager to partake of that lovely cake I saw in the drawing room."

Kitty gave a final sniff, then smiled and rose. She took the arm Mr. Yarby offered, and the two walked back inside where the celebration, although a bit muted from the earlier high spirits, continued in a pleasant manner.

Chapter 27

Three weeks later, all the awkward moments of the birthday party were nearly forgotten, and things were back to normal. Amelia and her brothers had been invited to family dinner at Longbourn House four times since then, and the evenings had passed quite pleasantly for all.

Mary was walking towards the parsonage in hopes of another Bible study session with Mr. Yarby. It was an unusually sunny and warm day for February—a bit of a false spring—and Mary was in a happy mood as she walked along the lane. She had decided on this visit to ask Mr. Yarby whether they could discuss some of the women of the New Testament. Her plan was to then steer the topic from their love of the Lord to a discussion of love in general. She felt it was past time for him to declare himself, and she was quite certain he only needed the right prompt to feel able to speak his own heart's feelings. After all, had he not comforted her tenderly when she was distraught after her father was shot? They had nearly kissed, after all—at least, Mary believed that was his intention. Would he have acted so if he did not care? Mary was certain he only needed the proper encouragement to declare himself.

As she approached the front door of the parsonage, she saw the rectory maid, Ellen, scrubbing the front steps. The girl looked up from her work.

"Beggin' your pardon, Miss Bennet. This weather is so fine, I decided it was a good time to scrub the winter's mud and muck off the stone steps. Have you come to pay a visit? Everyone is sittin' outside in the back, enjoyin' some cake and homemade wine in this lovely sunshine. Please go on through." She gestured for Mary to step over her work.

"Oh, Ellen, I should hate to place my dirty boots right over your nice, clean steps and add to your work. I shall walk around; I know the way."

"Thank you kindly, miss." Ellen smiled and returned to her work.

As she walked around the side of the parsonage, Mary tried to think of a way she could get Mr. Yarby away from his sister and brother so they could have a private meeting.

I would much rather be with him alone than just have this turn into a social call.

Mary could hear laughter as she approached the back of the house, then familiar voices. She knew she should not eavesdrop, but an odd feeling made her slow her steps, and then hesitate a moment to listen to the conversation.

"It is quite pathetic, actually, feigning such an interest in the Bible just to get close to you, Robert," Mary heard Amelia say. "Even if she has not done so of late."

"Now, now—don't be too hard on the poor girl, Amelia," Phillip replied. "She is only seeking what all young women want—a husband. Although personally, I must question her choice. After all, I believe we can agree I am far more handsome than Robert." There was loud laughter at this. "But at least he is respectable," he concluded.

"She may see it as an advantageous match, I suppose," Robert replied. "But I swear to you both I have given her *no* reason to think I see her as anything other than the daughter of my employer."

"I absolutely agree," said Amelia. "And I am proud that you have not been unguarded or careless in your behavior towards her at all. No one could call you out for toying with her affections; you have not compromised her one whit. Just take care you continue in such a manner. Otherwise, it could give rise to hopes and expectations that have no basis in reality and would just…complicate things. Well… perhaps she will give up this folly soon. You, of course, should pursue *your* choice of bride. When will you declare yourself to her, by the way? This constant mooning over her in private will not do!" she teased.

"I shall, but I must be certain of the lady's own affections," Mr. Yarby said seriously.

Amelia laughed. "Oh, there is little doubt of her feelings, I am confident."

"Then there is her father to consider."

"I can't imagine there would be any objection on that score," said Phillip. "Do not wait too long, little brother. That will clear the way for me, as well."

Mary clasped both hands over her mouth to keep the moan that seemed to rise from deep within her from escaping. Her entire body began to tremble, and she was barely aware of her own steps as she carefully backed away. Hardly able to breathe, she turned and began to hurry away, stumbling out of the side garden, and only nodding in reply when Ellen called, "Oh, are you not staying then, miss?"

Once she was safely alone in the lane, Mary broke into a full run and did not stop until she reached the little wilderness area towards the back of Longbourn. There she collapsed to the ground by a stone bench near a tall cedar tree and sobbed out her agony and humiliation until her tears were spent.

They despise me! They think me a fool! Why did I ever imagine a new dress or hairstyle would change anything? I am and always will be poor, pathetic Mary—the useless, plain daughter who will never find love or a husband. Oh, my heavens, how can I ever face them again? I thought Amelia was my friend, but she was laughing at me too. And in a few months, she will marry Papa and move into Longbourn? She does not care for me at all; she only pities me. And to know she is thinking that each time she looks at me? I could not bear it!

After a half hour of weeping, Mary got off the ground, pulled a handkerchief from her pocket, wiped her face, and blew her nose. Then she sat on the bench to think.

My only hope for happiness is for them to go. I must come up with a way to make Papa give her up and take the living from Mr. Yarby too. They must be made to leave Longbourn—somehow.

As she sat, the small kernel of an idea began to form in her mind. It seemed a good possibility; however, it involved an act that Mary abhorred above all things: lying.

Chapter 28

Her plan now set in her mind—and convinced there was no other way to preserve her dignity and future happiness—Mary went straight to her father who was, as usual, in his book room. He looked up with a smile, but on seeing his daughter in such disarray and so clearly upset, his countenance quickly changed to one of concern.

"Mary, my dear, what on earth is wrong? Are you unwell?"

"I am not unwell, Papa. But I am terribly distressed by something I have heard—" She broke off with a small sob and grabbed her handkerchief, pressing it to her mouth, struggling for control. Mr. Bennet hurried over and gently led her to the settee.

"Tell me what is troubling you," he urged, sitting beside her.

"Before I do, I must ask you to promise to have the carriage available for me tomorrow so that I may leave first thing for Pemberley. For I cannot bear to—" She took a shuddering breath. "*Promise* me, Papa."

"Of course, if you wish it. But what is so upsetting that you should desire to leave Longbourn? What did you hear?"

Mary looked at her father and felt a pang of guilt, knowing that the lie she was about to tell would ruin his hopes for happiness with Amelia. But she simply could not bear to have Mr. Yarby or his sister so near and see them daily, knowing what they really thought of her. She took a deep breath to tell her lie.

"I was walking over to see Mr. Yarby in order to ask about something I had read in the Bible. As I reached the house, their maid told me he and Phillip and Amelia were in the back. So, I walked around and as I approached, I...I..." Mary swallowed, nearly losing her nerve before plunging ahead. "They were speaking—of you, Papa, and how their plan was working perfectly to make you fall in love with Amelia. Then she laughed and said she did not care for you at all, but just wanted to live at Longbourn and secure Mr. Yarby's position here as rector. It is clear she does not love you, Papa. She only wants the riches of our home! You must break it off with her."

Mr. Bennet sat back, his mouth open. He stared at his daughter, and she felt him studying her. She lowered her eyes and was silent.

"Are you...are you *quite* certain of what they were saying, Mary?" he finally asked. "Perhaps you misheard them."

"No, Papa—I know what I heard. And now I recall that, early on, she pressed me to tell her where you enjoyed walking. It was clearly a plot to occasion opportunities to meet with you in an innocent way and worm her way into your heart."

Mary placed her hand on her father's, forcing herself to go on. "I am all too aware of how hard this is for you to learn. It is for me as well, for I have been just as deceived as you have. Amel—Mrs. Withers clearly took me into her confidence and pretended to become my intimate friend in order to get close to you. But it is all a sham. You *must* break with her. Thank goodness, nobody outside of the family knows of your attachment; we can avoid a scandal. And you must speak to the bishop about dismissing Yarby, for he clearly took this position under false pretenses and intended deceit!"

Mr. Bennet ran a hand over his face. "Not that I do not believe you, Mary—you are not one to tell a lie—but I wish to speak to her first. This is all so sudden and, frankly, completely unlike the Amelia I know. I must hear her side before taking such a dramatic step. This may just be some strange misunderstanding or confusion on your part that can easily be cleared up."

Mary tilted her chin defiantly. "Speak to her if you like, Papa, but of course she will only lie and use her charming ways to play on your affections and persuade you that I am…making this all up. But I am your daughter; you must believe me. I know what I heard!"

She reached for her father's hands. "Come away with me to Pemberley—and Kitty too. We shall all get away from this horrible fraud, and then you can write the bishop from there about dismissing Mr. Yarby. Then we shall return to Longbourn in due time and make a fresh start."

"I am so shocked. I must think long and hard about this news, Mary. What you have related distresses me greatly. I cannot believe Amelia would even say such…"

He gave himself a little shake and rose to pull the bell cord. "I shall order the carriage and tell Mr. Hill to accompany you tomorrow. Go and pack. Kitty and I shall stay here for now. Although, if what you have told me turns out to be correct…then we shall follow later." He gave a wan smile to his daughter. "Go along now, and leave me to think."

THREE DAYS LATER, MARY ARRIVED AT PEMBERLEY. WHEN THE carriage drove up to the grand manor, Barton, the butler, and Pemberley's housekeeper, Mrs. Reynolds, came out, expressing great surprise at Mary's unanticipated arrival. Told her room would be made ready as soon as possible, Mary was escorted into the morning room where she found Lizzy and Georgiana doing needlework. They both looked up from their work in astonishment.

"Mary!" exclaimed Lizzy. "I did not know to expect you. Did a letter advising us of your arrival go amiss?" She set her sewing aside and rose to embrace her sister and give her a kiss.

"There was no time to send advance word, Lizzy. Please accept my deep apologies for arriving unannounced. But I simply had to get away; the situation at home has become quite untenable and—" Mary broke off with a sob. "Oh, Lizzy, I am so unhappy!"

Lizzy enfolded her younger sister in her arms and comforted her while Georgiana rang the bell pull to order a pot of strong tea—the remedy for every crisis.

"So, OF COURSE, AS SOON AS I LEARNED OF THEIR DECEIT, I TOLD Papa I must leave Longbourn at once," Mary finished her tale. "I tried to persuade our father and Kitty to join me, but he wishes to remain for now."

"I am beyond astonishment at your report," Lizzy said. "Papa wrote not a word about his affection for Mrs. Withers. We had no idea!"

"Well, of course—he is still in full mourning, so he could not speak of it. Aside from Kitty and Mr. Yarby, no one knows of their attachment," Mary replied.

"How lucky for you to have overheard them when you did, Mary," Georgiana added, earnestly. "For the romance might have continued, and I should hate to see a man as kind and sweet as your father enter into a marriage under false pretenses!"

"Yes, and since it has not become public knowledge," added Lizzy, "Papa can speak to the bishop for approval to send them away and no one will be the wiser. We have escaped any hint of scandal. Well done, Mary. Oh, but poor Papa—I do feel sorry for him. If his heart was truly attached to Mrs. Withers, your news must have been a terrible and painful shock."

Mary dropped her eyes, feeling guiltier by the minute. One lie seems to have led to another, and she was amazed at how easily Lizzy and Georgiana believed her falsehoods.

I have always made it a practice to be honest above all things. I abhor liars, and yet, it appears I have become quite a skillful one. Well, once Amelia and Mr. Yarby are gone from Longbourn, I shall double my good works in the parish in penance, and I vow to never lie again. If only... there had been another way.

The faces of Amelia and Robert came into her mind, and Mary felt an ache in her chest that mingled with her guilt and the exhaustion of the long trip. What had she done? She had betrayed the man she loved and her only true friend. She gave a little moan and fell over in her chair in a faint.

Chapter 29

M r. Bennet sent a note over to the rectory, asking Amelia to please meet him at their usual walking place at the regular time and adding that he needed to discuss something of great importance with her. When she arrived, his heart ached at the sight of her, knowing that, if all Mary said was true, he would be forced to give her up. He sent up a quick prayer that it was a misunderstanding and he could still marry her.

After greeting each other, the two began their walk in a companionable silence. He caught her glance at him once or twice with a quizzical expression, but she said nothing. Finally, after they had traveled quite a distance, Amelia broke the silence and asked what Mr. Bennet needed to discuss with her.

"It is about Mary," he said, heavily. "Tell me truthfully, Amelia, for I must know. Do you care for her as a friend? Or, perhaps...was she merely a path to become close to me?"

Amelia stopped short. "I confess I find myself quite...perplexed by your question, Eugene. What on earth would make you think I do not care for Mary?"

Mr. Bennet did not answer her question, but repeated his again.

Amelia made a small sound of exasperation. "I am *terribly* fond of Mary; I don't know how you could think otherwise. From the very first time we met when you sent her to escort me around your property while you and Robert spoke of hiring him, she impressed me as a sincere and thoughtful young lady. Then, as she and I talked more following your late wife's passing, I perceived that she was feeling somewhat neglected in her family. You will recollect the conversation we had early on about the trials of being the middle child. I only wanted to try to help her and encourage her to better herself." She paused and studied his face.

"Is this what you are concerned about? That I overstepped my bounds in doing so? If I did, I sincerely apologize, Eugene, and shall evermore keep my opinions to myself. But please know that, whatever I did, my actions were sincere, and I only ever intended to help Mary."

"I want to believe that, Amelia, I do. But some information has come to me that makes me…question the haste with which our relationship has formed. This is why I ask whether Mary was a means to an end." He saw a flash of anger cross Amelia's face.

"What has been said about me? And by whom—was it that odious Mr. Collins? Is it not bad enough that he blackmailed Robert into giving him the curate position by threatening to spread malicious gossip about our attachment?"

"He did *what?*" Mr. Bennet's concerns over Mary's accusations receded to the back of his mind over this revelation. "Is that why Robert took him on? Your brother does not have a chronic health condition that warranted the need to bring Mr. Collins in as curate? That scoundrel! I shall demand he relinquish the position at once; else, I *will* report him to the bishop."

"No, Eugene, for my sake, leave it be." Amelia reached out to grasp his arm. "You are still in mourning, and if Mr. Collins retaliates in anger and spreads his vile gossip, his comments could still hurt us."

The two stared at each other a moment before Mr. Bennet nodded, muttering, "Very well. I shall do as you wish." They began to walk again, silently. Then Amelia pulled on his sleeve to stop him.

"Wait. If it was not Mr. Collins who planted doubts in your mind, who was it? What was said that makes you think I only pretended to like your daughter in order to get closer to you?"

"I...cannot say." He walked on.

"When did these accusations surface?" Amelia persisted, as she caught up to him.

"Again...I do not wish to reveal that precisely, but it was quite recent."

"But so very few people even know of our feelings." She stopped and turned to Mr. Bennet with a sorrowful countenance. "Was it Kitty? I know she is still not quite accepting of the idea of our marrying."

"Not Kitty, no."

Amelia furrowed her brow, concentrating. "Well, if it was not Mr. Collins, and it was not Kitty, and you say *you* have not informed your other three daughters about us, then that leaves...Mary?" Mr. Bennet did not look her in the face, clear confirmation of her guess. Amelia pressed a hand to her mouth. "Has Mary accused me of not caring for you? Because I do, Eugene, you must know that I do!"

"And yet, Mary is convinced you are only pretending to do so in order to live at Longbourn and secure your brother's position. To own it"—he paused and shook his head sadly—"she told me she overheard you say this."

Amelia gave a little cry and stamped her foot. "She could not have done so, for I never would say such a thing! I don't just care for you, Eugene; I *love* you! And as for wanting to marry you simply for Longbourn House, it would not matter to me if you were a duke or the Meryton cheese monger! It is your intelligent mind and your humor and kindness I love, not a house. I am beyond all comprehension of this!"

She angrily brushed back tears. "Where is Mary? I must speak to her so that I may clear up this misunderstanding."

"She left Longbourn for Pemberley. I do not know when she will return." Mr. Bennet studied Amelia's face. Her words were as sincere as he could hope to hear, but was it the truth? On the other hand, why would Mary make up such an outrageous fabrication? It made no sense. He sighed.

"Perhaps I have been a fool to think you could love me. There is a considerable age difference after all. Have I just persuaded myself into thinking this love is real?"

Amelia grabbed both his hands and pressed them to her bosom. "What does your heart tell you? Think back on all our conversations— our lovely walks. And recall where you said your mind went when you were shot—to me and to *us!* You know our love is true, and in your heart, you know what Mary says cannot be correct; you *know* it!"

"My heart says this love is real, Amelia," he said, and heard her sigh of relief. "But my mind—my mind is still quite confused." He shook his head. "I think we must not see each other for a time until I can figure this out."

She gasped and staggered back a few paces. Finally, she nodded, and the two walked slowly and silently back to the parsonage where they parted without a word or glance.

Chapter 30

After her fainting spell, Mary refused to leave her bedroom for the next two days and spent much of the time alone, often weeping. Lizzy and Darcy were confused and frustrated, unable to think of a way to help her. They even called in a physician, but he reported he could find nothing physically wrong.

"It just seems very odd that Mary is taking this so to heart," Lizzy said one evening as she and her husband settled into bed. "Indeed, I should imagine she would be crowing about her success in discovering Mrs. Withers's true colors before it was too late, yet she spends hours weeping as if deeply sad and refuses to speak to me about it further."

"Well, she must also feel betrayed by Mrs. Withers, clearly. After all, the two had become quite close, and your middle sister never has had many intimate friends, you know. For her to discover that she was just a pawn in a game to secure your father's affections must have wounded her terribly."

Lizzy nodded thoughtfully. "Yes, you are right, that is likely the key issue here. But the question remains, how do we help her?"

"All broken hearts heal in time, Lizzy. We shall just give her love and attention, and eventually, things will come around right."

"In the meantime, I should write to Papa and let him know we are glad he did not enter into an engagement with that Mrs. Withers. I did write that Mary had arrived safely, but I was reluctant to say anything about the recent events until I heard more details from my sister. But it is clear she is not going to say more—at least not to me." She leaned over to blow out the candle on the nightstand. "Perhaps once I write to Papa, I shall have a clearer idea of how to help her."

THE NEXT AFTERNOON, MARY SAT IN HER ROOM, STARING BLANKLY out the window when she heard a knock at her door. Although she did not wish for any company, she called out, "Come in." Perhaps it was just a maid bringing tea.

Instead, Georgiana entered, carrying Lavinia Jane. She smiled shyly at Mary and held the baby up.

"Miss Lavinia Jane is most displeased her auntie Mary has not been to the nursery to visit her yet on this visit," she said in a teasing voice. "She insisted I bring her to you." Georgiana walked over and set the baby firmly in Mary's lap. "She has grown quite a bit since you were last here, has she not?" she asked as she pulled a chair over to the window seat.

"Indeed," Mary murmured, offering a finger for her niece to grab. Lavinia promptly pulled it into her mouth, making Mary smile. She noted Lavinia was improving in looks. The pinched, angry face she recalled from before was gone, having filled out nicely. In fact, her overall appearance was plumper and healthy looking, and—heavens!—was that a dimple in her right cheek? It seemed her niece would be comely, after all.

"Are you feeling better, Mary?" Georgiana asked gently. "We are all dreadfully worried about your distress over the situation at Longbourn."

"My heart is still so heavy, Georgiana," Mary replied in a faltering voice.

"Well, of course—to learn that someone you considered a bosom friend should betray not only your father but you as well must be exceedingly painful. But can you not rejoice even a little in the fact that you made this discovery in time? Imagine the agony if the marriage had gone ahead only for your dear Papa to learn the truth too late. Then he would be trapped."

"The truth..." Mary bit her lip and squeezed her eyes shut. "The truth is so painful. But so are the lies."

Georgiana cocked her head. "What lies do you speak of? Do you mean those by Mrs. With—"

Mary broke in with a small sob. "I have always prided myself on being honest. I wish to always tell the truth."

"Well, and so you have—to the betterment of the situation despite this initial sorrow that accompanies it. You will feel differently in time I expect."

"I shall never forgive myself for ruining Papa's chance at happiness." Mary shook her head, then handed Lavinia back to Georgiana. "Will you please excuse me? I wish to lie down. I feel a headache coming on."

"Of course. But please say that I can persuade you to come downstairs soon to join me in some duets on the pianoforte. I have purchased new music I have been most eager to try, and your sister refuses to attempt them. However, I know you would be able to play them with me."

"Perhaps," Mary whispered, studying her hands in her lap.

After waiting another moment, Georgiana squeezed Mary's arm, shifted her niece onto her hip, and quietly slipped out of the room.

After returning Lavinia to the nursery, Georgiana went to her own room to think on her conversation with Mary.

Curious. Why does Mary say she cannot forgive herself? She has saved her father from a probable fortune hunter and a most imprudent marriage. That should make her feel pride—not shame. Unless there is more to the story. Could there be something Mary is not telling us? What could she have done that she thinks is so unforgivable?

Chapter 31

Amelia and Robert were in the parlor, quietly discussing the recent events and Mr. Bennet's decision to halt all communication with her for now. They wanted privacy for their talk, and when Phillip went out for a walk, it seemed a good time. But even after more than an hour, they were no closer to understanding why Mary would have told her father such falsehoods.

"I still do not comprehend it, Robert—why would she wish to sever the relationship between Mr. Bennet and me? He led me to believe she was happy to hear of our attachment. And she even assured me of her approbation herself, saying she looked forward to turning the household management over to me! I was so happy and eager to be a guiding influence on her once Eugene and I were married." She gave a start. "Could that be it? Is she jealous of me?"

"That does not seem like the Mary we know," Robert replied. "She is always considerate and kind. Why, more than once I have seen her taking soup or freshly baked bread to a tenant who is ailing. And when I complimented her on it, she merely said that she felt blessed to be a blessing to others. Hateful acts are simply not in her character."

"Perhaps we do not know her as well as we thought? Oh! I do not even have the ability to speak to her and try to straighten this out! I confess, Robert, I am quite vexed. I counted her as a dear friend—the first I made in this community. I know she has oft been lonely and that she feels unloved. Perhaps there is a broken heart in her past and she fears the same for her father? No, that cannot be it. She has never had a prior romance to my knowledge. Why, she has never even had a Season in London."

Robert shook his head with a soft chuckle. "A season does not seem like something Mary would enjoy. And personally, I should certainly hate to see her go through that ordeal—be paraded at balls and assemblies just for the thought of securing a husband? I know it is common for young ladies, but how can there be a true meeting of the minds in such a short time? I could not choose a bride based just on flirtation and dancing. Mary is far too cerebral to form an attachment based solely on a few smiles, compliments, and turns around the ballroom."

The door opened and Ellen walked in with a tray laden with a teapot, cups and saucers, and a plate of fresh scones. The sweet odor wafted over to Amelia and Robert as she set the tray down and began to arrange everything on the table.

"I agree," Amelia continued. "Mary is the sort of girl who might not make a good initial impression, but rather, she is one who improves upon acquaintance. And yes, she certainly is not one to attempt to catch a man by flirting."

Ellen gave a little giggle, then covered her mouth, lowered her eyes, and bobbed a curtsey. "I beg your pardon, Mrs. Withers, Mr. Yarby. I did not mean to overhear, but I have known Miss Mary for many years, and nobody would *ever* call her a flirt."

"That's all right, Ellen," Amelia said. "But please tell me—since you are better acquainted with her—have you ever known Mary to be the sort to spread false stories about anyone?"

This time Ellen laughed outright. "Gracious me, no! Everyone in Longbourn and Meryton knows that while Mary Bennet is no great beauty, she can always be counted on to be truthful, polite, and thoughtful. Why—just the other day when she called to visit, I was scrubbing the front steps and told her to go on in, but she said she wouldn't dream of putting her dirty boots where I had just washed and would walk around to the back. Now that's fine manners to my mind. But then, she is a gentleman's daughter after all."

Ellen, done with setting the tea things out, began to leave, but Amelia called her back.

"When was that, Ellen—that day you mentioned when Miss Bennet came by?"

"A couple days back. It was that sunny, warm day when you and Mr. Phillip Yarby had your wine and cake out in the back. But whatever she come for, she didn't stay long. Just a minute or so later, seems like, she rushed right out of the garden—hardly even said goodbye."

Amelia and Robert exchanged a stunned look.

"She rushed out, you say?" Amelia asked.

"Indeed, ma'am. Like the devil were after her, come to think of it. I thought she had forgot something back at Longbourn. But she did not return."

"That will be all, Ellen, thank you," Amelia said. When they were alone, she said, "Oh no. Robert, do you recall what we were talking about that afternoon?"

"I do—all too well. The three of us were making sport of Kitty's attempts to spend time alone with me with her faux Bible questions. You don't...you don't think Mary heard that, do you? And she is upset with us for laughing at her sister?"

"No, Robert, I think it is far worse than that. I believe Mary heard just *part* of our conversation and believed we were making fun of *her*. For she has also brought her questions about scripture to you several times, has she not?"

"Yes, but I welcome talks with Mary—they are lively and interesting. I admire the way her mind works." He sat heavily at the table. "So, you think she overheard some of our comments but did not stay long enough to realize we spoke of Kitty?"

"It must be. For I know, if I had been eavesdropping and heard something so…well, cruel— for there is no other word for it—I would have been utterly devastated to learn people I counted as friends were laughing at me, and I should have fled at once. And Ellen just said she had barely gone around back before she returned and departed! Oh, that must be why she has said such terrible lies about us! She is trying to salvage her dignity."

Mr. Yarby sighed. "I agree it makes sense. She must hope that, by telling these tales, Mr. Bennet will get rid of us both. For who could bear to be around people she thought were her friends, after believing them possible of such hateful words? I feel utterly wretched to even imagine we may have hurt her feelings."

"I must write her at Pemberley at once," Amelia announced. "I shall explain everything, apologize for making sport of Kitty, and assure Mary that our affection for her is steadfast and true."

"And what of Mr. Bennet?"

"First, I must make things right with Mary. Only then can there be a chance for Eugene and me to be happy."

Chapter 32

Finally, nearly two weeks after her arrival, Mary left her room more often and began to participate in the daily routine of Pemberley though she was still rather quiet and obviously low in spirits. One day, she and Georgiana were in the morning room after breakfast. Both were longing for a brisk walk, but it had rained every day for the past week, and it was simply too soggy, so they occupied their time with needlework while waiting for Lizzy, who was having her regular morning conference with the housekeeper, Mrs. Reynolds.

The door opened and both looked up to see a footman enter, bearing a silver salver upon which sat a thick envelope. He walked up to Mary, bowed, and extended the tray to her. She saw her name written on the envelope and picked it up, curious. Expecting a letter from her father or perhaps Kitty, she did not recognize the handwriting at first. Then she gasped and dropped the folded paper in her lap as if it had burned her.

"Mary, is something amiss?" asked Georgiana, pausing in her work. "Who is your letter from?"

Mary's heart was pounding so hard she was certain Georgiana could hear it. She took a deep breath and said in a strangled voice, "It is from Mrs. Withers."

"It may bear good news. Perhaps she has an explanation for what you overheard. It is still possible you were mistaken…is it not?" Georgiana asked gently.

Mary sprang up from her chair and went to the fireplace where she hesitated only a moment before throwing the missive in the flames. She stood there, fists tightly clenched, watching it burn. Then she turned to Georgiana with a fierce expression.

"I can have no interest in *anything* she will have written! And I shall treat any further correspondence from her in the exact same manner."

She returned to her seat and picked up her needlework, but discovered her eyes were so tear-filled, she could not see what she was doing.

"Pray excuse me, Georgiana," she muttered, laying it aside and rising. "I wish to return to my room."

Before Georgiana could reply, Mary rushed out. Georgiana quickly went to the fireplace to see if any of the letter could be salvaged, but found only ash.

TWO DAYS LATER, THE WEATHER HAD TURNED SO LOVELY THAT Georgiana persuaded Mary to go for a walk in the gardens though the grounds were still damp. After an hour or so of rambling on the gravel paths around the estate, and remaining mostly silent, they came to a bench by the pond and sat to rest.

Georgiana studied Mary for a time. Finally, she spoke.

"Mary, forgive me, but I must speak my mind. I am not even sure why I think this, but I have a very strong feeling that your unhappiness with the situation about Mr. Yarby and Mrs. Withers is not entirely about this plot to trap Mr. Bennet in a marriage. Is there, perhaps another reason you ran away from Longbourn and continue to be so melancholy? Could it be…something that impacts *you* more than your father?"

Mary's lower lip trembled a moment, then she bent over, covered her face and began to sob. "Oh, Georgiana, I lied—I lied about everything! There is no plot, there never was. Amelia and Mr. Yarby are not the wicked, conniving opportunists I painted them to be. Indeed, they are two of the kindest, most wonderful people I have ever known. And now I have ruined Papa's chance of happiness forever! Oh, what have I done?" Her crying became so violent she could not continue speaking. She rocked back and forth in agonized weeping while Georgiana patted her back and waited.

When Mary finally gained control of her emotions, she required the use of not only her own handkerchief, but Georgiana's as well. She sat, exhausted, with a numb expression.

"Can you explain why you lied about them?" Georgiana asked after a moment.

"I lied because my own pride was hurt. I *did* overhear them talking, but it was not about Papa; it was about me. They were…making fun of me," Mary's voice cracked, and she struggled to keep the tears from flowing again.

"Oh, that must have been very painful. But it is still not quite clear to me. Why should they make sport of you? If they are the kind and generous people you say they are, why would they behave in such a manner?"

"Because…" Mary's voice faltered a moment before she continued in a rush, daring to say the words out loud for the first time, "Because I so *desperately* love Mr. Yarby, and they have found me out. I believe I have loved him from the first moment I saw him in Papa's library when he came to interview for the living at Longbourn. And I thought, if he could appreciate my interest in the Bible, then he would know how smart I am and overlook my plain looks and fall in love with me too. So, every other week or so, I contrived to come up with scriptural passages that needed explanation and then visit him to discuss them. I…I so enjoyed our talks, and I naively thought he did, as well. But I was fooling myself. On that awful day, I walked towards the back of the parsonage and Mr. Yarby, his brother, and Amelia were there talking and I heard them." Her voice became anguished again. "They saw my feeble plot to get closer to Mr. Yarby for what it was and they were laughing at me! They called me 'pathetic.' That is why I left Longbourn and came to Pemberley. How could I ever face them again? To see Amelia every day when she marries Papa, knowing she thought me a complete and utter fool? I could not bear it."

Mary turned her face to Georgiana for the first time. "So, I lied. I fabricated the story of them trying to trap Papa into marriage and her not loving him. And then I fled here like the coward I am. I wanted my father to break with her and fire Yarby so they would be gone and my agony over—you see?"

Georgiana embraced Mary. Crying once more, Mary sank down, resting her head in her friend's lap. "I am so ashamed. There can be no excuse for what I did. I always have done my best to be a good Christian woman; instead, my actions show me to be the most selfish, hateful creature possible."

Georgiana stroked Mary's hair. "But you can still make things right, can you not? You can write your father and tell him the truth before it is too late and he dismisses Mr. Yarby. Then, in time, the pain you feel now will fade, and you can show your face to them again—perhaps even rekindle the friendships of before."

"Never! Such agonies of the spirit could never leave me!"

"Yes, they can and they will. Sit up, Mary, I wish to tell you a story."

Mary sat up, sniffed, and gave Georgiana her attention.

"Some five years ago, I was persuaded to think myself in love. I was only fifteen—a child! What did I know of love? Yet I heard his flattery, his kind words of admiration and love, and I believed them. But this man—I can't call him a *gentleman*—had an evil plan in mind. He asked me to elope with him when I was staying at Ramsgate with my paid companion, and I foolishly agreed. The elopement request alone should have been a sign to me that this was not an honorable romance, for who would want to marry in secret and in haste if the love was sincere enough to wait properly for the banns to be read? I have a considerable inheritance of my own, you see, and he wanted to get his hands on it. I was too young to realize his true motive was not my love but my money."

Georgiana gave a small smile. "Fortunately, my brother arrived unexpectedly to visit me in Ramsgate, and I told him of the plot, else I might have found myself saddled in marriage to a man with little in the way of honor, kindness, or reputation. And not only was my heart broken, like yours, but I also suffered the most terrible bouts of shame and humiliation—how could I have been so stupid not to have seen him for the disreputable fortune hunter he was?" She shook her head in remembrance.

"It quite put me off the idea of romance, I can tell you. It is why, at twenty, I have not yet had a Season in London. But, Mary, I relate this story to assure you that, while I still may have an occasional pang of regret over my actions, the pain has faded far away. Time does heal all wounds, believe me."

"But you were the victim of that sad story, Georgiana, while I...I am the *perpetrator* of mine! My behavior was reprehensible. I have acted against every moral code I grew up with—as a gentleman's daughter, as a Bennet, and worst of all, as a Christian. How can I ever find forgiveness?"

"Does the Bible not say: *And when ye stand praying, forgive, if ye have ought against any: that your Father also which is in Heaven may forgive you your trespasses?*" Georgiana patted Mary's hand. "If you can somehow find forgiveness for the hurtful things your friends said about you, then *you* will be forgiven for your lies. I do not say it will be easy, but there is a path if you will take it."

"That is from the book of Mark, chapter eleven," Mary murmured. "Oh, but Georgiana, my trespasses seem so very, very bad."

The sun had gone behind some dark clouds. Georgiana looked up and frowned.

"It is chilly, and it looks as if it may rain again. Let us return to the house, shall we? We don't have to talk about this further today. But I think you will see in time that you need to return to Longbourn and make things right."

"I do not think I have the courage. I should much rather stay here and be the maiden aunt to Thomas and Lavinia. It seems safer."

Georgiana laughed. "Oh, believe it, Mary, if you stay here, I shall make you endure the London Season next year with me. That daunting possibility alone might be enough to send you running back to Longbourn."

Mary gave a small laugh and nodded. Linking arms, the two young women made their way back to the house. When they entered Pemberley, an exhausted Mary went to her room to rest. Georgiana went to find Elizabeth.

"I AM ALL ASTONISHMENT AT YOUR TALE, GEORGIANA!" ELIZABETH exclaimed when Georgiana finished relating all that she and Mary had discussed. "I should have realized there was more to my sister's story. Now it makes sense why she has been so morose. I must speak to her at once and force her to rectify matters."

"I would caution you against that, Lizzy. She is in such a fragile state of mind just now. In fact, I do not believe you should even let her know that you are aware of the whole story—not yet at any rate. It might force her to run away again—and where would she go? She might put herself in terrible danger." Georgiana shook her head firmly. "No. I believe we should give her a few more days to come to her own conclusion over what she needs to do. In her heart she knows she must make amends."

Elizabeth made a helpless gesture. "I still cannot fathom it all! For Mary to tell such falsehoods—that harm not only her friends, but our father too? It is inconceivable. Mary has *never* lied!"

Georgiana gave Elizabeth a sad smile. "But, Lizzy—Mary has never had her heart broken."

Chapter 33

Mr. Collins sat in his rented rooms above a public house in Meryton, staring out the grimy windows. As his wife had predicted, the accommodation he could afford was only minimally furnished. But aside from the desk, a couple of chairs, and a bed for the occasional nap, what more did he need? The chimney did not draw well, so the fireplace smoked a bit, and that was vexing. But he reasoned he would not be using it much longer. Not only was the weather getting warmer, but he had every confidence that he would soon hear from Mr. Yarby's former employer and learn something that would be so scandalous, Mr. Bennet or the bishop would see no alternative but to fire him. With him would go his sister, eliminating any chance of Mr. Bennet fathering a son at his late age. That, Mr. Collins thought, would secure Longbourn for himself and his new son. In addition, Mr. Collins believed he could likely persuade Mr. Bennet to let him step into the vacancy as the Longbourn rector until he inherited. Newly refurbished and with well-working fireplaces, the cozy parsonage would no doubt make Charlotte quite content to move from her parent's home.

Having already finished reworking his sermon for next Sunday, Mr. Collins was a bit bored. However, he did not wish to walk back to Lucas Lodge quite yet. Since he was paying good money for these rooms, he felt a strong obligation to spend as much time in them as he could even though the view was minimal and the noise from downstairs occasionally excessive. In addition, he and Charlotte were getting along poorly of late. She had refused to come see his rooms, saying she could not imagine a reason to do so. And at Lucas Lodge, every time an issue came up or he made a helpful suggestion on a better way to do things there, Charlotte would side with her parents, which hurt his pride. She should take her husband's side, of course! In addition, Lady Lucas had begun to insinuated herself into every aspect of caring for young Alexander, which annoyed him. Another reason to find a better position and start anew with his family.

However, the job situation was looking bleak. He had sent applications to a few parishes where he had gotten word of a possible vacancy, but he had been thrice rejected, which stung. There was but one opening left for which he had applied: in the village of Haswell in County Durham. He almost hoped he would not get it. It was small, quite far north, and appeared to have little to offer in the way of diversions, from what he could tell. Dull farmers and shopkeepers for the most part, he mused—how tedious *their* society would be. Such a step down from the elegant rooms at Rosings Manor. The salary would also be quite modest—just thirty pounds above his current earnings.

The more he thought about his situation, the more imposed upon he felt. Thinking an ale would lift his spirits, he decided to go downstairs to the tavern below his room. Maybe that cute little serving girl—what was her name? Oh yes, Nancy—was working this afternoon. Curly red hair, freckles, and a saucy manner to match. She had definitely flirted with him the other evening. Though initially he thought she might have done so only in hopes of a nice tip, he reflected now that there was likely more to it, that she probably *did* find him of interest. He had never seen her in church that he could recall. Perhaps, he mused, he could offer to privately counsel her on the importance of a relationship with our Lord. As one of the local ministers, it would only be the proper thing to help bring her closer to God. Yes, he would greatly enjoy discussions with her.

Checking himself in the small mirror, he brushed his hair, then proceeded downstairs.

March 2

Dear Mrs. Withers,

You will, I hope, remember me from our meeting at the funeral of my mother, Mrs. Bennet, at Longbourn. I am writing you now in the hopes of healing the problems that recently arose at Longbourn House.

My sister and your friend—Mary—has been staying with us at Pemberley estate in Derbyshire since what I understand to have been a terribly sad incident some weeks ago, resulting in pain to parties other than herself. Mary has taken my husband's sister, Miss Darcy, into her confidence and related a day where she overheard you and your brothers discussing Mary's attempts to improve and deepen her relationship with Mr. Yarby through scripture study. Indeed, she said you were all ridiculing her for this. I do not write those words to chastise you but to help explain her actions afterwards.

You are, no doubt, aware of the untruthful stories she told her father about you and your brother. These were a direct result of her pain and humiliation, and they were said with an intention to drive you both away in order to salvage her hurt feelings as she found herself unable to be in your company any longer.

Yet, Mary now regrets her actions, and I am certain you realize how out of character they were for her. She knows she has caused pain not only to you but also to our dear father, and she is most sincerely remorseful.

But even yet, Mary is too ashamed to return to Longbourn and put things to right. Her humiliation over hearing your comments seems to have shifted into a shame about her own behavior, and at this point, she has not the courage to confront it. I am hopeful that, with gentle persuasion by Miss Darcy and me, her feelings will change, although how quickly, I cannot guess.

Miss Darcy also has informed me of another incident of which I must write. Upon receipt, Mary burned your recent letter to her without reading it, so whatever message you were trying to communicate was unsuccessful. She apparently vows to burn any future letters, so it seems there is no use for you to write again.

Pray forgive me for perhaps intruding in these matters, but my interference is kindly meant. We all love Mary, and nothing would make us happier than to see everything settled among all of you so that Mary will be able to return to Longbourn again, free of shame and, hopefully, to renew her friendship with you and your brother. However, it may yet take some time.

I give you permission to share this letter with my father, Mr. Bennet, so that he may be assured the rumors about you are just that—taradiddles that are wholly without foundation.

Yours most sincerely,
Elizabeth Darcy

"I CAN SCARCE BELIEVE IT!" DECLARED MR. BENNET UPON READING his daughter's letter that Amelia brought to him. Initially, he was somewhat suspicious that it was a forgery, or some attempt by the Yarby family to deceive him, but it was clearly written in Lizzy's hand. Furthermore, after Amelia recounted her and Mr. Yarby's new knowledge from their maid of Mary's visit and their belief in the conversation Mary overheard, he was convinced. He sat back in his desk chair and studied Amelia ruefully. "You were telling me the truth all along. I should have known you would not lie to me."

"Yes, but I am afraid the truth has also revealed a side of my family that is not very flattering. We should not have made sport of Kitty's attempts to endear herself to Robert. I can only say in our defense that we had been drinking—perhaps, a bit too much dandelion wine—and that, plus the warm weather, loosened our tongues as well as our sense of good manners and propriety. Please forgive me, Eugene. I am truly quite fond of Kitty, you know."

"It is I who should ask for your forgiveness, Amelia. I was too quick to believe the stories my daughter told, as outlandish as they seemed to me at the time. I should have shown better judgment and had all of us sit down together. Then, we could have sorted out this misunderstanding with fewer tears and heartache." He reached for her hand. "Can you excuse my behavior and believe that I do love you, despite the doubts I exhibited?"

"Any father would likely side with his child over someone he has known less than a year; it is only natural. I bear no ill will towards you or Mary, be assured. I am only happy we have cleared up everything at last."

Mr. Bennet glanced down at the letter again, his face showing his dismay. "To tell such falsehoods! It is so very unlike my daughter. She prides herself on always being truthful, you know."

"To a fault," Amelia said, and the two shared a small chuckle. "But please do not be too harsh with her. She was just so terribly hurt and betrayed by what she overheard—what she believed. To her, convincing you that I was a fortune hunter seemed the only solution and the best way to rid herself of us. And Mrs. Darcy *does* write that Mary now feels great remorse over her actions."

"Although, she does not yet have the courage to confront those she has lied about and beg their forgiveness." He sighed and ran a hand over his face, considering. "Well. What to do now? Lizzy writes Mary burned your last letter. It seems I must travel to Pemberley to speak to her and set things to right."

"My brother and I discussed this long into the night, trying to decide whether I should go to her or ask you to do so. In the end, Robert decided *he* would speak to Mary as her pastor and…friend. He left early this morning, in fact, and has every hope of bringing Mary home within a week's time."

"Will she even speak to him once he gets there?"

"I believe so. She is quite fond of him, you know."

"Yes, but now she must face the heartache that those feelings are not returned, must she not? That will be another painful trial for her."

Amelia smiled and clasped Mr. Bennet's hands. "Oh, I think we may all soon learn that Robert's feeling are not quite what most people, including Mary herself, may think."

Chapter 34

Lizzy was passing through the entry hall of Pemberley, on her way to consult with Mrs. Reynolds, when she heard a conversation at the front door. A man was speaking to the butler in what sounded like a most urgent manner. Curious, she altered her course and went to see who was there.

"What is it, Barton?" she asked the butler.

"This gentleman insists on speaking to Miss Bennet, madam, but my understanding is that she is not accepting callers."

Elizabeth looked at the handsome man. "And your name, sir?"

"Robert Yarby, ma'am."

Elizabeth smiled. "I think Miss Bennet will be most happy to see this particular visitor, Barton. I shall take him to our guest. If you will please follow me, sir."

She guided Mr. Yarby upstairs to a small sitting room, a favorite of Mary's because of the good light for reading. She knocked, opened the door, and poked her head in.

"Mary, you have a visitor."

Mary set her book aside, stood, and smoothed her dress, wondering who could have come to see her? Was it her father? A feeling of guilty dread washed over her. She nodded to her sister that she was ready, and could not help staggering back a step when Mr. Yarby walked in. Lizzy winked at her and departed, closing the door firmly behind her.

For a moment, the two stood, eyeing each other warily. Then Mary dropped her eyes, cleared her throat, and curtseyed.

"Mr. Yarby. You have come for an explanation of my spreading such dreadful falsehoods about you and your sister, I surmise," Mary said, softly. "I can have no excuse. My reprehensible behavior is unforgiveable."

"Miss Bennet, I am the one who must beg your pardon. It was quite wrong of my sister, brother, and me to make sport of Miss Kitty that sunny day in the garden. I am so terribly sorry you overheard us."

As the words sunk in, Mary's head snapped up. "Kitty? You spoke of my *sister* that day?"

"Yes. You see, we had—I beg your pardon, Miss Bennet, may we both sit down?"

Still a bit stunned at his revelation, she nodded and motioned to the settee. The two sat, though Mary perched at the far edge, keeping her distance and avoiding his gaze.

"That is better," Yarby said. "As I was saying, your sister was doing the very same thing you were—coming to me with Bible questions, although it became quite clear to me that her interest actually lay in… other matters. Still, she is a member of my parish and my employer's daughter, so I could not refuse her entry. I feel terrible that you heard our joshing and assumed it was you of whom we spoke. *Your* visits to my library to discuss the Bible have always been most welcome, let me assure you."

"I feel even more a fool now," Mary said in a choked voice. "All the damage I caused—and it was not even about me!" She raised her eyes to Yarby's. "Please believe me when I say I am so very, very sorry.

I did not mean to be hateful and deceitful about you and Amelia. I only did it because"—Mary took a deep breath—"because I care for you a great deal. And when I realized that you did not feel the same and heard Amelia encouraging you declare yourself to a lady...well, I could not bear it and fled."

A broad smile spread over Yarby's face. "Yes, we did speak of a woman to whom I wished to declare myself, as I recall. But I hesitated because I was not certain of the lady's feelings. Now I am. You see—that lady is *you*. It has always been you, Miss Bennet—Mary. My affection for you has grown slowly and steadily this past year, but I was so afraid to tell you, afraid to even *speak* of it because of what people in Meryton might say—me courting the daughter of my employer. I feared they would call me an opportunist. It is what made me hesitate to ask you for more than the one dance at the Christmas assembly, why I always carefully guarded my conversations with you and tried to keep a proper distance, even as I longed to hold your hand and kiss your lips."

"Truly?"

"Truly."

"Oh." Mary was silent a long while as she tried to process this remarkable confession. "Would you...would you like to kiss me now?" She scooted over on the settee, closing the gap between them, and tilted her chin up.

Yarby laughed softly, then leaned in and touched his lips to hers—at first, barely skimming them, then pressing in again with more deliberation. When he finally pulled back, his eyes searched hers, and he asked, "Was that all right, Mary?"

"Oh yes, Mr. Yarby—I mean, Robert. It was...quite nice." She leaned forward again, seeking the touch of his mouth, a sensation more exciting and marvelous than she had ever hoped or imagined.

After a time, they separated again, both just staring at each other with expressions of stunned joy.

"So, you truly love me?" she whispered.

"With all my heart."

Tears filled Mary's eyes and spilled down her cheeks, even as she continued smiling. Yarby gently brushed them from Mary's face, his finger trailing along her cheek back to her lips.

"Now that we have that settled, you must come back to Longbourn with me, and I shall speak directly to your father. That is—if your answer is yes."

Mary, never one to tease, still could not resist saying, "Answer? I don't recall hearing a question."

He laughed and slipped off the settee to one knee, holding both her hands tightly. "Miss Mary Bennet, will you please make me the happiest of men and agree to be my wife?"

At her accepting nod, he returned to his seat and pulled her close for another long kiss. At last, they sat, her head on his broad shoulder as he stroked her hair, marveling at this happy result.

"So, you did not think me foolish for bringing you my scripture questions?" Mary asked.

"Oh no. I looked forward to each encounter; you have such a thoughtful mind." He paused a moment, before continuing. "In fact, tell me now: What was it you wanted to discuss that dreadful day when you overheard us talking and believed it was you of whom we spoke?"

Mary pulled away, embarrassed. "Love. I...wished to talk about some of the women in the Bible who love Jesus—for there are not many mentioned, as you know—the woman at the well to whom Jesus speaks, the widow who gives her last mite, and Veronica, who wiped our Lord's face on his way to Calvary. "

"All wonderful stories of a woman's devotion. But do you know what my favorite quote about women from the Bible is?" he asked softly.

She shook her head.

"It is Proverbs 31:10: 'Who can find a virtuous woman? For her price is far above rubies.'" He kissed her again. "That is *you,* my dear, dear Mary. And all the rubies in the world could not persuade me to give you up."

Chapter 35

There was joyful celebrating that evening at Pemberley once everyone recovered from the shock of Mary's astonishing announcement that she and Mr. Yarby were now engaged. Of course, this was also after Mary once again took responsibility for the harm her lies had caused and assured her family that she would do everything in her power to make things right. That settled, Darcy ordered several excellent wines brought up for supper, followed by peals of laughter and many toasts to their happiness. Lizzy and Darcy insisted Mr. Yarby stay with them at Pemberley and sent servants to retrieve his belongings from the Lambton Inn.

After dinner, Darcy joked, "Mr. Yarby, I think we should discuss the Bennet family more over some brandy while the ladies go through to the sitting room. You may be their reverend, but I have far more experience with being connected in marriage to this family. I am happy to share my knowledge and advice."

"Just mind you also tell him of the great joy our connection has brought you," Lizzy replied tartly to everyone's laughter.

As the ladies separated from the gentlemen. Georgiana held Mary back a moment and whispered in a teasing voice, "I suppose this means you will no longer remain here at Pemberley as the 'maiden aunt' to our nephew and niece."

Mary gave a soft laugh. "No indeed. Perhaps Robert and I shall be blessed with children of our own; I can only pray so. But first, I must make amends to Papa and Amelia. I hope it is not too late for them."

"I am quite certain you will find all is well. In fact, Lizzy and I feel exceedingly confident of it," Georgiana said with a mischievous smile that Mary did not understand.

"Are you two coming, or are you going to gossip and share secrets there in the hall all night?" Lizzy asked, but her expression showed no annoyance, only warm affection.

The two linked arms and hurried in.

TWO DAYS LATER, DARCY PROVIDED HIS FINEST COACH TO TAKE the couple back to Longbourn. Lizzy sent along one of the underhouse-maids to serve as both a help to Mary and to act as a sort of chaperone since Mary and Mr. Yarby were still unmarried. Although that meant the two had to somewhat temper their adoration, they were both mindful of the propriety of the situation and did not resent it too much.

However, along the way there was still a great deal of discussion about their future.

"Will you miss Longbourn, Mary?" Mr. Yarby asked. "I mean, you can and will visit often, but the parsonage is considerably less grand than your home. And our budget is not lavish, as you know; economies will have to be made, perhaps, from what you are used to. In addition, after your father sadly passes, Mr. Collins is unlikely to keep me on, and we may have to move."

"Robert! Are you trying to talk me out of marrying you?" Mary asked with a teasing smile. Somehow, since they had professed their love, she found it easy to joke and tease in a manner she had never done before. Amazed at herself, she thought that, if she kept this up, her family would not recognize the new Mary.

He laughed. "Not at all! I told you I shall never give you up. But I simply want you to know what to expect."

"Living with you at the parsonage and yet within reach of my family?—I cannot imagine a happier arrangement. And once Amelia and Papa wed, all will be well." She turned away and wrung her hands in her lap. "But I must confess, Robert, I so dread having to tell Papa what I have done and said. I am sure he will be very angry with me. It all seems such a mess and wholly of my doing. But I must own to what I did."

"I am sure your father will forgive you. After all, Amelia and I are still here; he did not dismiss us as you had hoped, so there is no permanent damage done. Do you...do you wish for me to go in with you when we arrive at Longbourn?"

Mary shook her head. "Thank you, but I must do this myself." She gave him a smile. "Knowing you support me, however, will give me the courage I need."

DARCY HAD SENT AN EXPRESS TO ALERT MR. BENNET AND KITTY of Mary and Mr. Yarby's arrival, so they both came out to greet the carriage when it pulled into the sweep at Longbourn. Mary hugged her sister, and then her father, while Mr. Yarby hung back a bit, observing. He and Mary had agreed they would not disclose their engagement until she had smoothed things over with her father and Amelia.

"Mary, I believe we have much to discuss," said Mr. Bennet evenly. With a nod to Mr. Yarby, he went into the house, followed by Kitty and then Mary who first gave Robert a loving, lingering gaze.

Once alone with her father, Mary shed tears and begged for forgiveness. She explained the plot to convince her father to break with Amelia and fire Mr. Yarby, unaware that he already knew the particulars thanks to Elizabeth's letter. When she at last finished her sad tale and sat, sniffing a bit into her handkerchief, Mr. Bennet came and sat next to her, patting her back in comfort.

"There, there, dry your eyes, my dear. You are forgiven. Love is a strange and powerful potion. It can alter one's deepest personality traits and convictions. I believe we both have learned that lesson these past few months. It made me disregard the required mourning for your mother and allow myself to become deeply attached to Amelia. And it caused you to do something I believe I have not seen you do since early childhood: tell a falsehood."

"Yes—but, Papa, your feelings for Amelia did not cause anyone pain as mine did."

"That is where you are wrong. My indiscreet behavior with Amelia was witnessed by our cousin Mr. Collins, and he used that information to blackmail Mr. Yarby into taking him on as curate, threatening to spread the scandalous gossip about Amelia and me around Meryton if he was not hired."

Mary gasped. "How dreadful! And he a man of the cloth too!"

Mr. Bennet chuckled. "Sadly, beneath their clerical garb, men are men after all and can be subject to all sorts of temptation."

"But you will speak to the bishop and fire Mr. Collins at once, now that you know," Mary said firmly. The thought of her dear Robert being extorted in such a way infuriated her. "In fact, he should be publicly censured for his actions!"

Mr. Bennet raised an amused eyebrow. "Goodness, Mary, what of forgiveness? Does the Bible not exhort us to do so?" Mary looked abashed, but before she could speak, he chuckled. "I am only teasing you. I will most assuredly have a serious conversation with Mr. Collins when my period of mourning is over and he can no longer do any damage with his gossip."

There was a knock at the door. At Mr. Bennet's call to enter, Mrs. Hill popped her head in.

"Mr. Collins is here to see you, sir," she said.

Mr. Bennet gave Mary a wry smile.

"Talk of the devil."

Chapter 35

M r. Collins bustled in and made straight for Mr. Bennet, now seated at his desk.

"My dear Mr. Bennet, thank you for seeing me, and I do apologize for the short notice, but you will be glad I am come, for truly, I have the most shocking news to report…the most scandalous information regarding—" Mr. Collins, noticing Mary's presence for the first time, broke off his speech a moment to bow his head to her. "I beg your pardon, Miss Bennet, I did not see you there."

"Not at all, Mr. Collins," said Mary in a frosty tone. "Papa and I were just finishing." She nodded to her father and left the room.

"Won't you sit down, Mr. Collins?" Mr. Bennet's tone was only slightly warmer than his daughter's. "What news have you to share?"

"It concerns your rector, Mr. Yarby. I have had some suspicions of him for quite some time, you see, and therefore felt it my duty to take steps to inquire as to his background. I had a suspicion he was not all he purported to be. And you will be pleased to learn, I was correct! I was entirely correct in my apprehension of him."

"Will you please get to the point of the matter, Mr. Collins? I have much to do just now."

"Of course, of course. Well—as you may know, the reverend Mr. Yarby came here with very little experience—I believe he had been a curate—or rather, he *said* he had been a curate for but a year or two."

"Mr. Collins, I was the man who hired Mr. Yarby, so I am more than aware of his qualifications and background."

"But *are* you aware, sir? Are you *truly?*" Mr. Collins pulled out a handkerchief and patted his damp upper lip before neatly folding the cloth again and returning it to his pocket. "As I said, for some time now, I have worried that there was more to him than we know, and I became determined—oh yes, *determined*—to seek out the truth for the sake of all concerned!"

"Indeed? For *all* concerned—or just for *you?*" Mr. Bennet stared intently into his cousin's eyes.

"Well...well..." Mr. Collins was briefly flustered before plunging on again. "My point being—what do we really know of Yarby's background? Why did he come to the clergy so late in life?"

"As I understand it, he had a failed business venture then cared for his ailing father until that man's passing. It was then that Mr. Yarby found his calling. And judging from his popularity in the parish, I cannot help but think he made the right choice. His sermons are much to my liking."

"He may have a natural...talent for speaking, but when I show you this document"—Mr. Collins fumbled in his coat, brought forth a folded piece of paper, and waved it violently, punctuating his final words—"you will no doubt come to the same conclusion as I."

"Which is...?" Mr. Bennet took a deep breath, his patience rapidly coming to an end.

"That Mr. Yarby is a fraud. He has foisted himself upon your good nature to take this valuable living without any prior experience whatsoever!" Mr. Collins sat back, a bit breathless.

"Whatever do you mean? I received a very good reference from his former rector…a Mr.…Mr.…"

"Smethurst, correct?"

"Ah yes, that is the name."

Mr. Collins thrust forward the paper to Mr. Bennet with a look of triumph.

"Just you read *that,* sir, and learn the sad truth. For Mr. Smethurst has written a reply to my inquiries of Mr. Yarby that reveals he was *not* their curate! Indeed, Smethurst has never even heard of this Mr. Yarby—if that even *is* his true name. The entirety of his experience is a complete fabrication!"

Alarmed, Mr. Bennet opened the letter and began to read.

Mr. Collins,

I thank you for your recent letter asking about our curate—a Mr. Robert Yarby. I can state without hesitation that I have no idea of whom you are referring. There has never been such a person working in our parish, and anyone purporting to have been our curate here during the time you specified is being quite untruthful.

I know not by what means this Mr. Yarby has prevailed upon the good will of Longbourn parish to secure a position there, but please know that he is absolutely not someone who has worked here. Therefore, we would be unable to provide any reference for him.

Yours most sincerely,
The Reverend Thomas Smethurst

"I…cannot believe this," Mr. Bennet murmured, as he set the letter down on his desk. His mind was whirling. Had he been the victim of a nefarious scheme? Were he and Amelia who they claimed to be, or were they, in fact, liars and cheats taking advantage of him? But to what end? It is not as if he had a large fortune to swindle. But the letter appeared in every way to be authentic.

Have I allowed my feelings for Amelia to blind me to the truth? Have I been a fool, after all?

"This is most disturbing, Mr. Collins," he said softly. "For, if this is all true, it would appear I have been deceived in my trust of both Mr. Yarby and Mrs. Withers." He continued to stare at the letter in his hands.

"*If* it is true? My dear Mr. Bennet, how can it *not* be true? You will, of course, fire Yarby immediately and send them away without reference," gloated Mr. Collins. "My dear Charlotte and I shall be most happy to replace them at the parsonage as soon as you give word they have quit the place."

The thought of Mr. Collins as the permanent rector at Longbourn shocked Mr. Bennet out of his sad reverie.

"Your offer is a bit premature, Mr. Collins. I shall need to do my own investigation, if you please, before I take any permanent steps."

"But the proof! It is all right there written in the rector's own hand! How can you even think of waiting an instant before you speak to the bishop and do what you must?" Mr. Collins sputtered. "If I were owner of Longbourn, I assure you—"

"But you are *not* the owner of Longbourn—not yet in any case," Mr. Bennet interrupted, firmly. He stood, trying to signal an end to the meeting. "And until such time, I shall make the decisions I think best for the rectory; Longbourn's advowson gives me that right. I thank you for bringing this to my attention, but I must ask you now to depart and let me consider the proper course of action." He saw a sneer spread across Mr. Collins's face.

"No doubt, you wish to consult your heart as well as your head on this matter, Mr. Bennet. Oh yes, I am aware of your attachment to Mrs. Withers. But I assure you, the only option open to you is quite obvious: Mr. Yarby and his sister must go. Good day, sir!"

He gave a curt nod of his head and stomped out of the library.

A few seconds later, the front door loudly closed.

Mr. Bennet sighed and sat heavily, picking up the letter once more. A small tap at the entry drew his attention to Mary, who entered, shutting the door behind her before marching over to her father.

"Papa, I heard much of what Mr. Collins said. How can Mr. Yarby be thought a fraud? May I see this letter?"

Mr. Bennet's mouth fell open. "You were listening at the door?"

Mary made a helpless gesture. "Apparently, my morals have gone missing yet again, Papa, but after what you just told me of his blackmailing Mr. Yarby, I had a feeling Mr. Collins's visit here was not to bring happy news. So, yes, I listened." She held out her hand. "May I please see the letter he brought?"

Mr. Bennet passed it to her, and she quickly scanned it before slamming it down on the desk.

"And how do we know this is, in fact, a legitimate letter? Could it have been perhaps manufactured—and I deplore to even suggest such an uncharitable thing, but it must be said—by Mr. Collins himself?"

"It certainly looks authentic" was her father's sad reply. "You can see the postal mark for yourself."

"But you will give Mr. Yarby a chance to defend himself against such outrageous, slanderous accusations, will you not? Even if that letter appears…authentic?" Mary's voice cracked a bit at the end.

"I…don't know." He shook his head. "It might be best to simply end things now. Mr. Collins had one thing correct: we do *not* know all that much about the Yarbys. Robert was the least experienced of all the curate applicants last year, and when he visited, perhaps I was too easily swayed by his charming manners to do proper research into his background. Who knows what more may be revealed about him and…Amelia. No, perhaps I should send them both away."

"But it was the bishop himself who sent you Rob—Mr. Yarby's recommendation, is that not true? That must count for something. And you love Amelia, Papa! She has made you so happy, and your current feelings only spring from the fact that I made up stories so you would doubt them. Do not be so hasty to throw away the very thing that has brought you great joy of late. And Mr. Yarby is such a fine pastor. Please—for my sake? At least speak to him."

Mr. Bennet could see tears shining in Mary's hopeful eyes.

Oh, dear—she is so in love with Mr. Yarby. Perhaps as much as I am with Amelia. But despite Amelia's hopes, he cannot possibly return her feelings. I have not seen any sign that he favors Mary above any other. It would spare her heart if I just removed them both from our lives. And in time she would forget him. Still…

After a long pause, Mr. Bennet replied. "Very well, Mary. We shall send for both Amelia and Yarby."

Chapter 36

"Mr. Bennet has asked to see us, Amelia"—Mr. Yarby entered the sitting room, holding a piece of paper—"as soon as possible."

"What reason does he have; does he say?"

"He does not. His note is short and to the point. It merely reads: *Please come to Longbourn House as soon as you can, we have important business to discuss.*"

"What business could it be?" Amelia set her needlework down. "Perhaps Mary has confessed her lies, and he wants to assure us that all is fine?"

"Perhaps. But you and he have already settled things between you, thanks to Mrs. Darcy's letter."

"Then why should he ask to see us both?"

Yarby paused, considering. Then he smiled and nodded, confident of his answer. "I believe I know. I have a feeling Mary may have told him of our engagement even though we agreed I would speak to him first. He likely wants to congratulate us and give us his blessing."

Amelia smiled. "Of course, that must be it. Let me get my pelisse, and we can go right over."

"Where is Phillip?"

"Hmm, he walked into Meryton, I believe. I shall tell Ellen to let him know where we have gone."

MR. YARBY AND MRS. WITHERS ARRIVED AT LONGBOURN AND were shown into the formal sitting room, where not only Mr. Bennet waited but Mary as well, who kept her eyes fixed on her hands in her lap.

After exchanging greetings, everyone took their seats and waited for Mr. Bennet to begin.

"Thank you for responding so quickly, Mr. Yarby," he began. "I asked you here because I am the recipient of some information that has confounded me greatly."

"I do apologize for not speaking to you myself," Yarby jumped in. "I did not anticipate Mary breaking this news to you so soon."

Mr. Bennet stopped a moment, trying to process the reverend's meaning. He shook his head and continued. "Mary has nothing to do with this news; I do not know to what you refer. I speak of a letter from your former employer, the reverend Mr. Smethurst."

"Why should he need to write to you? I don't understand. Is he unwell?" Yarby asked. He and Amelia exchanged worried glances.

"No, that is not the issue. Rather…well, as you know, you were the least qualified of the candidates for the living here at Longbourn. You had scant experience, but Mr. Smethurst wrote so highly of you, and we got along so well in your interview that I was persuaded to hire you without any further investigation into your past."

"No doubt the news of your wife's unexpected passing played a part in that." Amelia spoke for the first time. "Everything was in such a state of confusion, and Robert took charge of matters in such a capable manner that you could see at once he was the man for the job. Why do you bring this up now, Eugene?"

"Because I have information that leads me to think you made up your entire story of being a curate in Dorset—that you never worked there at all."

For a moment, Mr. Yarby could only stare blankly at his employer in surprise. "I am quite astonished at your pronouncement, Mr. Bennet. Why on earth would you think that?"

"This letter from the reverend Mr. Smethurst is why." He pulled a folded paper from his vest pocket and held it aloft as he continued. "He claims you never worked there and, in fact, claims not even to know you! So, I ask you now, Mr. Yarby: Did you fabricate a story of working there, thinking it so far away that I would not bother to seek out more details?"

"But...this is preposterous!" exclaimed Yarby. "I worked there fifteen months, gave many sermons, performed baptisms, made parish calls. Amelia kept house for me. Whoever wrote you this letter is grossly misinformed!"

"Or an outright liar. You must write to Mr. Smethurst at once, Eugene," urged Amelia, "and get him to clarify this letter. I cannot understand why he or anyone would say such a thing! Or is it a forgery?"

"I do not think the response would say anything other than what I hold here in my hands, Amelia," Mr. Bennet said sadly. "And the postmark confirms it is from that parish."

There was a long pause. Mary gave a little sniff and dabbed at her eyes with her handkerchief.

After thinking a moment, Mr. Yarby said, "Mr. Bennet, may I please see that letter?"

After Mr. Bennet handed it to him, and he unfolded it and read it carefully. When he got to the signature, a small smile of relief came across his face. "I thought so. Mr. Bennet, this was *not* written by the reverend Mr. Smethurst."

"I knew it!" exclaimed Mary. "It is a fabrication by that dreadful

Mr. Collins to force you to fire Mr. Yarby, Papa."

"No, Mr. Collins did not write this," Yarby said. "I recognize the hand quite well. It was written by Mr. Smethurst's elderly father—also a reverend and now retired. He suffers from senility, you see. However, he still sometimes thinks himself the rector there and has been known to wander into his son's office when it is not occupied and attempt to do some work—answer letters and so on. You see here"—he pointed to the signature—"He signed it Thomas Smethurst. The reverend Mr. Smethurst who wrote my recommendation is *Charles* Smethurst. Thomas did know me, of course, but as I said, his senility was becoming rather pronounced. Things from the past were still fresh in his memory, but more current situations or people—such as me and my service—seemed to fade from his mind rather quickly."

"Wait a minute." Mr. Bennet hurried from the sitting room and after a moment, returned, holding a bundle of papers. "Ah! I knew I had not thrown out or burned your application. See here—the sermons you included and"—he pointed to another page—"the letter of recommendation signed by *Charles* Smethurst. And I can see now it is written in a very different hand than this page from his father. I cannot think why I did not consider checking these old papers at once when Mr. Collins showed me the letter."

Everyone gave a relieved sigh.

"Well. Forgive me for having doubts yet again, Robert, Amelia. But this letter arrived, and things have been so befogged of late—I fear I was far too quick to accept the letter as authentic," Mr. Bennet said sadly.

"What else could you think?" Yarby finished for him. "I understand your concerns, and pray do not give it any more thought. It seems our minds have been at sixes and sevens for some time now, but at last, I hope we can put any doubts to rest."

Mr. Bennet crossed over and extended his hand to Mr. Yarby who shook it firmly.

"I think we could all do with some tea," Mr. Bennet said, going to the bell pull. When he returned and sat, a puzzled expression crossed his face. "Just one more thing, Robert. When you first came in—what did you mean by your statement that you did not anticipate Mary breaking the news to me so soon. What news?"

Smiling, Mr. Yarby rose and went to Mary, taking her hand and kissing it. "That your daughter and I are engaged, sir. I asked Mary to be my wife while at Pemberley, and she has graciously accepted me."

"Is this true, Mary?" Mr. Bennet asked.

Mary looked up at her fiancé, her face glowing with joy before answering. "Yes, Papa. Robert loves me. We love each other! Oh, can you believe things would work out in this happy way?"

Before Mr. Bennet could reply, Mrs. Hill was at the door.

"What did you need, Mr. Bennet, tea for everyone?"

"Hang the tea, Mrs. Hill. We need two bottles of our finest wine—at once! We have an engagement to celebrate!"

Whooping with excitement, Mrs. Hill congratulated Mary and Yarby, then hurried off to retrieve the wine. By now, everyone was on their feet, hugging each other, laughing, and even crying with happiness.

"What is going on?" Kitty's voice cut through the celebration. Beside her stood Phillip Yarby. "Mr. Yarby and I were taking a walk, and when we got back to the parish, Ellen told us you were here. Is it Lydia? More bad news?"

"You have only to look at their faces, Miss Catherine, to see something quite special is taking place." Phillip grinned as he looked at Robert and Mary, arms around each other. "I believe my little brother has just become engaged to your sister."

Kitty screamed with delight and rushed to hug her sister just as Mrs. Hill returned with the wine. Mr. Bennet and both Mr. Yarbys helped fill the glasses.

"I was so afraid you would be upset," whispered Mary to Kitty. "For was he not a favorite of yours at one time?"

Kitty tossed her head, and giggled. "As if I would want to be married to a stuffy preacher—even one as nice as Mr. Yarby. No. My heart is set on another now, and Mary"—she lowered her voice to a whisper—"I do believe he feels the same."

The two hugged again, then broke apart to take the proffered glasses of wine.

"A toast!" Mr. Bennet cried. "To Robert and Mary. I am glad to know that my book-loving daughter will not stray far from my library but live contentedly next door."

"To Robert and Mary!" echoed everyone.

As they drank, Mr. Bennet and Amelia exchanged a loving glance. Words were not needed to know what they both were thinking: the time to reveal their secret love would come soon.

Chapter 37

As soon as his official mourning period was over in late May, Mr. Bennet called on Mr. Collins at Lucas Lodge. He considered inviting his cousin over to Longbourn in order to have their discussion in his own library, but this way, he could end the appointment and leave Lucas Lodge when he wished. The news he was about to deliver would be such that Mr. Bennet was certain Mr. Collins would begin to grovel and beg, which might be tedious at best. Better that he should state his piece and depart.

It had not been easy putting off the pushy rector for the past month and a half while Mr. Bennet waited for the anniversary of his wife's death and the end of his mourning period. He did not want to give Mr. Collins any opportunity to make good on his threat to expose his romantic attachment to Amelia and cause a scandal. The gossip was likely to be minimal, but he did not wish to hurt his future bride. Whenever Mr. Collins sidled up to him after church services and quietly inquired about the letter from Thomas Smethurst, Mr. Bennet merely demurred and begged patience, saying he was "still investigating, but no doubt the truth would be a revelation to all once he got to the bottom of it." Then he would pat Mr. Collins's arm and give him a bit of a wink as if they shared a great secret.

So, Mr. Bennet knew Mr. Collins would have no reason to suspect anything when the two sat down in the Lucas Lodge salon that spring day. Indeed, he noted that Mr. Collins had the appearance of one who eagerly anticipated hearing happy news.

"I so appreciate your coming to visit me, my dear Mr. Bennet," Mr. Collins began when the two sat down and he had ordered tea be brought in. "Your thoroughness in confirming what the reverend Mr. Smethurst's letter revealed is to be commended."

Mr. Bennet did his best to appear serious. "Well, such an accusation made against someone I hired must be fully investigated, as I am sure you know. One cannot take drastic steps without being absolutely certain of the guilty party, correct? And *any* behavior in a man of the cloth that reeks of deception and underhanded tactics should be punished properly, do you not agree?"

"We are entirely of one mind there, dear cousin," Mr. Collins assured him. "Entirely one mind! There is no question that such a man should be dismissed at once."

"I am exceedingly glad you agree with me. Then you can brook no opposition when I inform you that your tenure as 'curate' to Mr. Yarby has come to an end and you will have no further interference in his management of things at Longbourn rectory." He watched as Mr. Collins nodded his head in happy agreement before the words sank in.

Mr. Collins's mouth fell open, and he stammered, "I beg your pardon? You are dismissing *me?*"

"Indeed, I am. For as you just stated, any man of the cloth who blatantly lies should be fired, and at once. And since I am now aware that you blackmailed Mr. Yarby to take you on as curate by threatening to reveal the attachment between his sister and me, I can no longer have you in my church. For who would tolerate a man in the pulpit with a mouth full of scripture but a heart filled with deceit? Not I, most assuredly. You have taken a share of Mr. Yarby's salary long enough. I have written to the bishop to confirm my decision, but your time as curate ends now."

"But the letter I gave you—Mr. *Yarby* is the liar, not me!" Mr. Collins sputtered, flecks of spittle flying in his agitation.

"Sadly, I must inform you that the letter you received in response to your inquiry was written and signed not by Yarby's former employer but by the senior Mr. *Thomas* Smethurst, who suffers from senility." Mr. Bennet pulled out two pieces of paper. "Here is the recommendation for Yarby written by the younger reverend, Mr. Charles Smethurst, and here is the reply you received. As you can readily see, they are in two quite different hands. And just to be certain, I wrote Mr. Smethurst once again. He was most apologetic that his father's response to you had slipped past the housekeeper and into the post. They try to watch out for the poor old man, he wrote, but somehow, they missed intercepting his reply to you. I cannot fault you for being deceived, but I can indeed fault you for the motivation behind your actions. They were reprehensible and not those of a gentleman."

Mr. Collins's eyes narrowed. "Yet you *did* form an attachment to Mrs. Withers while still in mourning! That news can still hurt you, you are aware."

"As for even thinking of spreading gossip about me and Mrs. Withers, my full mourning ended today, Mr. Collins, and Amelia and I plan to marry in June. The banns will be read next week. Some may whisper about the suddenness of the attachment, but we care little for the opinions of village gossips. We are only determined to act in a manner that will shortly secure our mutual happiness."

He stood. "I wish you luck in finding a new position, Mr. Collins. May I suggest you apply yourself vigorously to that endeavor, seeing as you now have a wife *and* a child to support. Good day."

Mr. Bennet reached the door just as the housekeeper opened it to bring in the tea tray. Mr. Bennet stepped aside for her, then reached for the platter of warm scones. He picked one up.

"This smells quite delicious, thank you."

He took a satisfying bite. And without a backward glance, he walked home.

Chapter 38

And so it was that, on the third Saturday in June, the reverend Mr. Yarby happily performed the marriage ceremony for his sister and Mr. Bennet as friends and family looked on with great joy. After much debate in the Bennet household, Mr. and Mrs. Collins were invited. Since the Lucases were coming, it seemed impossible *not* to invite them, reasoned Mr. Bennet. Such a snub would have led to questions, and that might have required explanations that would surely have been harmful to the Collins family. And while he did not much care about Mr. Collins's reputation, Mr. Bennet did not wish to see Charlotte's feelings hurt. Amelia was in agreement, so all were asked to attend.

However, as it turned out, Mr. Collins was unable to be at the festivities as he was called north to interview for a position at a small parish in the town of Haswell in County Durham, and due to timing and the distance, as Charlotte explained, would be unable to return in time. Charlotte enjoyed herself at the reception, catching up with her dear friend Eliza and showing off her son, Alexander, who sadly continued daily to bear an increasing resemblance to his father.

If Mr. Collins still harbored any hopes that the haste with which Mr. Bennet and Amelia married would cause a scandal, he was disappointed. Over the past year, Amelia had endeared herself to many in and around Meryton, and the majority of people pronounced themselves "quite delighted" with the match. Such a kind and sensible woman would only be a good partner to Mr. Bennet, all agreed.

A honeymoon was delayed for the happy couple, however, as the following Saturday, Robert Yarby and Mary Bennet became man and wife. Yarby's former rector, Mr. Smethurst, journeyed to Longbourn to perform the ceremony and stayed on to substitute for him at the church the next two Sundays. Mr. and Mrs. Bennet hosted a grand wedding breakfast for the couple in Longbourn's gardens. Mary seemed to never stop smiling, and more than one guest was heard to note how "Mary has so blossomed this past year," and "who would have ever thought it possible?" Robert had eyes only for his bride, and it was clear his love was genuine.

Kitty and Phillip Yarby sat next to each other at the breakfast, and those who closely observed them wondered whether another wedding might be forthcoming. Phillip had set up his business in Meryton and was already doing well. He was hunting for a comfortable cottage in the area that would be suitable for a man in his position—one who anticipated taking a wife in the near future, it was rumored.

The next day, both newlywed couples left on their honeymoons. Mr. and Mrs. Bennet went north to tour the Peak District, where they anticipated many happy walks together. Walking was, after all, how their romance began in the first place. Mr. and Mrs. Yarby traveled to Oxford where they planned to explore that town's delights, including the many bookshops, museums, and libraries.

When the happy couples returned, they found that the servants had transferred all of Amelia's things to Longbourn House and all of

Mary's possessions to the rectory cottage in a near seamless transition. Amelia teased her new stepdaughter—or was it sister-in-law now?—that since Mary had helped her choose the new fabrics and wall papers, she could not be other than completely content with the parsonage décor. Of course, the Yarbys were invited to come over at least thrice weekly for family dinner, and Mrs. Hill was heard to remark that, in all her days at Longbourn, she could not recall so many happy dinners with so much joyful laughter ringing through the halls.

March 19

Dear Lizzy,

I write with such happy news! Indeed, I am so excited that I can scarce hold the pen, so pray pardon the blots. Amelia has been safely delivered of a boy—a baby brother for us all! James Robert Bennet made his appearance around midnight after a scant four hours of labor, much to everyone's relief. Papa chose the name himself. Amelia wanted to name him Eugene, but he said he preferred James. Robert was, of course, chosen in honor of Amelia's brother, (and I can report with complete authority that "Uncle" Robert is quite pleased about it too!).

James is as good looking a babe as one can expect for a newborn, and appears as if he will favor Papa greatly, though that could change in time of course. Perhaps he will have Amelia's hazel eyes. We are so grateful that the pregnancy was without trouble and the birth was not difficult. I can only hope Robert's and my child will come as easily. I expect to share word about your next niece or nephew in another two months although I already feel large as a house!

And even more news—our sister Kitty has just told us she and Phillip are also expecting a child—so soon after their Christmas wedding! It seems the Bennets/Yarbys are multiplying at a rather prodigious rate. Kitty is making over one of the smaller bedrooms in

*their house for the nursery and has kindly asked Amelia for advice.
I believe it is Kitty's way of making up for her previous disagreeable
attitude towards Papa's attachment to Amelia. I can assure you,
however, that all of that discord is long forgotten.*

*Papa is quite over the moon with happiness. Indeed, his marriage
to Amelia has been nothing short of transformative. He spends less
of the day alone in his library and more time out and about in the
community. He laughs often and truly seems joyous every minute of
every day. He already speaks of taking his new son for long walks and
teaching him all about the estate. When I remember how I might have
succeeded in my deceitful attempt to force Papa to fire Robert and
send him and Amelia away, I still cannot help but feel shame.*

*By the way, I owe a debt of gratitude to Georgiana. I recently
learned that she told you of our talk when I first confessed my
terrible lies, and because of that, you took the initiative to write to
Amelia when I was with you in February of last year. That letter
brought Robert to Pemberley where he told me of his love for me.
Had Georgiana not spoken to you, the happiness I feel every day as
Mrs. Robert Yarby would not exist.*

*We are all exceedingly joyful to learn of Georgiana's engagement to
Lord Godwin, and we look forward to the wedding this fall. It seems
her first season has secured her happiness for the future. Tell her I do
not regret in the least missing out on a Season in London with her. I
am quite certain I could not have had any happier success than I found
in my own back garden.*

*Finally, forgive me for passing on a bit of village news in case
Charlotte Collins has not already written it. Mr. Collins accepted the
rector position in Haswell and moved there last July, but Charlotte
and the baby are only now planning to join him. She told people that
she did not go north with him because she wanted to be certain the job
was a good fit for her husband, and also that she would find everything
in the tiny rectory as it should be. But others have whispered she was*

punishing her husband for having a dalliance with a serving girl in the tavern beneath the rooms he had temporarily rented. It may be just a rumor though, and I feel a bit guilty for even repeating it here. In either case, I do hope they find happiness in Haswell and make a good home for themselves, since they can no longer look forward to one day assuming possession of Longbourn House, now that Amelia has given Papa an heir!

Oh, Lizzy, when I think of how everything turned out for us all, it seems like a fanciful dream, yet I know it is all true, and I give thanks for it every day. I hope that Mama is smiling down from Heaven, knowing that all her daughters are finally wed and, above all, that Longbourn will remain—at least for the foreseeable future—firmly in the hands of the Bennets.

Much love,
Your sister Mary

THE END

Acknowledgments

Finding a home for *The Bennets: Providence and Perception* has been a dream come true. But it wouldn't have happened without the help of many people. First, thanks to my husband for his continual support. Many thanks to Meryton Press—Janet Taylor and Ellen Pickels—for all their help in shaping *The Bennets*. I am also grateful to my faithful beta readers: Nancy Jeu, Kathy Robinson, and David Withers for their feedback. Reading a rough draft is a feat not to be underestimated! Cindy Mancini was an ideal first editor, making sure my book was as clean and error-proof as possible for submission. And lastly, my dear friend Anne Timmons, who brought a vague idea out of my head and turned it into a beautiful cover illustration.

About the Author

KC Cowan spent her professional life working in the media as a news reporter in Portland, Oregon, for KGW-TV, KPAM-AM, KXL-AM radio, and as original host and story producer for a weekly arts program on Oregon Public Television. She is co-author of the fantasy series: *Journey to Wizards' Keep*, *The Hunt for Winter*, and *Everfire*.

KC is also the author of two other books: *The Riches of a City*—the story of Portland, Oregon, and *They Ain't Called Saints for Nothing!* in collaboration with artist Chris Haberman, a tongue-in-cheek look at saints. She is married and divides her time between Portland, Oregon, and Tucson, Arizona.